Ink, Fire, Beauty

By Jordan Renee

The moment he took power, Emperor Xórong declared himself a collector of beauty. He began to gather and hoard, binding his treasures for display like bundles of flowers in gold-dusted vases. His rule stretched across decades, rich and unchallenged, until the day one of his flowers left her vase, befriended a devil, and set fire to the Empire's edge.

Dedication

For my mother, who not only taught me to read, but more importantly, gave me space to imagine.

Acknowledgements

My first and greatest thanks goes to my parents, to my mom for her endless support, and my dad for reading more rough drafts than anyone should ever have to. Together, they have held me up through every success and disappointment, and never let me forget that no matter what I accomplished in life, they would always be proud of the person I'd become.

A big thanks to my siblings as well, Madison, Logan, and Emerson, who I love more than life itself and whose company not only inspires much of my work, but also brings me more joy than anything in this world.

Many thanks to my grandparents, who are some of my earliest and biggest fans, and who have supported my work through all the twists and turns of this journey. And of course, this book wouldn't have been possible without the excellent guidance of Dr. Evie Terrono, who both introduced me to Art History and whose teachings helped shape the ancient world my characters inhabit.

I am also endlessly grateful for Raichelle Johnson, a dear friend and fellow Art Historian who willingly accepted the daunting task of reading one of the earliest drafts of this novel.

For offering her mentorship and wisdom on all things writing, I must thank Jordan Rosenfeld, who convinced me to both push forward and be patient when I needed to hear it most.

I also thank Sue and Ritchie Watson and my Aunt Shari and Uncle Joe for their incredible generosity, and the Randolph-Macon College English department for stretching my love of literature to new heights.

I must also thank my church family, and last but not least, everyone at Pen It! Publications, LLC for making my dream a reality.

Table of Contents

ONE

"Too numerous to record are the men of ancient times who were wealthy and noble and whose names have yet vanished away."

The power of beauty lies, of course, in appearance. Beauty is the ability to hold the world's gaze, to steal its breath, to captivate and own.

When she'd heard otherwise, foolish claims that beauty exists in the viewer, in how they feel after experiencing something wondrous, Túlià had laughed.

There were feelings tied to beauty, she knew. Greed. Envy. Obsession. She knew them all. She had seen how beauty could twist a soul and taint a heart, so she only allowed herself the vanity of three things: her hair, her hands, and her name. All were gifts from her mother, so all were beautiful to Túlià. She didn't know if anyone else thought her three vanities to be beautiful both because she hadn't ever cared to ask, and because most people didn't look at her.

They looked at her paintings.

It was all anyone wanted to see of Túlià, which is why she always stood in the shadows behind her work at a viewing, her thick hair pinned out of the way and her long Painter's hands joined behind her back.

She hated this part, hated seeing the silhouettes of the wealthy move between her scrolls, fans, and painted banners, hated watching them trace her seal with their gold-dipped fingers. As if they knew Túlià, as if they understood how much of her soul, hers and her mother's, she blended into each brushstroke.

Túlià might have once enjoyed the soft gasps of approval that fell from the O shaped lips of someone seeing her work for the first time, but now she only wanted to be left alone, to paint quietly in her little Pavilion, to remember what she'd lost and forget the Emperor.

She hadn't told him, but this collection was for her mother.

After a year of suffering through her absence, Túlià wanted a way to both honor her mother's life and distract herself from the pain of memory, so she'd feverishly produced a number of works, all featuring what her mother had loved most, the Mountains.

Watching the Emperor enter, Túlià was glad she hadn't tried to explain the inspiration for her latest collection. He would never understand.

Emperor Xórong.

She hated him most of all.

He always insisted on being the last to see her paintings, forcing patience on himself, building his own anticipation to further sweeten the latest reveal of Túlià's perfectly arranged displays.

Xórong's wives went before him, then the Princesses. He had eight daughters, perfect in number and appearance. Every viewing, they did their best to outshine Túlià's paintings, and each time they failed. No amount of silk ribbons or jade hairpins could be arranged in a way that told stories the way a scroll could, at least not once that scroll had been handled by Túlià.

As the royal daughters passed her shadowed sanctuary, multiple pairs of perfectly arched brows flicked disdainfully

16

in Túlià's direction, the motion echoed by floor length sleeves, skirts, and skillfully braided hair. Such subtle indications of their hatred contrasted perfectly, as always, with the barely restrained glee of the man who entered the room last.

Emperor Xórong was handsome in the way of the wealthy. He held the glow of frequent pampering, dressed in the garb of a free-flowing purse, and boasted the belt loops of one who began looking forward to his second meal while still consuming the first.

He took his time, pausing to admire each painting with both fists tucked beneath his chin. As always, four Zānshì accompanied him.

Túlià rubbed the single pearl tied around her wrist when they passed, muttering a word of prayer. As if Zānshì were not already demon enough, Xórong insisted they accompany him in fours, the number of death. Bad luck for the Emperor, some said. Most said bad luck for his enemies. The two Zānshì on his right turned their white masks toward Túlià in passing.

We see you, they seemed to say. *No shadow can hide you from our eyes.*

Zānshì never spoke aloud. It was thought they couldn't speak at all, or worse, that they could, and only the Emperor's painted red seal over the closed lips of their masks kept some hellish language from spilling forth.

Lizards. Snakes. Dragons—all had been used in attempts to describe, from one neighbor to the next, just what made a Zānshì. Occasionally, a tiger or a hawk would find its way into the mixture, but most often the scales dipped toward reptilian. There was one word however, that all who knew of the Emperor's soldiers agreed upon: Devil.

17

Their nearness was Túlià's least favorite part of the viewings. Usually they moved on in just enough time for the breath she'd been holding not to send her to the floor, but today, Xórong stopped.

"Painter, come with me."

After a moment, she did, trailing behind the silent footfalls of the Zānshì and keeping her head down, less out of respect for Xórong and more to avoid accidentally meeting the gaze of the trench-deep eye cavities in the face of the nearest mask.

"I have reconsidered," he said, still wandering among her paintings, unbothered, as always, by his eerie companions.

Túlià swallowed, gripped her pearl, and forced herself to speak calmly.

"Reconsidered, Highness?"

He nodded, bending to study the bottom of a painted screen that stood taller than a man and spread twice as wide.

His fingers traced the smoothly mounded islands covering the foreground. Each bit of land bore a handful of dark bamboo stalks growing sturdily against the wind. A family of Mountains shadowed the space behind, towering over an ink-frothed expanse of ocean.

"You will go to Yán sè Falls and paint a portrait of Princess Kāì standing before them."

Túlià's heart soared at the name of the Falls on his lips, then dipped with confusion.

"Princess Kāì? I don't—"

"It is very nearly her twenty-first birthday," he continued, "as I'm sure you are aware."

"But Highness—"

Túlià's words choked off as her interruption sent one of the Zānshì's hands to the gleaming bone-knives strapped across his lower back.

"You will take a Zānshì, for the Princess's protection," Xórong said, smiling at her discomfort and nodding at the devil guard who had silenced her.

"Come. We will discuss the details of your journey in my personal chambers."

Túlià followed him silently past The Hall of Sincerity and into The Palace of Illustrious Administration, doing her best to ignore some of the more unpleasant decorations that covered the Emperor's most private space.

"You must realize my women do not leave The City," Xórong continued, lowering himself onto a bench smothered in pillows the color of dried blood.

"Yes, Highness."

"So this is a very special favor I'm granting you."

"Yes, Highness," Túlià repeated, keeping her eyes on the misshapen feet of the Zānshì standing just to Xórong's left.

"Then you understand the difficult position I am in. Yes? Tell me," he added, in response to Túlià's nod.

"You do not wish to be seen granting favor to a woman, especially a woman of the lower court."

Túlià didn't realize she spit the last few words through gritted teeth until she heard Xórong's sigh of displeasure.

"Exactly, a woman who should really be kneeling in the company of her Emperor, don't you agree?"

Grateful for the long sleeves covering her tight fists, Túlià knelt slowly and waited, reminding herself that after nearly a year of asking, the Emperor had finally granted permission for this journey. The least she could do was maintain a facade of respect until she left his presence.

"To keep my subjects from whispering," he continued, "I will send Kāì with you so that her birthday may serve as our excuse for such a gross breach in etiquette. The common people can hardly deny me the pleasure of doting on one of my daughters."

"Forgive me, Highness, but why Kāì?"

Túlià could hear the raising of Xórong's brows in his voice alone.

"You prefer to travel with some other Princess?"

Of course she didn't. Kāì was the only person of royal blood whose company Túlià enjoyed. So she held her tongue, praised her luck, and pretended to listen as Xórong went on with his instructions.

"Paint Kāì's portrait as my birthday gift to her and no one will be the wiser that your true reason for this trip is— what was it again?"

"For my mother," Túlià murmured.

"Ah yes, for your mother and her unfortunate loss. Now go prepare. You leave at dawn."

TWO

"It is only those who were masterful and sure, the truly extraordinary men, who are still remembered."

Kāì fussed impatiently at her hair while she waited in Túlià's quarters, her attention wandering between the ever present envy of her dear Painter's wonderfully thick locks, and the news she couldn't wait to share.

The news won out and burst forth when the envy-inducing locks and the person they belonged to rounded the corner, replacing Kāì's brief moment of jealousy with honest joy.

"Father has told you then," she said, standing and taking Túlià's hands. "You must be as excited as I am, and then more so," she added, remembering what the Falls meant to Túlià, what this journey would be for her.

"And you got to spend time in Father's private chambers as well. How lucky. I'll help you prepare your things if you tell me his every word."

"He instructed us to take a Zānshì, *for safety*," Túlià said, leaning back and resting both hands on her stomach.

"You shouldn't mock Father," Kāì scolded, barely hiding her smile. "But a single Zānshì? I thought they always traveled in groups of two, at the least. Father must think the road very safe to have only one join us all the way to—"

"The door, Kāì."

Straightening, Kāi continued to chatter as she followed Túlià's nod toward the soft knocking at their door.

"A gift from the Emperor," whispered the servant who waited just behind it, passing a load of what looked like at least a dozen gowns into Kāi's waiting arms.

"Oh Túli, just look at how *beautiful*. And thank you," she added, dismissing the servant with a tilt of her head.

Túlià watched as she laid out each gown in the glow of the last few drops of sun that slipped through the window.

"Our journey isn't going to be just blue skies and radiant gowns, Kāi. I don't care how safe Xórong imagines the road. Are you sure you truly wish to go?"

"Of course I wish to go. Oh I can't wait! The jasmine will be in bloom, and the farmers will have just begun..."

Túlià let her voice fade, trying to calculate the distance of the journey while also managing to do twice as much packing as Kāi, not that she was surprised. A distracted Kāi made for a nearly worthless Kāi.

They would have to cross the fields and farmland— two days by cart, then sail to the foot of the Sywán Mountains—another four days depending on the weather, then a day's climb to reach the Falls. Doubled for the return journey, Túlià would have to spend fourteen days in the company of a Zānshì.

Fourteen, unlucky.

Well, perhaps it would be more. Hopefully, it would be less. It hardly mattered that Xórong had only assigned one Zānshì. A Zānshì was a Zānshì, and he could easily suck the marrow from her bones without the aid of one of his devil brothers.

"Are you going to do a window prayer?" Kāi asked, interrupting her dark thoughts.

Túlià sighed. "It isn't called a window prayer, but yes, I am."

"Will you let me add a poem this time?"

"If your poem is appropriate," Túlià muttered, already beginning to gather supplies from around the room and arrange them across the floor beneath her open window.

"What was so inappropriate about the last poem?" Kāì demanded, holding up a small scroll for Túlià's approval.

"We are asking for protection all the way to the Mountains. Put that tiny thing back and pick a scroll worthy of the gods. And your last poem," she continued, pretending not to see the face Kāì made behind her, "was almost an insult."

"How can something be *almost* an insult? It is either insulting, or it isn't," Kāì countered, kneeling beside Túlià at the window and presenting her much larger scroll.

Spreading and pinning the delicate roll of silk, she arranged herself as comfortably as she could. Why Túlià insisted on creating her prayer-paintings while crouched on the floor like a little monkey was beyond Kāì, but she joined her all the same.

"You mentioned Emperor Xórong as though he were in equal power with the gods. Hold this."

"Well the one I have in mind today is much better. I've had more time to practice it since I knew from the moment Father told me about our journey that you would want to be *spiritually prepared*."

Túlià made a face of her own. Luckily, Kāì understood that once her brush touched the scroll, she was to be silent. It was perhaps the only piece of Túlià's prayer she respected enough to maintain quiet for longer than she was accustomed to. Túlià guessed it was less out of respect and

23

more because Kāì loved watching her paint almost as much as she loved her precious Emperor.

Focusing on the sound of birds, on the sweet breeze coming through the open window, and on the feel of her slow brush, Túlià prayed. She prayed to her mother, to their Mountain ancestors, to any spirit or god willing to watch over her and Kāì while they traveled.

Knowing her mother's pearl would magnify the prayers a thousandfold, she spun the little bracelet so it would rest against her pulse and lift her thoughts higher.

Guidance. Wisdom. Courage.

Kāì began to fidget beside her, nearly upsetting the inkstone.

Patience.

Túlià added, lifting her head and passing her brush to Kāì. She watched the graceful movements of her friend's hands as they added tall, neat rows of poetry to the scroll's outer edge.

Far away on cold Mountains, a stone path leads upwards. Among white clouds, people's homes reside. Stopping my cart I must, as to admire the maple forest at night's fall. In awe of autumn leaves showing more red than even flowers of early spring.

"Well, is this appropriate enough for your gods?"

Túlià nodded.

It was perfect. The words captured the same course as the miniature cart Túlià had painted crawling up the side of a snow-capped Mountain like an ant on a mound of white rice.

"Are we meant to fit in that little cart?"

"It is *meant* to show the insignificance of our people in the shadow of nature. I've told you a dozen times. Now hold back your teasing until I've finished."

Kāì made a show of pressing her lips together and held steady a large bowl while Túlià laid the scroll across it so the painted portion sank down into the bowl's open mouth. Carefully retrieving a lit candle from one of her many worktables, she lit the center of the painting with practiced motions and watched as the ink-decorated silk burned slowly out from the Mountain's painted center. When the flames reached the edge of the bowl, Kāì sprinkled water over them from a pitcher until the now useless scroll was cool enough to touch.

Following Túlià to the window, Kāì only managed to be silent long enough for her dear Painter to toss its ashen contents out into the air before her will gave way.

"Couldn't we have burned something with a more pleasant smell?"

"No, Kāì. The Sagà smoke was for my mother, asking her spirit to watch over us on our journey."

"Of course," Kāì murmured, solemn until a smile began nudging at her lips.

"What is it?"

"I was just thinking what she would say. *I've never seen two girls with more trouble in their eyes.*"

Smiling as well, Túlià finished the familiar words. *"Just be sure you use those eyes to look after one another.* How many times did she say that to us?"

"Not nearly enough, considering we've been weaving trouble all over The City since the moment we learned to walk. She would be glad we're doing this," Kāì added, returning her attention to the still empty chest she was meant to be packing.

25

"I know she would," Túlià agreed. "It was her dying wish."

THREE

"Xórong, an Emperor who faced ten thousand deaths with no regard for his own life, and went forth to rescue his nation from disaster was remarkable indeed!"

At dawn, as instructed, Túlià and Kāi waited at The Gate of Mounting Prosperity to meet their Zānshì and driver. Xórong's driver arrived first, bowed low, and began to load their things behind his oxen. The Zānshì didn't bow. And he didn't arrive so much as appear on the steps above them.

Zānshì who startled her pulse into madness like this often brought to Túlià's mind an image of the lizards that hid between reeds in The Garden of Refined Artistry. The tiny creatures could lay still enough that you failed to see them until they were nearly underfoot. This is how the Zānshì moved, or rather, didn't move. It was as if they managed to be so still that eyes simply forgot them.

Túlià couldn't guess how long their Zānshì had been lizard-still and watching before he chose to move down the steps, giving her a good look at his strange gait. Like all Zānshì, his legs were...something else. Hidden beneath spotless white wrappings, they bent and turned out at the knees like no animal she had ever seen. They appeared to be always crouching, waiting and poised to strike. Watching him walk, Túlià was oddly reminded of a snake, and she imagined with some certainty that if a snake had legs, it would move like one of Xórong's devil warriors.

The Zānshì regarded both women until, once again, Túlià had to force herself to choose between breathing and collapsing from the emptiness in her lungs.

Kāi mustered up a small bow and extended her pale hand toward the cart.

"Will you be riding with us, Master Zānshì?"

He took a single, odd-legged step backward and lowered the cart steps, mimicking her one handed gesture until both Túlià and Kāi followed his direction into the small, well decorated space. They both breathed an audible sigh of relief when he shut the door behind them and climbed up to sit beside the unfortunate driver.

"Well, he seems like a gentleman at least," Kāi said, opening both her fan and the window to chase away the heat of the tight wooden space.

Túlià's choked laugh melted into a sigh at the sight of one of her paintings behind Kāi's head. She tugged the scroll free and tried unsuccessfully to cram it through the mockingly too small window.

"Xórong even has to slather the insides of his carts with beauty," she muttered. "I wonder if he insists on only spreading the most beautiful honey across his bread every morning too."

"Don't speak poorly of Father," Kāi reminded her, still furiously fanning back hair she now considered a blessing in comparison to Túlià's much thicker mane. "It's not as if he hung your painting here simply to irritate you. Don't you think the Emperor has more important things to address?"

"No."

"Besides," she continued, correcting Túlià's slumped shoulders with a tap of her fan, "I rather like this painting. It reminds me of you."

"It's a crane," Túlià scoffed. "What are you saying."

"That you are thin and frowning."

"He isn't frowning. He's a crane. They don't have lips."

"Lips or no, it looks like he's frowning. Maybe you are beginning to lose your touch to old age," Kāì teased.

"Old age? I'm only twenty summers! You're the old maid between us."

"Honestly, I don't have more than an extra season on you."

"We should find you a husband on this trip," Túlià countered. Maybe that *gentleman* Zānshì who caught your eye."

Kāì gasped and struck Túlià with her fan in a decidedly un-Princess like way.

"Stop it, stop it Túli. He can hear us," she added in a whisper.

Both women went silent immediately and began trying to peer through the wooden slats behind their Zānshì, in the same way they knew he could pry through with his ears. They waited until their hearts stopped pounding, Túlià cursing her foolishness, before either dared speak again.

"Do you think he didn't hear then?"

"Of course he heard, Kāì. He likely just didn't care. He's a warrior, remember? I hardly think he'd bother with stupid gossip."

"He might," Kāì answered, still whispering. "Haven't you heard the stories?"

Yes, Túlià had heard the stories.

Once, when she was nearly eight summers, she had absolutely refused to go to sleep, and insisted on sitting at her mother's side deep into the night, watching her paint. On that night, her brush did not spin the usual white clouds weaving through Mountains and settling over water, but the white mask of something Túlià had only ever seen from a distance.

"Zānshì," her mother breathed low into her ear. "Do you know them?"

Túlià shook her head. "I have never been close to one."

"Be glad of that, Babèi. Those who come close to a Zānshì do not often survive. Unless of course, you are *the one.*"

"What one?"

The brush continued to move, filling shadows beneath deep eyes and twisted knees, turning what had at first looked like a simple soldier clad in white, into something from a place Túlià knew she never wanted to visit.

"The one they choose to live, to go on and tell the story of their might to all who will listen. During the day," she continued, standing to stretch her Painter's hands, slightly longer versions of Túlià's still growing fingers, "they fight for the Emperor, protecting him, his land, and his people. But during the night, they are free to do as they please."

"What do they do?" Túlià pressed, watching her mother hang the gruesome scroll on the wall and wishing she would take it down.

"I can't be certain, since I was never foolish enough to test them, but I hear they walk the streets, peering into windows and looking for naughty children who ought to be asleep."

Túlià's little heart began to move nearly as fast as her eyes, which couldn't decide between her mother's newest painting and the suddenly much more terrifying window it hung beside.

"I think I would like to sleep now Màmà."

FOUR

"His story began in the summer of the Ninth Empire, when the legitimate heir, Emperor Fùqun's son, died."

Túlià woke, eyes fluttering as the sound of voices and the slowing of wheels pulled her from sleep.

The novelty of leaving The City for the first time in her life had worn off once she'd realized the rest of Xórong's domain seemed composed of nothing but flooded rice stalks as far as the eye could see. She was not able, even, to admire her mother's distant Mountains, since an early morning haze had decided to visit and stay long past morning's end.

Túlià nudged Kāi awake and both women jostled for position at the small window, searching for whatever had interrupted their slow trip across the Empire's wide stretch of farmlands.

Three shadows lay in the dust beside their cart, the first shadow addressing those of their driver and Zānshì with flailing arms and an angry voice. He grew louder, and more shadows began to chime in.

"Do you want to handle this, *Princess* Kāi, or should I?"

"Handle what? Let the men take care of it. No—Túlià, don't go out there!"

"I want to see what happened."

"But they could be bandits."

"I've never met a bandit that stood any threat to a Zānshì."

"You've never met a bandit at all," Kāi grumbled, reluctantly following her out into the hot sun.

She was right. Túlià had never encountered a bandit, but neither had Kāi, or any of the Emperor's women for that matter, since their engagements were limited solely to the residents and visitors of Xórong's treasure-encrusted Palaces.

Túlià's eyes adjusted to reveal an overturned cart, a broken wheel, and a very angry group of farmers. Rice wine spilled from the wreckage, and by the looks of their ruddy cheeks, the men had sampled more than a sip of their wares during the long haul across the fields. They had probably been hoping to sell in The City. Now, the broken wheel had left their wines soaking up dust in the middle of the road, and they were not pleased.

Of the four farmers, one gestured wildly and roared insults at the Emperor's driver, requesting none too politely that he pay for the damage to both cart and wares. The driver had his palms up, doing his best to explain that he'd not touched the cart, and that something must have spooked the farmers' mules off the road.

The Zānshì simply watched.

And the remaining three men watched him. Emboldened with wine slowed blood, the farmers lacked the usual fear that turned even the strongest of men into weak-kneed children. Túlià followed their glossed eyes to the Emperor's devil soldier and guessed rather quickly what had spooked their mules.

He took no blame, waiting silently for the two drivers, theirs and his, to settle.

When Kāi emerged from the cart, the golden hem of her gown had hardly touched the ground before the eyes of every man settled on her.

34

With her moon-pale hands, long lashes, and dainty, slippered feet, Kāi was easily the most beautiful sight on the fields, and likely the most beautiful woman these farmers had ever seen. They moved past their awe the moment they realized what such beauty meant: property of the Emperor. And that meant Kāi had money and power, both of which they foolishly believed could right their cart and restore their wares in mere moments.

They moved toward her, clamoring for attention, begging for assistance. One, in his drunken stupor, dared to clutch her sleeve.

The farmer's hand vanished.

It took Túlià a long moment before the specks of blood on the man's whitening face told her that his hand had not truly disappeared, it had been removed, quickly and cleanly by the bone-knife of the Zānshì behind him.

The farmer only managed to scream once before a body slumped at his feet, soon joined by a second, then a third.

It took another moment for him to realize he had now lost not only his cart and his wares, but his traveling companions and his hand. He stood still, stunned, watching the blood flow from their bodies and mingle with his rice wine in the dust.

When the Zānshì approached, he flinched, falling to his knees with a hundred nightmares in his eyes. But it was not a knife of bone that touched the remaining farmer this time, only a band of white cloth, wrapped tightly around his stump by the surprisingly gentle hands of the Zānshì.

They stood together, and when the white mask dipped toward the horizon, a clear signal for the farmer to go, he ran, stumbling and clutching his ruined arm to his chest, weeping over this new luck that balanced precariously on the rim of his misfortune.

"He will never make it to The City," Kāì whispered between trembling breaths, holding her own hand to her chest as if she felt his pain.

"Of course he will make it," Túlià murmured. "Someone has to tell the story."

They watched their Zānshì mount behind the oxen and tilt his mask expectantly at the Emperor's driver, who still stood in the dust, watching blood soak through his sandals.

He began to shudder, looked at Kāì's beautiful face for a moment, as though searching for something to give him strength, then turned and ran for The City.

The Zānshì's eyes locked onto his retreating back at the sound of the driver's first footfall. His mask swung slightly between the two fleeing figures on the horizon, farmer and driver. Tipping his head, the Zānshì made a decision, overtook the driver with long, twisted strides, and slit his throat.

It was a quick death, still, Xórong's demon had already returned to the cart and cleaned his bone-knife long before the last beat of the poor man's heart.

Gesturing toward the cart with a single, white-gloved hand, much the same way he had when Túlià and Kāì first boarded, the Zānshì invited both women to take their seats inside.

He shut the door behind them, sealing a space that seemed even smaller and hotter now that the smell of blood hung heavy in the air. Taking up the reins himself, he began to guide the oxen. Their slow, heavy tread just failed to cover the weeping that spilled through the fine cracks in the Emperor's cart.

Túlià held Kāi's trembling shoulders well into the night. Between murmured prayers for the spirits of the bodies they had left behind, she seemed unable to stop wondering how the Zānshì had managed to keep even the smallest drop of blood from landing on his white robes.

FIVE

"But Fùqun's favorite concubine, Méigi, had given birth to a son, Xórong."

It took until nearly dawn before Túlià's need to relieve herself overcame her fear at having to address the beast who drove their cart.

Kāi had made an effort to clean herself up, and nodded weakly in answer to Túlià's false-bold decision to knock at the roof.

"Zānshì. We wish to stop."

The cart stopped, and the door opened.

Both women descended the steps and kept their eyes on the Zānshì's misshapen feet.

"We only need a moment," Túlià said, struggling to keep her voice even.

She began to lead the still mostly numb Kāi toward the shelter of a nearby dove tree, faltering when she noticed a now familiar shadow trailing close behind.

Did he mean to *watch* them?

Fear melting into disgust, Túlià whirled on the Zānshì and held up her free hand, the other still clinging tightly to Kāi.

"I said we need a moment."

Nothing. No response. No indication that he'd heard at all.

She tried again.

"Master Zānshì. We must take care of our needs. In private."

His head moved from the two women to the dove tree, and back again. Was he...hesitating? Túlià had never heard of this happening before, but it hardly surprised her that Xórong had failed to include female needs in the training of his devil warriors.

Finally, blessedly, the Zānshì turned his back and held up two fingers.

Two minutes.

Two minutes to be free of his gaze and breathe normally for a change.

Túlià tugged Kāì the rest of the way to the dove tree, offering to stand between her and the Zānshì while she took care of herself. Kāì returned the favor, pulling a single petal from the branches and gifting it to Túlià when she finished.

"Look. Your mother's favorite."

"Yes but we don't pick them Kāì, remember. She liked to let them be."

"I'm sorry," she whispered, her lower lip beginning to shiver. "I forgot."

Letting the petal fall, she suddenly took Túlià by the wrists hard enough to make her gasp.

"You shouldn't have spoken to him like that Túli. He could have killed you. I might have left you in the dust like our driver when he...passed," she finished weakly.

"He won't kill me, Kāì, and he certainly won't kill you. You're a Princess, remember?"

"I don't think I want to be a Princess any longer."

"Then we should turn back," Túlià murmured. "This was a silly idea anyway. It's only the Falls..."

Kāì lifted her gaze from the petal she'd dropped, wiped her eyes, and straightened her spine.

"No. No, it's not just the Falls. It's Yán sè Falls. Your mother's Falls. We came all this way, and we will continue."

"It's going to be dangerous Kāi. You saw what he did. The Zānshì—"

"Won't hurt either of us," she interrupted firmly. "He killed Father's driver because he'd already let one man go and because he knew he could guide the oxen himself."

"But—"

"Túlià, is the Zānshì a Painter?" Kāi demanded, pulling back her shoulders and taking advantage of the height in her royal blood.

"No."

"And is the Zānshì a Princess?"

Túlià almost smiled.

"No."

"Then he won't hurt either of us, will he, because both a Princess and a Painter are needed for this trip. You need a Princess to paint in front of the Falls, and I need a Painter to paint me in front of the Falls. As long as we stay together, everything will be all right."

Túlià did smile then, and the lightness in her step stayed even when the Zānshì's shadow rejoined itself to theirs on the way back to the cart.

This time, before shutting them in, the Zānshì delivered a basket of food from their provisions beneath the driver's seat. It was as if they had reminded him with their momentary stop, that unlike a Zānshì, they were human and needed to rest, eat, and relieve themselves.

Kāi's shoulders were still strong as she gracefully accepted the basket and thanked him with a cold nod.

The door closed, the cart began to move again, and the two women ate in silence until the wheels beneath them stilled at the sight of the moon.

SIX

"Xórong was young and his mother was lowly and had no standard of conduct."

"Do all common people sleep on the ground?"

"Of course not Kāi. I'm sure they have straw mats at least, similar to these."

"I never imagined straw to be so scratchy."

"Well I know you can't be foolish enough to imagine it sliding like silk."

Kāi smiled briefly before her eyes darted across the fire to where their Zānshì stood watching. Her smile vanished.

"I don't think I will find much sleep tonight Túli."

"I won't either."

"Well, tell me how your viewing went."

"Ghastly, as always," Túlià muttered.

"But it was for your mother. I'm sure she would have loved it."

"I could hardly think of her, could I, with all of *them* there."

"Honestly Túli, You can't hate everyone in The City."

"I don't hate you."

"And I am honored, or course, but—"

"Kāi, did you *see* what Princess Xiàná was wearing?"

Kāi sighed. "How bad was it this time."

"Let's just say I am amazed it stayed on her body."

"She only wants to make Father happy."

"Any father happy to see his own child, who can't be older than twelve summers might I remind you, dressed like *that*, should be cast off the nearest cliff."

"Túlià," Kāi hissed. "You can't threaten to throw the Emperor from a cliff in front of—"

The Zānshì lifted his head, cutting her off. He looked at Túlià until her mother's pearl seemed to burn like coal against her wrist, then turned his back on them to survey the dark horizon.

Túlià laid down, and heard nothing but cicadas and stars until Kāi's irritation overpowered her fear.

"Princess Xiàná only wants to please the Emperor. You can't hate her for it, because I am the same way."

"No," Túlià countered. "You write Xórong poems and pick him flowers, which is a far cry from powdering your body and wearing as little clothing as possible."

"Even so, you've hurt my feelings."

"Well then do tell me, fair Princess, how I might appease your wounded heart."

"Hmm…tell me a story, one of your mother's."

"Which one?"

"My favorite."

"Which is your favorite?"

"Túli, you have known me longer than I've known myself. If you honestly don't remember my favorite story, I'll throw *you* off a cliff."

"Of course I know your favorite story, The Children of the Sun and Moon."

Kāi nodded against her straw mat and waved for Túlià to begin.

"Long, long ago, the Eastern Sky God had two wives, the Sun Goddess and the Moon Goddess. With the Sun

Goddess he had ten sons, and with the Moon Goddess he had twelve daughters. The family lived together in a Mountain-sized mulberry tree where they cared for their children with much love. When the children were old enough, their mothers began to instruct them on the proper way to appear in the sky.

The Moon Goddess was strict but gentle. She made certain her daughters were ready before sending them into the night, one at a time. Because of her worry, she never slept when one of her daughters lit up the sky. Whenever one returned, the Moon Goddess would bathe her in the Eastern Sea, hang her in the mulberry tree to dry, and send the next daughter out among the stars. Because of their mother's gentle care and attention, each daughter always behaved and came back to her safely.

The Sun Goddess, however, did not have such control over her sons. Perhaps because she was lazy. Perhaps because the sons were more difficult to guide than the Moon daughters. The people didn't know. They only lived on, unaware of the mischief brewing in the mulberry tree.

One day, the sons decided to have a trick and a laugh, appearing all together at once in the sky, ignoring their mother's instructions to never do so. While they played, the people below began to suffer from drought, and prayed for mercy.

Outraged, the Eastern Sky God called for his best marksman, who notched his mighty bow and felled nine of the sons, leaving only one alive. The suffering of the people ended, but the Sun Goddess would forever water the mulberry tree with her tears of mourning, watching while her last remaining son warmed its branches with his light."

Túlià was nearly asleep by the end of her own telling, and Kāì watched her for a bit, thinking on the story, on the mothers, sons, daughters, and angry father at its end.

She thought of her own father, wondering if he would be capable of such a thing, wondering what it would be like to shine in the sky as his last remaining sun.

Would he look at her the way he looked at Túlià's paintings? Would being his favorite feel the same if it took being his only to reach such a position of honor?

Studying Túlià's thin face, which presented a proud frown even in sleep, Kāì shook her head and closed her eyes.

No.

All the favor in the world couldn't fill the well of loneliness her life would be without Túlià.

SEVEN

"All the high ministers feared that Xórong would become the heir."

The Xórong Sea, called so because the Emperor claimed it as his own to irritate a neighboring Rajah, was beautiful in many ways. Its blue-gray waters stretched long fingers between the Sywán Mountains, which served as a stunning backdrop for the sun to rest on every evening.

This same sun watched expectantly as the Emperor's little cart, filled with its recently roused inhabitants, began moving steadily closer to their next destination at the Sea's edge.

To reach Yán sè Falls, one could go around a particularly long finger of seawater, or one could go across, and by doing so, shave as many as three days from the journey. Such a maneuver would also remove the need to stop for extra supplies in the Rajah's Capital, and better still, allowed travelers of the Empire to avoid moving through rival territory altogether.

Because the Sea belonged to the Emperor and the Mountains were considered neutral ground, aside from the odd pirate or bandit, Kāi's claim that Xórong thought the road to be safe was most likely accurate.

When they reached the Sea and were once again directed down from the cart by a white-gloved hand, Kāi and Túlià nearly ran for the large but simple home of the Dockmaster who would board them for the night.

Túlià remembered at the last moment to walk behind Kāi with her head down, displaying a respect she wasn't used to maintaining around her childhood friend.

Their knock was received by a handsome, aging face, and a rather impressive cluster of children, all clamoring with wide eyes and sticky fingers to get a glimpse of the Princess.

The sight of their reaching hands twisted Túlià's heart, reminding her how they had left the last man who dared to touch even the fabric of Kāi's robes. But their Zānshì seemed content for the moment to oversee the care of his recently acquired oxen.

"He's probably going to eat them later," Túlià muttered.

"I thought we just agreed, Zānshì don't eat. Now behave yourself," Kāi whispered over her shoulder, somehow managing to quiet the children, accept Dockmaster Mātu's invitation to dinner, and scold Túlià all at the same time.

When the evening meal arrived and their Zānshì still had not shown himself, Túlià delivered a single raised eyebrow across the table to Kāi, who frowned and pretended to spit rice at her while their hosts were distracted by a spilled glass of wine.

As if he'd heard their thoughts, one of the older children at the table asked his father permission to speak and inquired after the Zānshì.

"What is he like, Highness? Are the stories true?"

Before Kāi could open her mouth, the table began to echo with snippets of tales the children had likely gathered from past visitors to their home.

"I heard the Zānshì have dragon claws!"

"No, dragon claws wouldn't fit into their gloves, Dàshēg."

"I think they have goat feet and big curving boar teeth. That's why they must wear hoods, masks, and silly shoes."

"They cover up because of their skin," an older looking girl asserted with the authority of someone who imagined themselves nearly an adult. "It's diseased and covered in sores. The Emperor makes Zānshì hide their skin so the sickness doesn't spread to his people."

"That's silly Jiāoà. You've never even seen a Zānshì."

"Neither have you."

"I have so. And I saw his eyes too."

"You did not! Father, Wèyiú is telling fibs again."

"It isn't a fib. I can prove it. I know it happened because when I saw his eyes, the Zānshì took my soul," Wèyiú finished, returning to his plate with a look of absolute victory.

This drew a handful of chuckles from around the table, though Kāì and Túlià remained silent. Trading gossip about the Zānshì had lost its thrill the moment they'd witnessed the ever present bloodlust of Xórong's demon warriors firsthand.

Noting his guests' discomfort, Mātu quieted his children and sent them to prepare for bed, instructing his wife to show Kāì and Túlià to their chambers for the night.

The woman was quiet and pretty in the way only a mother can be. After apologizing affectionately for the behavior of all twelve of her offspring, she asked about their Zānshì as well.

"Where will it be staying tonight, Highness? Forgive me, I ask only for the sake of the children. They don't know any better."

49

"In the stables, I assume. With the oxen," Kāì added, daring Túlià to comment with a slight narrowing of her eyes.

"I will go check on him now if you wish," Túlià offered.

"Oh please don't, Painter. Not alone, not for my sake."

Kāì nodded in agreement. "Of course not Túlià. Don't be foolish. I am certain the children will be fine," she added, dismissing their hostess with a slight bow.

She waited until the woman's small footsteps rounded the corner before giving Túlià a well-deserved pinch.

"What are you thinking? It's nearly dark and you want to go wandering about the stables with a Zānshì?"

"My supplies are in the cart, which is with the oxen, in the stables," Túlià explained, rubbing the place where Kāì's gold edged nails had nearly broken through her skin.

"You want to paint? Now? But you can't even see the Mountains, not with all this fog."

"The sun is setting over the Sea."

"I don't care if the sun is setting over the moon. I forbid it."

"You forbid it?" Túlià scoffed.

"Yes."

"You can't forbid me from doing anything, Kāì."

"I can. I'm a *Princess*, in case you've forgotten. Now let's go to sleep. I can't remember the last time I was so—"

Her voice melted away, covered by the creak of the door as it swung open to reveal their Zānshì standing perfectly still between two well-dressed beds. He looked as if he'd grown roots into the floor, and clearly intended to keep watch there all night.

Kāì yanked the door shut and took a deep, calming breath.

"Actually, I think painting the sunset is a wonderful idea."

EIGHT

"They said they hoped an older and worthier one would be selected from among Fùqun's sons to be made heir."

"Is he still watching?"

Kāì opened her eyes and lifted her head from the spare bundle of cloth she'd been using as a pillow.

"Yes. He's still watching."

"You're the Princess. Tell him to go away."

"You tell him to go away. I'm sleeping," Kāì murmured, sinking back down into the thick grass, which she found to be far softer than a straw mat over dust. "Haven't you finished painting by now? It's too dark to see."

Yes. It was too dark to see. But Túlià was far from finished.

She needed this. She needed time to do what she did best, to let herself melt into the ink and spread across the curling paper. Each new coat covered her like a blanket woven from memories of her mother. Painting was the only thing that gave her peace anymore. And after days spent in the constant presence of a nightmare come to life, her coats had cracked and rubbed thin.

Túlià didn't need to see the scroll either. She could paint with her eyes closed, and often did. It was the action of painting that was perfect to her, not the finished piece. Her mother had explained it many times, but Túlià had never been able to put it into words herself until she'd come across a poem on a much older painting that hung from the walls of The Hall of Earthly Wisdom.

Trees just releasing green, streams begin to thaw. Towers and pavilions where immortals reside, in the highest register. No need for willow and peach trees to embellish the space. In spring Mountains, morning sees Life rising like steam.

Painting was about nature and thought, a meditative task that, if done right, could actually capture and convey the essence of *Life* in something as simple as ink. This was why looking at a painting after its completion was nothing in comparison to the act itself, the true moment of connection between nature and painter and ink and scroll and the flow of *Life*.

When her mother painted, Túlià had watched her hands, hardly taking the time to study her newest painting before badgering her to begin the next one. The pleasure was in doing, not in viewing.

It was for this reason that Túlià hated the royal viewings, hated seeing how people consumed her work. Because they could never know what it cost her, or what she gained, by creating. They couldn't imagine the bittersweet pain and heartrending joy of the memories she poured into her creations. They would never understand the feeling of nature and man meeting at the tip of her brush.

The experience of Túlià's viewers was like tasting a dish, something set before them without a word of explanation. They could marvel at the flavor, briefly, but they didn't know how the dish was made, or why. They didn't know how far the ingredients had traveled or how the tools of preparation cut into the hands of the creator. Most of all, they didn't know the mixture of pain and pride that came from kneeling before another and offering up the latest dish like an unbroken heart.

Even Kāi, who had been with her through the time of her mother's death, did not fully understand. So Túlià knew that to anyone who looked, her paintings were simply something beautiful.

She hated it. She hated it almost as much as she hated the Zānshì still standing a few paces behind her. Túlià refused to look at him, and simply painted until it was so dark that turning to search for his silent shape wouldn't have mattered.

The Zānshì could certainly see her though.

And if she had turned to look before the last streaks of sunlight melted away, Túlià would have seen the white petal of a dove tree held carefully between his thumb and forefinger.

NINE

*"Moreover, he loved Xórong's mother and wanted to establish him,
but he dreaded speaking about it."*

The crisp snapping of sails in the wind woke Túlià at
dawn. Brushing grass from her hair, she frowned at the
still fog-hidden Mountains and roused Kāì. They spared a
moment to step inside and wash their faces and hands
before readying to leave.

The Zānshì oversaw their things being moved from
cart to ship, a task that stopped for a moment when Kāì
decided to give the Dockmaster's children a few small treats
for their hospitality.

There was a hairpin or bracelet for each little girl. And
rather than being disappointed by Kāì's lack of marbles and
miniature kites, the boys were instead overjoyed by the
discovery of an entire basket filled with sticky rice cakes,
which were divided up between them and consumed within
minutes.

Túlià gave her many-layered painting of the sunset to
their hostess, whose quiet hospitality she found refreshing
in comparison to the smothering servants at The City.

"Thank you," she said, receiving it with a deep bow.
"This is such beautiful work."

Túlià managed a smile, endured an incredibly sticky
embrace from the smallest of the Dockmaster's children,
and boarded the ship at Kāì's heels.

As they turned toward the Mountains, Túlià nudged Kāì sharply and dipped her chin in the direction of the stables.

"Look."

"At what? I don't see anything."

"Kāì, where are the oxen?"

"Stop it Túlià, that isn't funny."

"I'm serious. I don't see them."

"He didn't eat the oxen!"

A few deckhands looked their way, causing Kāì to nervously adjust her dark braids. One of the many reasons she differed from her sisters, and so one of the many reasons why Túlià loved her, Kāì did not particularly like to be stared at.

"He was with us the whole night," she continued with significantly more control. "I won't hear another word about this."

"Fine. If you don't mind amusing yourself for a few moments, *Highness*, I'm going to make sure my inkstones have been properly stored."

When the only answer she received was an excellent view of the back of Kāì's head, Túlià left, huffing about the dramatic nature of royalty.

Her supplies were tucked into the far reaches of the hold, carefully wrapped in bits of cloth to ward off the jostling of first the cart, and now the ship. She unwrapped and rewrapped each item, sorting them into piles and making sure nothing had been left behind or damaged.

Sorting soothed her in a different way. It was one of Túlià's oldest memories. Long before she had been allowed to touch brush to silk or paper, the time she spent in her mother's Pavilion was a time of sorting. She loved separating the different tools into piles that made sense only to her.

Brushes for example, were not arranged from shortest to tallest, or tallest to shortest, but in the order she would be most likely to use them.

Halfway through placing the finely tipped brushes in close company, Túlià saw something familiar but out of place nestled between two cakes of ink.

A dove tree petal.

Had Kāì placed it there to surprise her? A petal certainly couldn't have found its way into the cart, much less into her tightly packed supplies on its own. She had only unwrapped a few of her things the previous night while painting the sunset, and there had been no dove trees nearby then.

Tucking it into her pocket, Túlià had just resolved to ask Kāì about the petal later when she heard a noise. It sounded like...retching.

She stood, peering between stacked chests and boxes until a flash of white sent her stumbling backward, dropping one of her precious inkstones to crack against the floor.

The Zānshì, seated on a crate, clutching his stomach, and leaning over a shallow pail.

Ship-made shadows surrounded him, muddling every part of his body but the mask, which seemed to capture and reflect more light than the hold contained.

A Zānshì with ship sickness? The stories had never spoken of such a thing.

As she watched, the mask turned, rose, and came toward her.

Túlià ran.

A fist caught in her hair, yanked her back, and forced Túlià to her knees. She tried to scream, but a bone-knife at her throat turned the cry for help into a whimper. The blade bit slowly deeper until she felt blood running down across her collar bone.

"Please," she choked. "I'm sorry. I saw nothing. I'm-"

The blade stopped. The Zānshì released her hair, but kept his bone-knife at her throat. Túlià choked on a second scream at the sight of his white glove in front of her face.

The Zānshì pressed a single finger to her lips, and left.

TEN

"But Fùqun was old, and he loathed any talk about the matter of succession."

Túlià emerged from the ship's hold with teary eyes, blood-stained robes, and no idea why she had been allowed to live. She was certain, at first, that the Zānshì would kill her. She had offended him somehow by seeing him in such a vulnerable state, and those who offended a Zānshì never drew breath for long after.

So why did she have nothing but a weeping red necklace to show for her insult?

Kāì nearly fainted when she saw her, but upon realizing there was no healer aboard, gathered herself together and began tending to Túlià personally.

She didn't ask who was responsible for the damage to her friend's throat. If it were one of the deckhands, Túlià would have called for help and let the Zānshì handle him. But the clean, purposeful wound, combined with Túlià's silence, told Kāì everything.

The incident with the farmers, followed by their poor driver, had shown a side of the Zānshì that her protected City life had never exposed before. She had imagined her father's soldiers off fighting in grand wars, protecting the land and its people. Kāì knew his Highness also kept a handful of guards nearby for personal protection, but always thought they were more for show than anything. What could possibly threaten him within the walls of his own City, after all?

Witnessing a Zānshì bloodbath out in the fields had opened her eyes to their true ferocity, but it wasn't until now, with Túlià's blood staining her sleeves, that she realized how dangerous and unpredictable the devil warriors could be.

She had thought them only a danger to those who were not in favor of the royal family. To Kāì, there was a clean line between enemy and friend. After the Emperor's driver, and now his Painter, Kāì understood that Zānshì drew no such line.

Her father must have been incredibly powerful and clever to maintain control of the Zānshì, but without him here, the demon she had been assigned for protection seemed to be growing more and more violent.

"From now on," she murmured, delicately winding cloth around Túlià's ruined throat, "we don't leave each other's side."

Túlià nodded, wincing at the pain it produced, and squeezed Kāì's hand.

"K—hmm."

She frowned and tried again, this time managing only a wet sounding cough.

"Túlià, what is it?"

When her friend didn't answer and only pressed both hands to her freshly bandaged throat, Kāì began to cry. Túlià joined her, tears and blood mingling on the crisp silk of both women's robes.

They held each other, weeping over demon-inflicted cruelty for the second time in two days, wondering why they had ever agreed to undertake such a dangerous journey. The moment they resolved to instruct the Captain to turn back, shouts rang out among the crew.

Someone had spotted a leak.

ELEVEN

"In Autumn, Emperor Fùqun became ill."

When Túlià imagined a leak, she thought of a chipped vase or cracked teacup. She wasn't familiar with boats, but she knew enough to see the looks on the faces of the crew and understand that this leak was far worse than a bit of broken porcelain.

Kāì took charge, guiding her to the Captain and asking just how serious the problem was.

"Not a problem, not a problem Highness," he said, giving a practiced smile and raising his hands placatingly. "We will have the leak fixed very soon."

Túlià coughed and gestured back toward the still-visible shoreline in the distance.

"She's right," Kāì agreed. "We should turn back. We are only half a day into the journey after all."

The Captain shook his head. "I'm afraid we can't. The current and winds take us toward our destination, away from Master Mātu's docks. Turning back would mean fighting against both. We have a better chance of reaching the shore ahead than the shore behind."

"What do you mean by *a better chance?* You said the leak wasn't a problem!"

Hearing the control in Kāì's voice melt into a near shriek, the Captain took a step back and began looking around for someone to assist him. When no one appeared, his head bowed under Kāi's demanding gaze, and he spoke the truth.

"Forgive me. The leak is significant and all attempts to patch it have failed. I am unsure how something like this could happen, but we have men rotating through the hold to draw water out in buckets. If the wind and currents stay in our favor, we will make it to the shore in another day and a half. Our only chance is to keep bailing the water out until then and hope we can keep up with the leak."

He bowed and left, not waiting for the possibility of another un-Princess like outburst from Kāi. But she was quiet. None of her lessons had prepared her for something like this, and her hands were hardly made for carrying buckets.

Nonetheless, she had already begun rolling up her sleeves when another cough from Túlià stopped her.

"Nn—no," she managed, nodding in the direction of the hold. When her next attempt to speak failed, she simply formed a makeshift mask with her fingers and covered all but her eyes.

"The Zānshì is in the hold," Kāi murmured, understanding at once. "Not to mention all of those deckhands. It wouldn't be safe for me down there alone, and you can hardly stand upright after all the blood you've lost."

Túlià nodded carefully and pointed to a space at the front of the ship, far from the growing clamor of men moving to and from the hold. The best they could do for the moment was to stay quiet and out of the way.

So they did.

TWELVE

"He ordered his advisors to set up Xórong as heir and to drive out other noble sons and move them away."

By sunset, the men were exhausted.

They had turned to throwing everything that was not of necessity overboard. Kāì bravely volunteered the majority of her things to this cause, keeping only a spare sash and a few hair pins that she tucked into a purse and tied around her waist. She absolutely refused to let anyone touch Túlià's small chest of painting supplies however, for which Túlià was inexpressibly grateful.

She absolutely hated not being able to speak.

Every turn of her head and every swallow brought tears to her eyes. There were no herbs aboard to ease her pain, and even if there were, no one within leagues had the proper knowledge to administer them.

So she was forced to suffer in silence, squeezing Kāì's hand much too hard while both women observed the endless stream of men and buckets who dragged themselves up from the hold, dumped their load, and returned.

Each man looked more wet, cold, and tired than the last, and watching them, Túlià had never felt so helpless. When the first deckhand collapsed, Kāì began to weep again.

They still had all night and another day to go. They wouldn't reach the shore, and everyone knew it. Quiet fell across the ship, as from bow to stern, men set down their buckets, many of them suddenly aware of the fact that they had never learned to swim.

The silence was broken by a soft cry, then a thud, as the man responsible for the noise stumbled backward over some loose rope and fell to the deck.

The Zānshì who had startled him stepped out calmly from behind the main mast, gathered up the rope, and took a handful of his strange strides to a nearby crate. Hoisting it onto his shoulder, he carried the crate, whose contents had recently been thrown overboard, to a bare spot on the deck. He brought another, then another. Once he'd gathered six crates, side by side in two rows of three, he began lashing them together with his rope.

Soft murmurs rolled around the ship as he finished, stood, and held out a hand for Princess Kāì.

The Zānshì had built a raft.

Murmurs of confusion became hopeful as one man after another realized what this meant. By the time Túlià and Kāì made their way down to the Zānshì, three other rafts were being constructed, with shouts of encouragement echoing from every sail.

When the sun began to rise the next morning, the men had been divided into groups and assigned to a raft. And with their hope providing new energy, they began bailing again, this time in two shifts. One to rest while the other worked. Still, it was slow going, and the ship sat much lower in the water than when they departed.

Túlià spent many hours in prayer, holding her pearl and sending silent wishes to the gods. For the first time she could ever remember, Kāì failed to tease her for what she had always referred to as outdated superstitions and joined her quietly. When the wind picked up and land appeared on the horizon, the two friends shared a smile so wide that Túlià wondered how it didn't pull open the new smile at her throat as well.

Renewed once more by the sight of salvation, both sets of men began bailing together as one, with even the Zānshì joining at Kāi's insistence. His knee-twisted gait looked more out of place than usual in a line of sturdy sailors, and his presence obviously made them wary, but the addition of just one well rested set of arms, human or not, helped to keep up with the steadily gushing leak below deck.

When they were within shouting distance of the docking point, an unpleasant scraping sound filled the air as the little boat ground to a halt on the seabed, its rim nearly level with the lapping waves.

Fortunately, a handful of fishermen on the bank were kind enough to use their small crafts to shuttle the contents of the Emperor's ship: passengers, Princess, paint supplies, and all, to the waiting shore.

The near-collapse deckhands seemed more than grateful not to make use of their hastily assembled rafts, even to cross the short distance to solid ground. Some of them thanked the same gods Túlià had just finished praying to, sending a flutter of familiarity through her fingertips that would only grow stronger as she approached her mother's mist-shrouded Mountains.

THIRTEEN

"When Emperor Fùqun expired, the heir Xórong was invested and he became Emperor."

Túlià, Kāì, and the Zānshì took shelter with a wealthy family who had long held favor with Emperor Xórong. Both women were happy to spend most of the day and all of the night resting after such a terrible voyage.

They didn't know where their devil guard had gone, as they had not seen him since he tried to follow into their room, only to have Kāì slam the door in his masked face.

Túlià gave her the most grateful cough she could muster before collapsing onto the nearest bed and sleeping for hours on end.

She woke to find Kāì curled up beside her, leaving the second bed in the room empty. Normally she would have berated her friend for this behavior, since Kāì knew full well that Túlià hated to be touched while she slept. It usually made her feel smothered, but for once she was grateful for the warmth and company, especially since she was fairly certain the Zānshì who had cut her throat and taken her voice stood just on the other side of their locked door.

As if a lock could stop a demon.

Shivering now, Túlià stood, checked her paint supplies, and took a few sips of water from the basin at the window. Her throat still burned like a hot knife, but the healer who had looked her over the moment she arrived, at Kāì's prompting of course, told her she was lucky to be alive, that all she truly needed was to be sewn up and well rested, and that her voice would likely return to her once the skin had fully knit itself back together.

She was grateful, certainly, but the healer's next instructions nearly drove her mad.

No talking. No sounds at all until her throat scarred. The more she tried to speak, the longer the healing process would take, and the more she risked her voice never returning at all.

Fine. Túlià would paint instead.

She knelt, spread a small scroll across the floor, raised her eyes to the window, and—

The Mountains. Oh…the Mountains.

Túlià could see them, as clear and shining in the light of the moon as the pearl tucked against her wrist.

The very air around their soaring peaks seemed to sing with age. Shadows spun across the surface, mapping the Mountains like dark veins that held memories instead of blood.

Túlià wept. First with joy, then pain, then frustration.

Joy at seeing her mother's ancestral home for the first time. Not blocked by the Emperor's walls, not shrouded by fog, but bold and full and overwhelmingly *alive*.

Pain that it had taken a lifetime to reach this place. Pain that her mother wasn't there to see the Mountains with her. Pain that they'd been separated too soon.

And frustration, because even with her scroll open, her ink ready, her fingertips itching, Túlià knew she couldn't paint the Mountains, not yet, not like this.

She needed to be *there*. The place where her ancestors walked. The place where they lived and loved and brought her mother into being. There with the Mountains beneath her and the spray of Yán sè Falls against her brow, she would kneel, and Túlià would paint.

FOURTEEN

"As Emperor, Xórong examined the wars and events of the past and investigated the principles behind their success and failure, their rise and decay."

"Túli, are you awake?"

Túlià shook her head and rolled over.

"Yes you are. Turn back here. Don't think just because you're wounded that I must be kind to you."

Túlià laughed and pressed a hand to her throat, wishing she hadn't. Rolling back slowly, she raised her eyebrows at Kāi in question.

"We need to discuss the Zānshì and our path from here on. Blink once for yes, and twice for no. Alright?"

One blink.

"Good. Do you wish to return to The City?"

Two blinks.

"But Túlià, your throat. It's another day's climb to reach the Falls and— "

Her words ended abruptly as Túlià took hold of her chin and turned her eyes toward the window.

"Oh my."

Satisfied that Kāi had been won over by the beauty of the Mountains, as she had the night before, Túlià tucked back into sleep, only to be prodded awake again.

"What should we do about the Zānshì? You can't wish to travel with him any longer."

Túlià blinked twice.

"Of course not," Kāì sighed. "But convincing him to remain behind will be no easy task…"

Trailing off into thought, she let her gaze slip back to the window, to the Mountains, to Túlià's eyes, and finally, to her ruined throat.

"Wait here," she said firmly, standing and adjusting her sleep-flattened braids. "I will arrange for a guide to take us up the Mountain, hire a few local swords for protection, and purchase a set of mules to carry you and your supplies so you won't tire so easily."

Túlià raised a single eyebrow.

"Fine, yes Túli. The mules will carry me too. Princesses aren't exactly meant to climb Mountains on foot you know. Now," she added, "all that's left is ridding ourselves of that horrid Zānshì."

When she moved for the door, Túlià stood, giving her a squeeze on the wrist and a pointed look.

"Right. We stay together. Of course."

And of course, their Zānshì waited just on the other side of the door. Clearing her throat, Kāì addressed him with all the commanding power she could manage.

"Master Zānshì, my Painter and I will continue on this journey without you. Your services and protection are no longer required. You may return to the Emperor."

The mask stared first at Kāì, then at Túlià, bowed, and left.

Both women's eyebrows raised in unison at the sight of his retreating, snake-legged pace.

"Well," Kāì whispered, "that was remarkably easy. He even bowed. Have you ever seen him show such respect before?"

Túlià shook her head and returned to their room, selecting a few things to bring into town.

"You're ready to go now? I thought you might rest first."

Túlià pointed at their unmade bed, indicating that she had, in fact, already rested.

"Alright, but I will need another nap when we return," Kāì said, making an effort to straighten the bedsheets. Pausing, she held something up for Túlià to see.

"Túli, is this yours?"

A dove tree petal.

Túlià's hand went to her pocket. She remembered putting it there just before the Zānshì cut her throat. The petal must have worked its way up to her pillow while she slept. It amazed her that such a tiny, delicate thing could survive all the trouble she had endured over the last few hours.

Head cocked, she returned her mother's flower to the paint chest beneath the window and took one last look at the Mountains, finding great pleasure in knowing they would be there for her to enjoy any time she wished.

Out of habit, both women cautiously peered through their cracked door before exiting, and were relieved to find the hallway empty. It seemed their Zānshì had finally left them in peace.

FIFTEEN

"He dangled bait before the mouths of his enemies, brazenly challenged the powerful Huns, and faced an army of a million strong."

The seaside town of Gāngko, which rested crookedly at the foot of the Sywán Mountains, was something of an in-between place. Visitors loved being able to stand with their back to the Sea and face the Mountains, then vice versa for an equally spectacular view. Aside from the land, there was also a sense of being in-between people, since the neutrality of the Mountains encouraged visitors of all sorts to gather there and trade.

The Sywán people, the Rajah's subjects, and the Emperor's citizens could all meet in relative safety. And since Gāngko had been cobbled together over a period of many years, no one was quite sure who owned it. This meant none of the three groups had sent in warriors to maintain their claim on the land. The visitors themselves were responsible for keeping the peace, and since most spent their days trying to buy or sell, shop owners were not only polite, but welcoming.

Expecting hostility for being so close to the Rajah's enemy lands, Kāì and Túlià were pleasantly surprised by those who saw them wearing the Emperor's colors and waved, bowed, or best of all, offered discounted prices.

They paid a young man to handle their needs for the Mountain journey and spent more than a few hours wandering through the hastily erected shops.

Kāì bought a salve for Túlià's throat from a medicine woman who claimed it could do all, from disinfecting a cut to curing infertility.

Túlià smiled and shook her head at Kāì's foolishness.

"What? You believe in your silly superstitions but you don't believe in the power of herbs? Honestly Túli, what am I to do with you?"

The medicine woman laughed and lifted a pale scarf from the depths of her stores.

"I'm afraid this is all I have in the way of superstitions."

"What is it?" Kāì asked, studying the scarf's intricate embroidery.

"Those, Highness, are the Five Poisonous Creatures. A lizard, spider, snake, centipede, and frog. They symbolize power over illness."

"But how can poison ward off illness?"

"I believe the idea is that poison attacks poison," the medicine woman explained before waving her hand at a cart just down the street. "If it's more superstitions you're after, you'll need to stop and see Tùfú. Tell him I sent you. He's desperately in love with me," she added with a wink.

Stifling giggles, the two women hurried on to the cart she'd indicated and began sifting through its odd collection of wares.

Tùfú, who looked decidedly younger than the medicine woman they had just left, leaned out over the cart and shook his fist.

"You'd better stop sending me all these pretty women, Yīxé, or I'll leave you. I swear I will!"

Kāì returned the good natured smile he offered his two newest customers, watching as his hand swept outward in a way that somehow managed to capture all of his wares and Yīxé's cart as well.

"I see you beauties have already met my lovely wife."

"Your wife?"

Tùfú shook his head in answer to her next round of giggles and placed a dramatic hand over his heart.

"I love her more than life itself, but she thinks the handsome face I've been blessed with gives me reason to chase after every woman who crosses my path. She sends beauties to my cart to try and catch me in the act, but she never will!" he added, loud enough for Yīxé to hear.

Her shouted answer was enough to turn even Túlià pink, which sent Kāì into another fit of stifled laughter.

"Now beauties, on to business. What can I provide for you today?"

"Yīxé said we should come to see you about my dear Painter's rampant superstitions," Kāì explained, selecting something that looked like a tiny turtle dragon and holding it up to the light.

"Ah yes, a Painter riddled with superstition. There's nothing worse, in my opinion. Superstition turns to worry, and we don't want worry tainting your beautiful work. Your mind needs to be set free. Perhaps something like this."

Pulling a small talisman from the depths of his stacked trinkets, Tùfú dangled it just in front of Túlià's nose for a moment before placing it in her palm.

She studied the symbol carefully, a single dark eye painted on glass the color of the Xórong Sea.

"That, my beautiful Painter, is from distant lands. Here, we call it the Xié. Wearing this will protect you from any negative energy sent your way. But it does not absorb the energy, oh no. Then you would have to carry all that negativity with you. Instead, the bad wishes will simply bounce off and return to the enemy who sent them."

Túlià studied the simple design, unconsciously tracing the bandage at her throat with a single finger.

The demon who plagued her thoughts was far more than a scrap of negative energy, but she couldn't seem to return the trinket to its place on Tùfú's cart. He showed her many others, copper calamus leaves, gilded bear claws, pouches of dried gourd, but the little eye stayed in her fist as she shook her head at each one, declining them all.

When Túlià opened her purse, she was met with lifted hands and bowed head from the cart's owner.

"Please, please, I could never accept payment for such a small trinket from a beauty like yourself. Just promise you will tell Yīxé I behaved myself, should she ever come asking."

In answer to his conspiratorial smile, Túlià slapped down twice what her talisman was worth onto the cart and stalked away, forcing Kāì to nearly lift her skirts and run.

"Túlià, that was rude."

Her accusation was waved aside and ignored, but Túlià did stop to let her friend catch up while pausing to tuck the little Xié deep into her paint-streaked hair, fastening it just behind her left ear.

"He was kind to us, Túli. Why are you behaving this way? You have your silly trinket, after all. Isn't that what you wanted?"

Túlià gave Kāì a look too layered to decipher, even for a person who likely knew her better than the gods. They walked past three more carts before the answer came to her.

"It's because he called you beautiful, isn't it Túli."

When she received no answer, Kāi purposely let the distance between them grow, allowing her Painter to be a good twenty paces away before shouting after her.

"Túlià," she called, her face burning pink when those nearby turned to look at her, "I think you are beautiful, the most beautiful Painter I have ever met."

Túlià spun, her own face a mixture of surprise and exasperation as she took in the sight of Kāi's attempt to appear collected under the gaze of so many strangers.

Forgetting for a moment that she wasn't supposed to speak, she tried to shout back and managed only a garbled "hmph."

But Kāi brightened at the sound, taking it as acceptance, and this time did gather up her skirts to reach her friend, raising a few eyebrows from those who had never seen royal garments so casually lifted.

SIXTEEN

"For ten days and more he did continuous battle with the Huns."

"Did you buy that for our Zānshì?"

Túlià nodded and removed the talisman for Kāì to study, tossing it across the small space between their beds.

She had insisted they sleep separately this time, knowing she would rest more soundly with greater room to stretch out. They would both need all the sleep they could manage, since their climb began just after sunrise the next morning.

The arrangements had all been made. Eight mules waited to carry themselves, two guides, three hired swords, and their few provisions up into the Mountains. It would be a day's worth of steep climbing, and as much as Túlià wanted to rest, Kāì seemed content to talk the night away, spinning the Xié above her head and nudging Túlià's eyes open with her soft, rambling voice.

"But why did you buy this one? He showed us so many, after all. I would have taken the Sichan powder. That at least you could throw in a Zānshì's eyes and run. What good is this little bit of glass? It's just a symbol."

Túlià fluttered her long fingers, making Kāì look at her, and mouthed the words until she understood and read them from her lips.

"Yes, I know Túli. *Symbols have power.* You've told me enough times. It hardly matters though. The Zānshì is gone.

We haven't seen him since I ordered his return to The City. That means this silly thing," she added, waving the little blue eye at Túlià before tossing it back, "was a waste of Father's money."

And with that lovely reminder of her dependency on Xórong, Túlià closed her eyes and tried for sleep, imagining the day she would be free of him.

She had often wondered what it would be like to simply leave, to go where she wanted, paint what she liked, and sell to whoever she deemed worthy, leaving the Emperor, and perhaps even the whole Empire far behind her.

Quite honestly, she'd never had the courage.

It was dangerous, as she'd been told, and since learned firsthand, for women to travel without escort. And even if she safely reached whatever destination she chose, Túlià would be at equal risk for the rest of her life simply by living alone and unmarried.

There was also the matter of finance. Painting supplies were expensive. Her mother had explained this enough times when Túlià had, with the carelessness only a child can possess, tipped over more than her fair share of inkstones growing up. And depending on where she lived, wealthy patrons would be few and far between. It wasn't as if the odd noodle maker or roadside fortune teller could afford to purchase a painting when the exotic materials used to create it cost more than a year of his salary.

Especially after carting through leagues of Xórong's fields, witnessing with her own eyes the thin people who worked the land and the equally thin walls they took shelter in, Túlià was beginning to understand that lower class citizens of the Empire made little in the way of profit. Their lives were spent harvesting in support of The City's lavish lifestyle, meaning they kept almost nothing from the fruits of their own labors.

So for all her displeasure at the exquisitely arching gates, well trained warriors, and ever-flowing moat that separated Túlià's life in The City from the rest of the world, she remained very much aware that her position gave her the means to do what she loved most, to paint.

With Kāì silent at last, Túlià drifted off, and dreamed of Tùfú crawling through her window and asking her to run away with him. She agreed, and spent the rest of her days painting eyes on tiny slips of glass the color of the Xórong Sea.

SEVENTEEN

"Soon, the number of enemy killed became so great that the Huns did not have time to rescue their dead or carry away their wounded."

The sun offered a beautiful shine for their climb the next morning, so with mules, guides, and painting chest in tow, Princess Kāì and her Painter set off for Yán sè Falls, arguably the most beautiful place within a hundred leagues of The City.

The Sywán believed the Falls came about when the Four Rivers were created. During a drought, the people prayed for water. Hearing them, the gods pulled the Mountains up into the sky to kill four flying dragons. When their bodies fell to earth, they formed the Four Rivers. Out of pity, the gods allowed one dragon, Sóng, the one who loved to fly highest and fastest, to lay across the Mountains as he died. In this way, when his river tumbled over Yán sè Falls, Sóng's spirit could recall the sensation of flying.

Túlià loved the story, but she wasn't here for Sóng. This climb was for her mother. She could still hear her low voice sharing the account of how Túlià's grandparents had met and fallen in love in the shadows of these very peaks.

Your Gégé was a Painter from The City, your Nana, a Sywán Silk Spinner. One day, Gégé decided to climb the Sywán Mountains and capture them with ink.

With his journey upended by rain and mud that halted every mule in his small company, Gégé took shelter in a spacious cave that he quickly learned was already inhabited by what the Empire then thought of, and mostly still does, as the backward Sywán Mountain people.

Surprised by their generosity and warmed by their welcoming nature, Gégé stayed a full day after the rain stopped, and in that time, caught the eye of your Nana, a Silk Spinner with hands that could move like the Falls themselves.

She offered to join his company and direct Gégé through paths his own guides knew nothing about. They reached the Falls easily enough, and Gégé began to unpack his inks. Nana fell in love with him the moment he touched brush to paper. She returned with him to the Empire, and soon after, I was born.

Both of your grandparents did beautiful work, and they often conspired to create pieces that joined their talents and the unique traditions of their separate peoples. To your Gégé's delight, I took to painting much more quickly than to your Nana's gifts with silk.

When word spread of your grandparents' abilities, reaching even the ears of the young Emperor, he visited us personally, bringing three carts. The first he filled with painted scrolls, the second with silks, and in the third, he placed me.

My parents knew Xórong came for beautiful things. Had they known he would take more than ink and thread, they would have hidden me away...

Before she died, Túlià's mother had spoken often of her one wish, perhaps because she knew it could never happen, and simply found joy in feeling the name of the Falls on her lips.

Pointing to the Mountains in the distance, whose tips could just be seen over the Emperor's walls from their little Painter's Pavilion in The Garden of Refined Artistry, she would say, *One day I will go there. One day I will visit the place they met. I will paint Yán sè Falls in honor of their memory and their love.*

Túlià knew her Gégé used to have his own painting of the Falls hanging above the door of her mother's childhood home, since she would finish each telling of the story by solemnly indicating the empty space above the Pavilion's entrance, saying *There, there is where mine will hang as well. Then you will see the Falls as I did, Túlià. You can walk beneath them each day and remember your people. We must never forget where we come from.*

Túlià hadn't forgotten. She hadn't forgotten the painting, or her people, or her mother, or the Emperor who took her. This journey was her chance to reclaim everything she knew about herself, to honor her mother's dying wish, and to spit in Xórong's face all at once.

She would, of course, return with a painting of Kāì, simply to keep anyone who inquired about her trip from asking too many questions. But for herself, she would not leave this journey without a treasure to hang in the empty space above her door.

EIGHTEEN

"The Hun chiefs, clad in felt and furs, began to tremble with fear."

By midday, the sun they had enjoyed so much in the morning had become an object of resentment. Kāi's pale cheeks were now in a permanent state of flush, and she was obviously making an enormous effort not to complain. She knew every reason Túlià had for taking this trip, and would rather throw herself from the Mountainside than suggest they turn back now.

She had only suggested retreat before because she feared for the lives of herself and her friend, especially after seeing what the Zānshì had done to Túlià's throat.

But the Emperor's demon was gone now, and Túlià had been using Yīxé's ointment. In just a few days, her throat would be marred by nothing more than a rather unfortunate scar.

"You should consider yourself lucky," she had told Túlià while carefully helping her apply the medicine. "Not only to be alive, but lucky that you can still paint. The Zānshì must have known it's what you love more than anything in the world. He could have taken your fingers."

Even more than she was jealous of her friend's thick hair, Kāi wished for her skill. She had seen how her father's eyes lit up at the sight of Túlià's work, how it made her sisters' faces twist with envy.

She had certainly never twisted her face at Túlià's success, but she did wonder how it would feel to have the Emperor's eyes admire her the way they did his Painter's beautiful work. Kāi had even jokingly suggested one evening that Túlià simply strip her down and cover her skin with ink as if she herself were an open scroll.

Túlià had laughed for some time before saying, "Well that would *certainly* get his attention."

Aside from refusing this foolish request, Túlià had looked after Kāi as much as her busy schedule would allow, and Kāi had done her best to return the favor. Though hard as she tried, she knew her efforts fell short. Aside from providing a listening ear or shoulder for tears when the hatred that burned in Túlià's heart became too much for her to bear, what other gifts could she possibly offer someone who possessed such skill?

The helplessness Kāi experienced in the presence of her pain-filled friend sometimes grew into a shell of inferiority she wore around her heart like a slowly cracking egg.

She knew Túlià believed she had taken up poetry simply to please the Emperor, but in truth, the greater reason had been to please Túlià. The moment Kāi learned her father liked to add poems to his Painter's creations, she threw herself into poetry in the hopes of adding a few lines to Túlià's works herself.

She wanted to be good enough for Túlià, perhaps even more than she wanted to be good enough for her father. So when she heard him insist that she take this trip with his Painter, and realized how much it would please both of them for her to participate, the shell around her heart had split and fallen away, pushed free by the sheer joy filling her blood.

This journey was all Túlià had ever wanted, and now that such a wish was in her power to grant, Kāì intended to do so if it killed her.

NINETEEN

"They then summoned their Wise Chiefs of the Left and Right, mobilized men who could draw bows, and the entire Hun nation together attacked and surrounded Xórong."

Kāì did not leave the world at the exact moment the thought left her head and settled into her heart. That would have been quite an accomplishment on the part of fate. No, Kāì's last breath would not abandon her body for at least another hour, perhaps a bit more.

It was an arrow that took her life. No one saw it coming but the Zānshì who crouched just a few dozen paces away, careful to remain downwind of the mules' delicate noses. At such a distance, he could only see the arrow, not do anything to stop its flight.

So he shouted.

The echoes of his voice ruined his every effort not to spook the mules, and spook they did, scattering riders and paint supplies across the path before bounding back the way they had come.

One guide split his head on a rock after being thrown and did not get up. The second guide was shot from behind as he ran for safety. The hired swords circled Kāì protectively, failing to notice the arrow already buried between her shoulder blades. They soon joined her in the grass, speckled with arrows from throat to navel.

It took Túlià three heartbeats to find her bearings after being thrown, and another single beat to find Kāì. She saw the arrow, and the blood, and her Painter's hands began to shake.

The ground began to shake as well, the pounding of angry footsteps nearly upending her already unsteady legs. Still, she made it to Kāì before the archers descended from their rocky perch above the pass.

Túlià ignored them, simultaneously cupping Kāì's chin and tearing through her friend's robes for Yīxé's cure-all mixture. If the herbs could reverse infertility, then surely they could reverse an arrow.

The thundering of footsteps grew louder, joined by shouts as the archers switched out their bows for clubs and spears.

Had Túlià not been distracted by the foolishness of a final hope, she would have felt the familiar prickle at the base of her neck of something less than human passing through her shadow.

The Zānshì, his snake legs moving nearly too fast to follow, had fixed himself between Kāì and the approaching bloodlust of nearly a dozen attackers.

At the far edges of her mind, Túlià heard the grunts of every man he killed. The last man's screams faded just as Kāì's eyes began to dim.

She squeezed Túlià's hand.

And then nothing.

Even after Túlià found Yīxé's medicine—even after she'd poured it, weeping, onto Kāì's bloodstained robes, her tears mingling with the herbs—even after the bottle was long past empty, though Túlià's tears were far from it, Kāì failed to stir.

She was dead.

Kāì was dead.

And though fate may be cruel, this time, it was kind enough to let Kāì's spirit leave the earth without knowing that Túlià would never paint the Falls, and that her beloved Emperor wouldn't lose a drop of sleep over her death.

TWENTY

"Xórong's army continuously fought for a thousand leagues until their arrows were all used up, and they had no avenue of retreat."

Ānjìn had taken three vows over the course of his life. The first two, made by every Zānshì just moments after being selected, were blood oaths whispered into the hem of their Emperor's gold-edged robes. After slitting his palm and spreading the source of life over his own mouth, Ānjìn swore to never remove his mask and to remain silent until his dying breath.

He had never broken his vow of silence, but his mask had come off once or twice, when he was young and wished to remember what it felt like to breathe freely again. This could only be done at night, under cover of darkness, in the safety of the room he shared with his new Zānshì brothers at the far corner of The Hall of Imperial Reinforcement. If anyone alive saw Ānjìn's face, they were to be silenced, immediately and permanently.

He'd taken his third vow much more recently, but he'd known at the time he swore it that this vow was no less important than those he'd made at the start of his service.

Bring the Princess home safely.

He'd promised his Emperor, who had smiled strangely when he did so. A smile of relief, Ānjìn decided, wondering how it felt to have someone worry for your safety.

Now, the Princess was dead, he'd broken his vow of silence, and his mask lay at the Painter's feet. One of the Mountain archers had managed to tear it off as the spasms of death wracked his body.

Careless. Ānjìn had been careless.

Careless to put so much distance between himself and the Princess, careless to let the archer's grabbing hands reach his mask, and careless not to kill the Painter the moment it landed beside her.

She knelt by the Princess, weeping, with her back to him. She only had to turn to see his face, and when she did, he would kill her as he had been trained. In that moment, it seemed to be the only part of his training Ānjìn could uphold, the only promise left for him to keep, so it was what he would do.

He stood, silent, knives raised, waiting for the Painter to finish a mourning that seemed far too long for someone who claimed to hate the royal family as much as she did.

TWENTY ONE

"Relief troops did not arrive, and dead and wounded soldiers of Xórong's Empire lay heaped in piles."

Túlià did hate her family, hated them more than anything in the world, hated them now most of all as she sat knowing it was their father's ridiculous insistence that sent Kāi's blood spilling over her hands.

I will send Kāi with you, Xórong had said, grinning at his own cleverness, filling their rooms with gowns and servants to help her look the part of a Princess.

Too proud to let people see him granting the favor of freedom from his City to a mere Painter, the Emperor chose instead to fashion the journey as a birthday gift fit for a Princess. But of course he would never allow one of his delicate flowers to travel such a great distance, so he had dressed Kāi to go instead.

With her hair braided up into crowns and her body covered in fine silks, Kāi was nearly as beautiful as a Princess, and certainly beautiful enough to fool any common folk they crossed paths with outside the walls of The City.

Beauty.

The Emperor's greatest love, and perhaps, his greatest weakness.

It was why only the eight most beautiful of his concubines' daughters earned his favor and the title of Princess.

Not being one of the eight, Kāì had served as Túlià's Attendant and companion for most of her life, never once complaining over her misfortune or questioning the Emperor's selection.

Túlià knew she was plain in comparison to most of the Emperor's daughters, just as she knew it was her paintings that had caught Xórong's eye and let her remain in The City after her mother's death. Where her sisters dabbed beauty onto themselves with expensive powders and sweet-smelling oils, Túlià brushed beauty onto silk and parchment. She had to work much harder than the eight to earn her place, but as her own private rebellion, she introduced herself as the Emperor's Painter, not his daughter.

After a while, people started to believe her, and then, to forget her, until all that remained were her paintings, most of which echoed Mountains and waterfalls of every kind, though they were mere shadows of the true Falls she had only heard of in stories and wished to one day capture with ink.

Túlià had been nudging Xórong toward letting her make the long journey to Yán sè Falls since the day she accepted her mother's passing, hoping to fulfil their only shared dream, but such a wish seemed childish now that she knelt in a spreading pool of Kāì's blood.

Her sweet companion should have been safely tucked away back at The City, and Túlià had Xórong to thank that she wasn't.

Ancestors forgive this hatred.

With her Painter's fingers unsteady for perhaps the first time in her life, Túlià carefully closed Kāì's eyes and stood, her foot catching on something in the dusty earth.

A white mask.

She picked it up, studying the carefully painted seal of the Emperor where its mouth should be. The mask was heavier than she'd imagined, made of something unfamiliar to her. If she were a sculptor or potter, she might be able to guess, but ink was all she knew. Turning the mask over, Túlià was surprised to see the shine of moisture covering its smooth, inside edges.

But the Zānshì didn't sweat.

She couldn't be sure of this, but it felt right, at least until she looked at his true face.

Her Zānshì, the assigned protection for this journey, the one tasked with their safe return, the one who had let an arrow take Kāì, was most certainly sweating.

TWENTY TWO

"But Xórong with a single shout encouraged his troops, and there was not a single man who failed to rise up weeping."

Ānjìn watched the Painter pick up his mask with long, delicate fingers. They were still covered in the Princess's blood, and left pink prints where her skin made contact with the white glaze. Then, the Painter looked at him.

It took exactly four beats of his quickening heart for understanding to fill her eyes, for her to realize what their Emperor had done. He watched her disbelief, watched her insist on searching his face for what he knew she wouldn't find.

Ānjìn had heard the rumors of course. Curling teeth, diseased skin, eyes even a dragon couldn't meet. He knew them all, just as he knew the one thing that people who spread such gossip didn't know: their source.

These rumors, these stories, the fear, awe, and respect they granted him, all came from one man. The people spoke true when they said the Emperor thought himself clever, but the greater truth lay in knowing that he *was*.

Incredibly clever.

Dangerously clever.

Clever enough to take orphaned boys off the streets and train them to be exceptional warriors. Clever enough to cover their faces and make them into a weapon that harnessed the most powerful sort of fear, that of the unknown. Clever enough to spark rumors, to send whispers to the ears of the most accomplished gossips, the drunken storytellers and frustrated mothers who used tales of the monstrous Zānshì to shock their shipmates and scare their children to sleep.

In this way, the story spread to every kingdom, and respect for the Emperor grew as fast as the mounting fear of his elite guard, his untouchable ghost army, his all powerful Zānshì, who in truth were nothing more than street boys with masks over their faces and bone-knives in their hands.

Túlià realized enough of this in time to understand why the boy lifted his knives above her head, preparing to bring them down into her death-broken heart. No one could know he was just a boy, a boy with plain dark eyes, shorn black hair, and a perfectly normal mouth. No one could know the Emperor's greatest secret.

"The Princess is dead."

He *could* speak, though his voice, rough from lack of use, came nearly as chipped as hers.

The Princess? Túlià's mind danced in near madness, spinning to tether pieces of things she knew to things she didn't.

He thought Kāi was a true Princess. He'd said so.

To him, Kāi's death would mean his failure in the eyes of the Emperor.

According to legend, Zānshì who failed the Emperor were to take their own life in the only way their life could be taken, by a double bone-strike to the heart. It had to be done with human bone, which is why some said the Emperor allowed his demons to carry such gruesome weapons, as a constant reminder of both their strength and what would happen if they failed him.

This boy meant to kill her for seeing his face.

Then he would kill himself for failing Xórong.

"Wait."

He did. Neither of them understood why, but Ānjìn did wait.

With both hands over her aching throat, Túlià forced the words out past her lips.

"Kāi...is not—a Princess."

The boy seemed to become even more still.

"What?"

"She—is an Attendant. My Attendant," Túlià continued, eyes spilling over with the pain of each word.

"But she called our Emperor *Father*."

"Xórong is...her father—and mine. Her mother—was a concubine. My mother was his...Painter."

"Blood daughters."

Túlià nodded. Blood daughters. The offspring Xórong didn't claim as Princesses, named so because they possessed his blood alone, not his favor or his love.

"You deferred to her," the boy went on, confusion weighing the tips of his bone-knives. "You treated her like a Princess. She dressed like a Princess. And you don't call our Emperor *Father*."

"Because I hate him," Túlià spat, whimpering when the angry words tore at her throat in new places. She needed at least a dozen careful breaths to recover before addressing the distraught boy again.

"Kāi and I did...what we were told. She was to be a Princess—for the entirety of the journey, and neither of us was...was to breathe a word otherwise."

When she finished, the boy passed both bone-knives to a single hand, raised his arm, and struck Túlià cleanly across the temple. She managed one last thought before darkness took her.

Why had a Zānshì charged with protecting a false Princess not been told Kāi's true identity?

TWENTY THREE

"Faces spattered with blood, they swallowed their tears."

When Túlià opened her eyes and tried to sit up, there were two kinds of pain, the second much worse than the first.

Her body ached all over, her throat especially.

And Kāi wasn't there.

When she remembered the events of her bloody passing, Túlià realized her throat felt nearly as raw from crying as it did from the Zānshì's blade.

The Zānshì.

Túlià looked around, searching the small, dark space for any sign of the demon charged with protecting her, and Kāi.

Struggling to see through a fresh wave of tears, Túlià found little relief in noting the Zānshì's absence.

She hoped he was dead.

Why wasn't *she* dead? He was going to kill her, the Zānshì-boy. That was the last thing she could remember, his dark eyes studying her with a frightening indecisiveness.

A fire burned in the cave, near the mouth. Though small, the flames were agonizingly cheerful.

Túlià stood, finding just enough strength to stamp it out before returning to her place at the back of the cave.

She laid down, regretting that she had smothered her only light source when something pressed into her spine. A few careful sweeps of her hand revealed a crate, splintered but still intact, with a small collection of achingly familiar objects piled on and around it.

Her paint supplies, or at least, what was left of them after the Sywán attack.

Why had they attacked?

Túlià's tears seemed as endless as the Falls themselves.

It didn't matter why a supposedly peaceful people had attacked them. The fault fell on Túlià regardless. It had been her desire to take this trip. She had put Kāì at risk by allowing her accompaniment. She knew the dangers. She should have insisted Xórong choose another to travel with her. Kāì should be waiting for her back at The City, safe and bursting with questions about her journey.

Instead, Kāì's *Tián* had passed on, leaving the other half of her spirit trapped on earth without a proper burial.

Forgive me.

She wanted to get up, to move, to find Kāì and care for her as best she could. But her throat hurt too much to breathe, and her legs seemed far away, heavy, useless.

Sleep. She needed sleep. In the morning, Kāì would receive as close to proper burial rites as Túlià could manage.

TWENTY FOUR

"Drawing empty crossbows, braving the naked blades of the enemy, and facing north they fought to the death against the foe."

Ānjìn watched the Painter.

He watched her sleep. Then, he watched her wake up.

It felt strange to look at her again through the holes of his mask now that he had seen her face without it cupping the edges of the world away.

The Painter took much too long to rise.

Her eyes seemed stuck; her movements slow.

She was in pain.

It made her frown, or he made her frown.

She sat up, finally, looked at his mask, looked at him, and made a rude gesture with her hand.

Ānjìn didn't move. Neither did the Painter.

When she tried to speak, her throat made a sound like flaking bronze.

She coughed, hands at her scar, and coughed again.

He watched her.

She hated him.

Hated him for taking her voice. Hated him for letting them take Kāì. Hated him for putting his ridiculous mask back on.

She managed to speak the next time she tried, massaging the word from her throat with long fingers.

"Water."

Again, Ānjìn didn't move.

Had someone managed to remove his mask a second time, it would have revealed the same uncertain expression on his face that had so frightened Túlià the moment before he struck her.

Zānshì were never indecisive. The proper action always came to them, immediately and without thought. Their training prompted the response that would best please their Emperor, only now, Ānjìn was no longer certain what that response should be.

His Emperor would not be pleased that Ānjìn had let the Princess die.

But the Princess had not truly been a Princess.

His Emperor would not be pleased that the Painter had seen his face.

But the Painter said she was one of the Emperor's daughters, a member of the royal family, though not a Princess either.

Ānjìn had been told by a General, who repeated orders directly from the Emperor, that the one called Kāì was a Princess and that the one called Túlià was nothing more than a Painter.

Would the Emperor care that Kāì, the false Princess, had died under his watch?

Would the Emperor care if Ānjìn killed Túlià, the Emperor's own blood?

A member of the royal family had never seen a maskless Zānshì, not to Ānjìn's knowledge. Were they to be killed for such an offense in the same way as the common folk?

And why, why had Ānjìn not been told who he was truly protecting?

I don't think I want to be a Princess any longer.

You can't forbid me from doing anything, Kāi.

He'd heard them speak of it. They knew the truth. He should have known as well, or should have reached such a conclusion on his own. But he hadn't.

He should have seen them, not as a Princess and a Painter, but as two members of his Emperor's lower court. They were only blood daughters, not chosen as Princesses, but shared royal blood all the same.

The Painter, still massaging her throat, spoke again, a bit more clearly.

"Take that…off," she coughed, pointing at his mask. "I—know."

She was angry, and she wanted water.

Ānjìn could get water.

Or he could kill her.

If he failed to get water, would she die on her own?

The Zānshì stood and left the cave, pretending not to hear the soft clink of the Painter pulling a scrape-knife from the pile of battered art supplies he'd collected while she slept.

TWENTY FIVE

"Until finally, the lords and ministers of the Empire could all raise their cups and toast Xórong's victory, which even the famous generals of antiquity could not surpass."

When Túlià woke again, it was light outside, though she couldn't guess if she had slept only a short while or all through the night a second time.

The Zānshì-boy was still there, his mask still on, and he still watched her.

Water sat in a cup near her knees.

She drank it greedily.

"More."

He took the cup, left, and returned, leaving again three more times until Túlià was satisfied.

"How many days...since we were—attacked?"

The Zānshì-boy held up two fingers. She wanted to strike him.

Why didn't he just speak to her? She knew he could. And why did he not remove that awful mask now that she'd seen his face?

Túlià thought of Xórong, his Zānshì, his lies. She didn't know most of the details, but she didn't need to. It had become obvious to her the moment she saw the Zānshì's maskless face that the Emperor was nothing more than a charlatan who dressed his warriors up in silly costumes and

117

spread lies about their monstrous nature to scare his subjects into submission.

She hated him.

He should be dead in Kāi's place.

Oh, Kāi.

Túlià tried and failed not to let tears fall in front of the Zānshì-boy.

Two days, he'd said. Two days of Kāi's *Táng*, the earthly half of her spirit, waiting for proper care.

Túlià put a hand on her throat, used her other hand to steady against the wall, and stood.

"Take me to her," she rasped.

He didn't move.

Túlià tried again, rasping louder.

This time he stood, but instead of leading her through the mouth of the cave, blocked it with his body.

Fresh angry tears mixed with the wet sorrow already sitting on her cheeks.

"She needs tending. A burial."

The Zānshì-boy shook his head, his shoulders tightening when Túlià pulled the scrape-knife from her hair. He pointed at the fire, which he'd rekindled while she slept.

"Let me through."

He pointed again, indicating the glowing embers with barely noticeable frustration.

Well past frustration, Túlià advanced on him with clumsy legs and knife outstretched.

He's only a boy.

Boys bled if you stuck a knife in them. The Zānshì-boy would move or bleed. Kāi needed her.

Túlià aimed for his throat, just under the chin of his mask, hoping he might suffer as much as she had. When her blade was a hand length away from the white cloth that covered every inch of his skin, it disappeared.

A pluck and toss that happened too quickly for Túlià to see, given away only by the plink of the knife settling back into its little pile of painting supplies.

"I burned her."

Túlià blinked through unshed tears and confusion.

"You what?"

"I burned the false Princess," he said again, his rough voice muffled beneath the mask.

Túlià went still.

Burned. Kāi had been burned. Not buried. Burned. By a Zānshì.

She struck him.

Or rather, she tried to.

And instead found herself in the same position as the day she'd lost her voice, knees to the floor, hair in his fist, a bone-knife at her throat.

"Don't," he said, sounding more irritated than angry. "Don't do that."

He let go, and Túlià collapsed, shaking.

"How could you *burn* her?"

He stowed his knives. "It is the Zānshì way."

Túlià tried to weep, she wanted to this time, since tears were the only mourning she could offer Kāi now, but it seemed her tears had finally run out, leaving her with nothing more to do than think of Xórong's awful, sharp cleverness as she returned to her place at the back of the cave.

Of course Zānshì bodies must be burned. Xórong couldn't risk some curious enemy digging up a Zānshì grave pit and learning his wicked army was made of nothing more

119

than human flesh. A dead Zānshì could still give away the Emperor's secret if someone removed even a single mask.

Yes, they had to be burned, or Xórong would burn.

How she wished she could burn him, him and all his Zānshì-boys.

TWENTY SIX

"Now Xórong rose and the world was united."

Did all Painters sleep as much as his?
Ānjìn selected a smooth pebble and tossed it.
She grumbled.
He tossed another.
Her eyes opened.
"Are you throwing *stones* at me?"
Her voice sounded better. The water must have helped.
Ānjìn nodded. "You don't like to be touched."
The Painter stared at him, open-mouthed for a moment, before barely concealing a shudder.
Of course he knew that.
He watched her sit up. She rummaged through her paints for a bit, emerging with a bundle of sticky cloth. Rice cakes she'd tucked away what felt like ages ago.
"What should I have done?"
She looked up sharply, hating his mask.
"Done?"
"For the false Princess."
"Stop calling her that!" she barked. "Her name is Kāì."
"What should I have done for Kāì?"
"Why do you care? It hardly matters now."

Ānjìn didn't answer. The Painter finished her cake, wiped her mouth, and began to draw in the soft earth of the cave.

"A Mountain," she murmured, tracing the single, proud hump of earth. "Kāì deserved a Mountain grand enough for any queen. Inside, rivers of mercury would surround her like the rulers of legend. Her coffin," she continued, adding a slender box amid the winding rivers, "would be layers upon layers of gold, silk banners painted with her story between each shell. And for protection, a suit of jade to keep out evil spirits and an army of clay soldiers to guard as many riches as it takes to fill the Mountain."

Ānjìn leaned in to study the dusty drawing for a moment, frowning under his mask.

"I wanted to keep the birds away."

"Birds?"

"Yes. The birds and animals took everyone else."

The Painter said nothing for a long while, staring at her little Mountain tomb, then nodded.

Both remained silent, until with a rasping sob, Túlià asked the worst of the many questions that had been eating at her heart since Kāì's passing.

"Why did they attack?"

Her grandmother's people. Her mother's people. She couldn't fit the image of the vicious men, their arrows and blades, with the stories her mother had shared. The Mountain people were meant to be peaceful.

"The Sywán are not peaceful," Ānjìn muttered, echoing a twist of her thoughts. "We were always told so."

"Told by who?"

"The Generals."

"Generals?"

"They train us, lead us."

Túlià swallowed around her scar.

"Would the Generals have told the Emperor?"

"Yes."

The question confused Ānjìn nearly as much as the Painter's dust drawing. Of course the Generals reported directly to Emperor Xórong, and received their orders directly from him as well.

"He knew then," she whispered, clutching the cloth of her sleeves in long, dirty fingers. "Xórong knew the Mountain people had become a danger and he encouraged this journey regardless. He *knew.*"

Ānjìn was unsure how to react to this.

It couldn't have been an oversight on the part of his Emperor. He didn't make mistakes. And he did all things for the betterment of the Empire. Ānjìn didn't know how sending a pair of blood daughters into enemy lands would better the Empire, but it wasn't his place to ask such questions, only to serve.

Perhaps his Emperor had simply thought Ānjìn would be protection enough from the Sywán.

Then he failed. It seemed whatever the case may be, Ānjìn had failed in some way or another.

He knew what a failed Zānshì was meant to do, since in failing his Emperor, he had failed his only purpose and lost his right to breathe. His Emperor usually made such commands himself, however, wanting to witness the Zānshì's final punishment.

Ānjìn had been foolish to consider ending his life so early, panicking at the realization that the Painter had seen his face. After all the ways he had failed, he needed to kneel before his Emperor, receive his sentence, and take his own life properly.

"We can't stay here, Painter."

She stood. "Where should we go?"

"Back to Gāngko. You need food and rest, yes?"

"Yes."

Ānjin pointed over her shoulder at the splintered crate and all its contents.

"Your painting supplies?"

She looked for a long moment before turning her back. "Leave them."

TWENTY SEVEN

"Once he had achieved his ends and fulfilled his desires, Xórong believed that there had never been anyone like him."

It should have taken half as long going down the Mountain as it had to travel up, but without food in her stomach or a mule to carry her, Túlià was very much aware of each and every step she took.

The Zānshì-boy never looked back to see if she needed assistance or to make sure she kept up. He likely didn't need to. A boy he may have been, but a well-trained one, with ears better than any mule. The sounds of her breathing and the steps of her swollen feet were all he needed to track the movements of her body.

About halfway through their descent, Túlià briefly considered collapsing, but the thought of the Zānshì-boy carrying her replaced the dizziness in her eyes with a fierce stubbornness that would have made Kāì shake her head.

There's no shame in accepting a man's help, Túli.

"He isn't a man," Túlià muttered out of habit, forgetting briefly that he was in fact, only a man. A man who could hear her, she remembered too late, when his mask did turn back. He didn't answer though, neither in confirmation or contradiction to her mutterings, and continued forging ahead.

Forging was perhaps the wrong word, since no part of the path seemed to get in the way of his snake legs. Túlià wondered if this strange sort of walking was another insistence on Xórong's part. She shuddered, watching the white-wrapped limbs twist around and over the rocks on the path, convincingly monstrous in every sense of the word.

They stopped at a Mountain-chilled stream and Túlià watched, curious to see if he needed water as badly as she did, wondering if he would remove his mask to drink. But he seemed to know just what she wanted, and waited until she felt she'd die unless she knelt and drank. If he joined her, Túlià would never know, since he stood just as still when she rose to leave as he had when they first reached the stream.

Gāngko's jumble of seaside structures came into sight before they had taken another ten steps, and Túlià nearly wept at the thought of spending the night in a proper bed, not curled into the cold of a dark cave with nothing to warm her but the breath of a false monster on her back.

Not long after, Túlià's feet moved from broken bits of rock to the packed earth of civilization, giving her a burst of strength that left the Zānshì-boy behind her. She would have forgotten him completely if not for the downcast eyes of those who passed them, avoiding his mask, the reach of his hands, his creeping shadow.

Such behavior seemed more than strange to Túlià now that she knew the Zānshì secret. How could people show this choking mix of terror and respect to a boy only a year or two past his first shave? She wanted to laugh, but couldn't. There was nothing funny about what Xórong had done, forcing his people to live in fear of the very soldiers that protected them.

It wasn't right.

Túlià wondered for a moment what would happen if she turned, pulled off the Zānshì's mask, held it high for all to see, and shouted Xórong's secret as loudly as her ruined voice could manage.

The Zānshì-boy would kill her, of course. He would kill her and probably everyone in Gāngko, leaving no one better off for her sacrifice.

So Túlià ignored her ever-present Zānshì shadow and walked to the nearest respectable house. The moment she stood in the shade of its earthen walls, she stopped, legs threatening to crumble under the weight of her most recent realization.

She had no coin to pay these people, nothing to give in return for food and lodging. In fact, she had nothing at all in regard to possessions, aside from the robes she wore and the paintbrushes in her knotted hair.

"Well, that looks like one of mine, and to see such a pretty miss wearing it—"

The man's words were cut short as two bone-knives came to rest on either side of his heart. He went still and white, his hand frozen halfway to the Xié in Túlià's hair.

It took a moment for her to recognize the face of the man who sold her the little blue talisman, as it looked so different now without the cheer he'd displayed at his cart.

"Forgive me, Zānshì," he whispered. "The Painter has come onto my property and I did not know she was under your protection."

The bone-knives waited for Túlià to wave them away before their holder retreated to whatever shadows he'd been hiding between when the cart owner came around the corner of his home.

"Yes, I remember you," Túlià rasped. "But your name I can't recall."

"Tùfú," he said, managing a smile as he rubbed at the fresh pricks in his ribs. "You met my sweet wife and came to visit my cart a few days past. I see Yīxé's herbs have done wonders for your wound," he added, nodding at her scar necklace. "But if you don't mind my saying so, the rest of you looks as though you were rolled down the Mountain like a cart wheel."

Túlià nodded wearily and almost smiled at the accuracy of the statement. When she gave no answer to his questioning look, Tùfú moved to take her arm, then thought better of it, gesturing toward his home instead.

"Would you care to come inside? Yīxé doesn't often let me bring such pretty girls to visit, but she never turns away a traveler in need of a meal and a bath."

No longer trying to cover her exhaustion, Túlià accepted his invitation with a nod and followed his tall frame into the simple but clean home. Yīxé looked up from stirring two identical pots with a long-handled spoon and began shaking her head at Tùfú's wide grin.

"You've brought me a girl?"

"And a rabbit," Tùfú countered, passing his wife the freshly skinned animal.

She accepted it with a *hmph* of contentment, and after studying the two pots for a moment, tossed the rabbit in the left-most brew.

"Where is the other then?"

"Other?"

Yīxé raised her brows and spoon at Túlià.

"The other girl you traveled with."

Túlià suddenly couldn't think of anything but the pink flesh of the rabbit turning round and round in its stew, and barely made it back outside before spilling the single rice cake she'd consumed onto the earth.

The Zānshì-boy was at her side in an instant. She saw his shadow before she saw him, and was amazed to hear Yīxé shooing him away from over her shoulder.

"Go on devil. This is woman's work. I'll look after her."

Túlià let Yīxé's sturdy hands half carry her back into the house, and didn't have the strength to complain when the Zānshì followed. Her hostess seemed more than unhappy with his company, but even Yīxé's inner fire seemed to have its limits. She ignored his white form in the corner and fussed over Túlià with a manner that somehow managed to be both rough and gentle.

After checking the scar at her throat, she brushed Túlià's hair, cleaned her nails, gave her a few spoonfuls of blessedly rabbit-free broth, and made her up a bed of blankets near the hearth.

Like everything else in the space, the blankets were old and worn, but had been carefully scrubbed clean. She lay there, dozing, while Yīxé prepared her herbs and Tùfú sorted his wares. They spoke softly to each other, sharing and jesting in a way that Túlià had never seen between two people. It reminded her a bit of the way she and Kāi had teased one another, and her heart ached.

Just before she reached the deep sleep she'd been craving since her first awful night in the cave, talk turned to the Emperor.

"...a deckhand said he's more than certain."

"You know how deckhands talk, Tùfú. Their tongues are as good with gossip as their hands are with rope."

"But I heard the same from a merchant's wife who stopped at my cart the following day. There is unrest in The City."

"Unrest," Yīxé scoffed, rolling another set of herbs between her palms. "I shouldn't say I'm surprised."

"And in the outlying towns and fields as well."

"Hmm."

"The people are whispering."

"Yes, I'm sure they are."

"Grumbling."

"Of course."

"They are called ungrateful by the Emperor's supporters."

"Ungrateful? How so?"

"They should appreciate all the Emperor has done."

"Such as?"

"He chose the language and measurements."

"Made my old scales worthless you mean."

"He's already begun work on the Grand Wall."

"Not sure what good that will do."

"And the roads are better than they've ever been."

"You make him sound like a god."

"He isn't. There are no more gods, remember? He did away with them all."

This jest pulled quiet laughter from both their throats.

"Of course," Yīxé chuckled. "The Emperor banished all religions to be replaced with his own. What is it he calls his new form of rule?"

"*Legalism*, which claims absolute control by the Emperor, clearly defined punishment as the means of enforcement, and destruction of anything considered *socially unproductive*," Tùfú recited, finishing with more laughter.

"Apparently taxes are not considered socially unproductive, since I hear they have reached new heights under Emperor Xórong's rule."

130

Tùfú nodded in agreement, but froze when the Zānshì stood slowly from his crouched position in the corner. Túlià realized her hosts had forgotten his presence, their eyes moving past him just as he wished, until they spoke more freely than they ever would in the face of what they believed to be a demon warrior.

Tùfú shifted his position a bit to place himself between the Zānshì and his wife, who gripped her spoon much more tightly now.

Túlià sat up, wanting to tell these kind people not to be afraid, that she knew what they were thinking, and that the Emperor didn't really possess the power to bind devils to his will.

Half asleep, she forgot the dangers of sharing such a secret, and the lives of Tùfú and his wife were saved only by a groaning at their door.

TWENTY EIGHT

"This was the moment for demonstrating authority and proving one's merit as a ruler, laying the foundation for lasting peace in the Empire."

"**D**on't let him in, Yīxé."

"Of course I'm not going to let him in, stupid. I never do."

"Yet you always open the door."

"Only to throw him food," she grumbled, retrieving a bit of bread and moving toward the source of the groaning sound.

The Zānshì made it to the door before she did, one hand on his bone-knives. Túlià watched, wide awake now, wondering if she would have to stop him from hurting someone again, wondering if she *could* stop him. Her kind hosts had done nothing to deserve any punishment, but Túlià knew such a thing was trivial to the boy beneath the mask.

"Who is at the door?" she asked, remembering to clear the worst of the sleep thickness from her voice so they could better understand around her scarred throat.

"A Tattoo," Tùfú answered, pausing to draw a protective sign across his chest.

Standing now, Túlià drew in a soft breath of disbelief, feeling suddenly grateful for the Zānshì's presence.

"Stay there girl. Tùfú will open the door, I'll toss the bread out, and the door will shut. This whole mess should end quickly and you can return to your sleep."

Hearing what they planned to do, Túlià's Zānshì moved away from the couple and back toward her, knives pointed at the door.

Their hosts exchanged a look, readying themselves before drawing back the latch.

The door burst open, knocking aside Yīxé's bread and husband. Something man-shaped came through the opening, snuffling a bit until it saw the bread. Crawling across the floor, he paused over it, hunkering and snatching and eating with obvious delight.

This time, Yīxé, spurned by anger at the intrusion into her space, reacted more quickly than the Zānshì, and began beating the thing across its head with her mixing spoon.

It wasn't until he raised his arms to defend himself that Túlià felt her stomach sicken for the second time that day.

The skin of his arms, his face, and according to legend, the rest of his body as well, was crawling with creatures too vile to look upon. Runes and beasts and words of death writhed across the surface of his body, so covered in ink, it was hard to tell where his skin stopped and the creatures began.

Yīxé's frantic strikes knocked back the once-man's hood, and the sight of his eyes, spinning with madness and surrounded by the gaping, inky mouths of the Four Evil Creatures of the World, drew a whimper from Túlià that pulled those eyes straight to her.

They sparked with recognition, and the once-man spoke.

134

"Painter, Painter. Brushes in your hair. Brushes and scrolls. I remember you. At The City. Yes, at The City. Didn't he kill you though, didn't he?"

An ink-darkened hand stretched toward her, reaching for the brushes in her hair. Túlià couldn't take her eyes from his, as the words spilling from his rune-covered lips twisted around her ears.

She had never met this creature. How could he remember her? And what had he meant about someone being killed?

"Pretty Huàjā with your pretty paintings. Pretty pretty."

The Zānshì drove a bone-knife through each of the man's reaching palms. His shriek of pain woke Tùfú, who stood, clutching his bloodied head, and added a handful of poorly aimed kicks to the spoon strikes still raining down on the Tattoo's body. The combined assault of husband, wife, and Zānshì became too much for the creature, and clutching his bread between bleeding hands, he scuttled out into the night.

Túlià followed him.

It was madness, she knew, but the words he'd uttered seemed to be eating a hole through her chest that made breathing next to impossible.

Her mother. This Tattoo, this once-man, knew her mother's name.

He had seen the brushes in her hair and confused Túlià with Huàjā.

And he said someone had killed her.

Following the Tattoo was easy. She stayed just far enough behind to both keep him in sight and keep him from seeing her under the moon glow of the late evening. Boldened by the Zānshì shadow melting into hers, Túlià trailed the once-man down streets she never would have braved on her own.

For whatever reason, the Zānshì-boy had decided it was still his duty to protect her, and as much as she hated him, Túlià would take full advantage of that duty, despite knowing his loyalties could change at any moment.

So she chased the Tattoo's tainted skin further and further, studying him with eyes and ears as she walked, desperate for another morsel of information about her mother.

He stopped once, crouching beneath a candlelit window to wrap strips of tattered robe around his hands. Túlià forced herself to look away from his evil markings and search elsewhere on his person for some hint of his identity.

Shoeless, filthy, and mostly covered by the robe, he gave away so little that Túlià had nearly given up when she noticed what covered his head. A simple cap, knotted at the back with two slips of cloth hanging freely against his neck.

A Scholar. This once-man had once been a Scholar.

A Scholar to the Emperor, no less. He would have lived in The City, at The Hall of Earthly Wisdom. That would explain how he knew of her mother. But what of her death? Túlià crept closer, barely stifling a shriek when gloved fingers closed around her wrist.

"It isn't safe here, Painter."

"I know that," Túlià hissed, pulling herself free.

"Then why do you stay?"

"Because—"

She paused wondering how much to tell him, knowing he couldn't possibly understand.

Because she'd lost her mother a year ago.

Because it had supposedly been a terrible accident.

Because a maddened Tattoo had just suggested otherwise.

"It's none of your business, demon. Follow if you like, but don't get in my way."

He nodded, and vanished into the shadows.

Túlià's eyes returned to the once-man just in time to see him slip through a doorway, the sight of which made Túlià swear across every vile being she knew.

A Hovel. It had to be a Hovel.

She only knew of the wretched lìngdìng houses through City gossip, since some of the royalty liked to indulge occasionally and would send runners out to acquire the incense for them once darkness came.

Túlià had mistakenly wandered into a lìngdìng gathering once, when a few servants had gotten hold of the expensive drug and almost died from overconsumption in a storage room. She had gone to retrieve another set of jars to hold her mother's brushes, and returned with swimming eyes and a sickened stomach.

She recognized the smell now, and knew to cover her mouth and nose the moment she passed through the doorway.

Tiptoeing around limp bodies, Túlià swam further into the smoke, searching for the Tattoo through downcast eyes. Her whole body shook with the wrongness of this venture. A woman of her status had no place here. If not for her Zānshì, she never would have—

An uncertain sort of coughing turned Túlià's gaze back in the direction she'd come. The Zānshì-boy stood slightly behind her, his head tipped in a way that made him look more boy than devil, even with his mask. He took a step toward her, wobbling a little, and dropped one of his bone-knives.

Realizing his trouble, Túlià filled with frustration. A boy indeed. The fool hadn't thought to cover his mouth, and the hard edges of a mask were no help against a vapor that could twist through your nostrils and straight into your mind.

The Tattoo had vanished among the numbed bodies, and Túlià knew she had no hope of finding him unless she were willing to lift the head of every wasted figure in the Hovel and check their faces for ink. And now it would seem, her protection had vanished more quickly than a curl of smoke.

With panic tightening in her chest, Túlià made for the door, reluctantly taking her Zānshì by the arm and half carrying his useless weight out into the street. She hoped to get him back to the home of their hosts, to let him lie there for a while until he could breathe in enough free air to wash the lìngdìng from his body.

"Would you...let me call you Túlià?" he murmured. "Túlià. Túlià. It sounds better than Painter."

She shushed him, worried what would happen if someone heard the lìngdìng-slurred speech of a Zānshì. Her worries flared to worse when she heard drunken voices around the next corner.

Burdened by the Zānshì's clumsy weight, she could only stand beside him in the near middle of the street as four, foul smelling men wearing the colors of the Rajah stepped into their path.

They leered at her, taking in the sight of her knee-buckled Zānshì, laughing and sloshing whatever liquid had dulled their minds and soured their breath.

When she was pulled from his side and the first fist sent blood running out from beneath her Zānshì-boy's mask, all Túlià could think was *four men, death*.

TWENTY NINE

"So Xórong said — As from the stump of a felled tree there are sprouts and shoots, Heaven will perpetuate its decree in our favor in this new City."

When Ānjìn woke, he knew he wasn't moving because it hurt too much to do so, yet he was moving, or something moved beneath him. A cart?

His face was bare.

He opened his eyes, already reaching for his bone-knives, and finding them missing, had his tied hands around the Painter's throat before her familiar smell held him short.

"Off," she grunted, pushing her feet into his bruised chest, until, wheezing, he retreated to his corner of the cart, where they studied each other warily.

She had his mask in her hands, bound as well, and looked ready to batter him with it, so her next words surprised him.

"How is your pain?"

Ānjìn shifted a bit, testing his limbs and searching for the worst wounds.

"Zānshì don't feel pain."

An odd smile pulled at her lips and she began to turn the mask over and over with long fingers.

"Liar. I watched them beat you and I know you suffered."

139

Ānjìn shook his head. "I don't remember. Did I speak?"

"No. They don't know your secret if that's what you're truly asking."

The men driving the cart, yes. He could smell them now too. Their scent was just familiar enough to stir free the events of the previous night. He had smelled something strange then, something new. The world had started to dance, and the Painter was all he had to hold onto. The men took her away and beat him, then put him in a cart.

"Where are they taking us?"

"They didn't say. Not in our language, at least. But they wear the colors of the Rajah."

Ānjìn nodded. "Then they are taking us to the Rajah. Prepare yourself, Painter. We will most likely be tortured," he added.

"Tortured?

"Yes."

She clutched his mask to her chest, and for a moment he considered asking for it back. As much as he enjoyed breathing without it, his naked face felt strange to the air's touch. For reasons he couldn't explain, however, he liked the sight of the mask in her hands, and decided to let it there.

These men would want to know his Emperor's secrets. He'd kill himself before that happened, but taking his life wouldn't keep the Rajah from taking his mask. He needed to stay alive to make sure his face remained covered for as long as possible.

"Painter, protecting our Emperor is what matters most. If these men learn his weaknesses—"

"To Judgement with the Emperor. I'll tell the Rajah where Xórong keeps his royal soap if that's what he wishes to know. The Emperor has done me no favors. I don't owe him protection."

Then Ānjìn should kill her.

But he didn't want to.

Maybe they wouldn't torture a woman.

"Why do you hate our Emperor?"

She shook her head and held something up for him to see.

"Why do you carry this in your pocket?"

The petal. So she had been near him while he slept. The thought made him strangely warm.

He shook his head. "That isn't mine."

A lie. The first true lie he had ever told in his life. And he couldn't fathom why.

"I found it on you, and I've found it before. How did it get in your pocket?"

"It must have been the wind."

The second lie. It was already becoming easier.

She frowned and flicked it at him.

"I don't want it."

"Why not? Is it beautiful?"

The Painter went silent. She didn't seem to know how to answer. Ānjìn took advantage of the quiet to test his pain again. The worst of the bruising fell across his face and ribs. The Rajah's men hadn't done much damage.

"They didn't take off my mask."

The Painter shook her head. "No. I'm not surprised they didn't."

"Why?"

"Fear."

They both nodded and grew silent again.

For the rest of the rumbling cart trip, Ānjìn thought about the mask in his Painter's hands and the petal he'd secretly returned to his pocket. Túlià thought about the prospect of torture and did her best not to stare at the bloodied, naked face of the Zānshì-boy across from her.

When the cart finally stopped, it jerked them both awake, and Túlià barely managed to shove the mask across to her Zānshì before the doors opened and they were pulled roughly outside.

It was evening again, and just light enough for Túlià to see how much Xórong's demon swayed when the Rajah's men checked the bindings on his hands. He was most certainly in pain, and it was her fault. She had insisted on entering the Hovel. But she couldn't have known he'd be so stupid to the effects of lìngdìng.

They were led to a stable at the back of a rich dwelling and left like horses in one of the stalls. Much like horses as well, they had no hope of understanding the jabbering language of the Rajah's men who taunted them from afar.

Sober now, they seemed less willing to handle the Zānshì, and still made no effort to remove his mask. The same men who had spit on him between sloppily aimed kicks the night before, could now barely raise their eyes above his twisted knees.

Túlià was glad of it, and strangely glad they had been allowed to stay together as well. Crouching alone in an enemy horse stall was uncomfortable enough to make even the company of a Zānshì-boy more appealing.

She still hated his mask though, and even after the men left them for the night, he still refused to speak to her, at least until the next morning when he woke her with tossed bits of grain.

"They've gone," he murmured, just loud enough for her to hear.

"Gone? They have been gone since the past evening."

He shook his mask. "They stayed near enough last night, watching and listening."

So that's why he hadn't spoken to her. "But how did you know they were nearby?"

"If they are close enough to hear me, then they are close enough for me to hear them."

Túlià frowned. "Are you certain you aren't a demon."

His mask shook again. "We were trained to be this way. I spent many hours in a dark room listening to the drip of water until I was able to toss a stone into each drip before it reached the floor."

She tried not to look impressed, but noticed his chest puffing out a bit at the sight of her face. So Zānshì-boys weren't so different from any other boy. Wonderful.

But maybe she could use that to her advantage.

"What else can you do?"

No answer. He had returned to silence, either to protect Xórong's secrets, which he obviously cared very much about, or because the Rajah's men were close again. Túlià wouldn't know until they came and dragged him from the stall, leaving her in silence. When they brought him back many hours later, his white wrappings were covered in blood.

Her Zānshì-boy laid very still that night.

THIRTY

"The great inheritance of the former kings will be continued and renewed."

Ānjìn hurt, nearly all over, and his Painter could tell. Her face wound up and pinched when she watched him try to move, so he kept still, waiting until the Rajah's men circled far enough away for him to whisper to her in the darkness before sunrise. He'd overheard a few scraps of information from two horsemen, who being slaves from the Emperor's lands, both spoke his language, and true to the custom of his people, were unbearable gossips.

"We are at the edge of the Rajah's domain, in the stables of a Lord's summer home. The men here serve him, and they captured us to earn his favor. Word has been sent to him and he should arrive in a few days. Until then, they will try to break me. But I have been trained for it," he added when the Painter's face pinched even further. "And I believe they will leave you alone."

"Couldn't we run?" she whispered back. She'd heard the cracking of whips the past day, and judging from the blood on Ānjìn's body, she knew they must be bringing him immense pain.

"No. I am too weak to fight more than three men, and there are at least twenty here, some caring for the horses and some warriors. We would have to cut through our ropes, get by them, and run to the nearest village, which also lies under

145

the Rajah's rule. I might be able to manage on my own, but you are terrible at sneaking, and fighting."

The Painter narrowed her eyes, ignoring the momentary softness in her heart that had been brought on by the sight of his blood. She settled into silence, frustrated with his words and her helplessness.

Ānjìn wished she would hold his mask again. The sight of it in her long fingers comforted him somehow. But even if he were stupid enough to remove it, passing any item between their hands would have been nearly impossible since both were tied to horse bars over their heads.

Every time the Rajah's men came to take him to his next beating, they would untie Ānjìn's hands from the horse bar, but keep them tied together while they walked him to the room filled with whips, knives, and cattle rods. When they finished, they dragged him back to his Painter and re-tied his still bound hands to the horse bar.

Ānjìn never screamed. He didn't want his Painter to hear it. He didn't want to see her pinched face when he returned. And he didn't want the Rajah to learn that Zānshì had voices. His Emperor's face would be more than pinched if that happened.

Ānjìn tried to imagine his Emperor's face pinching at the sight of him, but couldn't. The thought made him feel sick. He wouldn't fail, wouldn't twist his Emperor's face with disappointment.

And he didn't fail, not for three days. On the fourth day, the Rajah's men took an iron cattle rod to his knees. Then, Ānjìn did scream.

When Túlià heard him, she cried openly. She'd never heard his voice so loud, and it frightened her to know that only something truly excruciating could pull such a powerful sound from him. He'd always been so quiet, so soft. Now they'd broken him, and it was her fault. Just like Kāì, he was here because of her, because of her stupid desire to go to the Falls.

They beat him well into the night this time. She could hear them laughing. The sound, coupled with her Zānshì-boy's echoing screams, hurt so much that Túlià began knocking her head against the wooden stall. She watched her tears fall onto the straw and thought of him alone in a dark room, listening to the drip of water. He was alone again, and there was nothing she could do about it.

So Túlià closed her eyes and knocked her head until a sharp pain added her own cry to the mix. Maneuvering up onto her knees, she angled herself carefully so that her tied hands could reach the mess that had become her hair. She felt blood, a paintbrush or two, and a scrape-knife. She'd forgotten she had stored one there to use against her Zānshì. Perhaps now, she could use it to save him.

Thanking her ancestors for the long fingers she'd been gifted, Túlià worked the pitifully small knife from her hair and began sawing awkwardly at the ropes that bound her. The task was long and hard, and set her arms to aching after only a few minutes, but it was a blessed distraction until the screams stopped.

Knowing the Rajah's men would return soon with her Zānshì, Túlià put the knife back in her hair and positioned her hands to cover the frayed rope as best she could.

When voices mixed with the whimpering of a wounded animal filled the stables, she was shaken to see the Zānshì-boy being carried, not dragged. Túlià felt an odd sense of relief at finding his mask still on, but her heart shivered when she realized what they had done to him.

The Rajah's men had found the Zānshì's weakness, not in his mask, but in his legs. Her Zānshì's poor, twisted legs had been battered, mercilessly, with careful attention paid to his bowed knees. Swollen and bloodied, it seemed as if his white wrappings were all that held skin to bone. He whined like a street dog when they dropped him in the straw. They didn't bother to retie his bound hands to the horse bar.

Túlià's Zānshì wouldn't be walking anywhere that night, and she was too far away to help him, so she went back to work, drowning his whimpers with the scratch of knife on rope until her aching wrists broke free.

She went to him, taking off his mask and reaching for his hands in the dark. The cold sweat on his palms, the smell of blood, and the sounds of his pain brought back memories of the night she'd lost her mother, but she shoved them away. She had been helpless then. She wouldn't be now.

Her Zānshì had said there were horsemen here who came from their lands. They may not be quick to help a Zānshì, and pleading had never been her strong suit, but she would try. Now, how to get their attention? Túlià couldn't leave the stables for risk of being seen. She would only be tied up again if caught, her knife taken away, right back where she'd started.

If she knew how to write, she might send a message. But who among the horsemen would even be able to read it? Not a message then, just some way to catch their eye, to bring them nearer.

One of the horses grumbled a bit in its stall, and an idea began to take shape in her mind.

It took a bit of coaxing to remove the Zānshì's grip from hers, but she stood, mask in hand, and crept down to the stall of the nearest horse. Pulling free the pin that secured him, Túlià began to make a soft hissing noise, like a snake in high grass. Through her ruined throat, it sounded even more impressive, and the horse started to dance. Lifting the mask

148

for a finishing touch, Túlià turned it just so to catch the rays of moonlight coming through the open doorway. The horse's dance became more frenzied, until his discomfort was enough to send him running from the familiar warmth of his stall.

Túlià ran back to her own stall, replacing her Zānshì's mask and waiting for the voices she hoped would follow. It took longer than she would have liked, but soon, the mixed sound of human and horse returned to the stable. Túlià waited until she heard the stall's pin slide home before speaking up.

"Mercy, please. Water. Water. Have mercy."

A weary, suspicious face appeared above her, and blessedly answered in her own language.

"We give water to the horses only. Not to Zānshì and their women."

"Please, he attacked me. He captured me, just before the Rajah's men took us. Look, see here," she added, pulling back her hair to reveal the long scar at her throat.

The man let out a low whistle of disbelief, his eyes darting between her neck and the finally silent Zānshì behind her.

"I ask only for water, please. To cool my nerves and soothe my throat."

Again, Túlià was strangely grateful for her ruined voice, which both added proof to her story and earned pity from the horseman.

He nodded, left, and returned with a bucket and ladle.

"Keep this tonight, but be sure you've thrown it into the next stall before they come in the morning. I don't want my time here to be known. But it's not right to treat a woman so," he added, inclining his head respectfully while she drank.

149

"Why do they keep me here? And what do they want with a Zānshì? Why have they not simply killed him already and set me free?"

"They wait for their Lord," he whispered, looking anxiously over his shoulder. "They sent word that they have captured a Zānshì of the Emperor and are waiting on their Lord's arrival. He will decide what to do with both of you."

"What will he decide?" Túlià asked, the shake in her voice hardly needing embellishment this time.

"First," the man said, nodding in the direction of her Zānshì, "He will have that mask taken."

"Why has it not been done well before now?"

"They fear it, the Lord's men. Even beaten and broken they fear it. They all know the tales, diseased skin and devil faces. They won't touch the mask. But the Lord is not a demon-fearing man. The first thing he will do upon arrival is strip that Zānshì to his skin, and I will be far away when he does so," the man added.

"Do you know when he will arrive?"

"The evening of tomorrow. I am afraid the demon will be left with you until then. The Lord's men are busy preparing for their Master's arrival. They won't have the time to beat him."

Túlià made herself look downcast, and formed a protective sign against her chest.

"Then may the ancestors watch over me."

She thanked the man for his kindness. After reminding her to toss the bucket away before morning, he left.

THIRTY ONE

"Tranquility will be secured to the four quarters of my Empire."

The moment she found herself alone with the Zānshì-boy once more, Túlià began washing him as carefully as she could with water from the bucket, hoping it offered him comfort.

The water was cool at least, against his fever-hot skin. The few times he managed to open his eyes, Túlià gave him sips from the ladle before he returned to sleep.

She learned quickly not to touch his knees. Even the lightest brush made his back arch against the straw, but dripping cool water onto them from a cloth seemed to give him some relief, so that is what she did, well into the night. Soaking her rag, washing his face, running water over his knees, and ladling small mouthfuls onto his half-awake lips. And she thought.

There was much to think about.

The arrival of the Rajah's Lord. The Zānshì. The Emperor. Her mother.

Where was Túlià's place in all of this?

If Xórong ever possessed a scrap of her loyalty, it had vanished with the doubt the Tattoo placed in her mind.

If her mother's death was not an accident, but an arrangement, a murder, or an execution, someone with significant power in The City would have given that order. Túlià could think of no one who would have any reason to wish her mother dead, but anyone with such power would have been in the Emperor's higher circle. This meant Xórong likely knew of it. Túlià had no way of knowing if he approved such an order, simply ignored it and turned a blind eye, or even made the order himself. Regardless, her loyalty to him was irretrievably gone.

Now, what did that mean for the Rajah?

Túlià owed him no loyalty either. She knew very little about him. Only that he had resisted Xórong's attempt to join a single nation, and that Xórong had graciously allowed him to remain sovereign of his own lands, provided he paid hefty taxes and conformed to the same measurements, road systems, and written language as the ones he applied to his own people. Facing the threat of a demon army, the Rajah had grudgingly agreed, and tensions had been growing between the two lands ever since. It was no wonder the drunken men in Gāngko had attacked her Zānshì on sight.

Perhaps Túlià could use that hatred to her advantage. What if she told this Lord the Zānshì's secret, the Emperor's secret? It would weaken Xórong's Empire significantly once everyone knew him to be a liar with nothing more than an army of boys dressed as devils.

And if the Lord saw her Zānshì as only a boy trained to do the Emperor's bidding, he may stop these terrible beatings. He may let them go.

But what would the Rajah do with such information? If he knew the truth about the Emperor's army, would he attack?

It was certainly possible, and the more she thought on it, the more Túlià realized such an attack would be inevitable, if not from the Rajah, then from one of Xórong's many other enemies. He had been neither gentle nor fair when handling his conquest of the warring states, and so anyone who learned of his secret would be more than tempted to bring their army to the Emperor's doorstep at the earliest possibility.

And many would die.

Túlià had not been alive when Xórong became Emperor and began shaping his Empire, but her mother had, and she occasionally shared stories of the bloodshed, of burned farms and starving citizens. War would not be kind to anyone, and as much as she hated Xórong, Túlià had no desire to see his City, its people, and the outlying farmlands go up in flames. It wasn't what her mother would have wanted, it wasn't what Kāi would have wanted, and so it was not what Túlià wanted.

Then what did she want? If not to see the Emperor on his knees, weeping in the ashes of his City, then what?

She wanted to be free. That was why the sight of a broken Xórong, a dead Xórong, appealed to her so much. With him gone, she would be free to do as she pleased. No more of her work would be made for him, hung for him, enjoyed by him. She could paint what she pleased, hang it where she liked, and sell to who she wanted.

Passing the ladle over her Zānshì's lips, Túlià realized she now had the one thing that would let such a dream happen, even without the Emperor's death.

The world was dangerous to a woman alone, but for a woman with a Zānshì, the world would cower. Of course, once they'd run far enough from the Empire, her Zānshì could live without his mask. They could work a farm, raise goats in the Mountains perhaps, and she could paint in the evenings. Finding buyers might be difficult but—

Túlià stopped, her hand hovering over the Zānshì's gloves. The Zānshì, the Emperor's Zānshì. He had no loyalty to her. His protection had been by order of Xórong, who owned him in body and soul. The Zānshì knew where his loyalties resided, and it was not with a Painter he met only days ago. The moment they were free, he would run back to his Emperor with her in tow, wouldn't he?

She didn't know. And since he was in too much pain to wake, much less speak, she couldn't ask. Túlià wondered if she would even be able to form such a question under the gaze of his dark eyes, which had come to unsettle her more than the dark holes of his mask.

The Emperor, the Rajah, the Zānshì, herself? Túlià needed to decide who had her loyalty and what she would do about it, quickly, before the sun rose. Then, she would only have until sunset to act on her choice.

She dipped her rag into the bucket, watching as the water fell onto her Zānshì-boy's legs, mingling with his blood. And she had an idea.

THIRTY TWO

"And Xórong's blessings flowed boundlessly."

Ānjìn had never known pain like this. But with the pain, he felt something else, soft and strange, and a bit cold.

"Don't move, Zānshì."

His Painter. He could smell her now. She was doing something to his shoulder, the cold soft thing.

"When the Rajah's Lord comes for you at sunset, will you be able to stand?"

He didn't answer.

"Zānshì, I need you to be able to stand."

Ānjìn tested his legs.

They hurt worse than anything the Rajah's men had done to him, throbbing like a second and third heartbeat.

He shook his head, and in doing so, realized his face was as bare as his chest.

What was she doing to him?

Sighing, she took hold of his chin, turned his face, and dipped something into a bucket.

"Just be still. Rest and listen for the Rajah's men. If they come near, I need to know."

So he closed his eyes again, took a deep breath, and focused on willing the pain to spread throughout his whole body. It was an exercise he'd been taught very young, most often after a broken bone. By spreading the pain, it lessened, like a drop of blood in clear water.

His Painter needed him to stand at sunset, so he would. Ānjìn had failed his Emperor and his Zānshì brothers already. At the very least, he wanted to serve his Painter.

The Rajah's men had broken him, and he hated himself for it. Ānjìn had always known his knees to be tender, but no one had ever taken a bar to them like this.

He remembered being trained to walk in the way his Emperor wished, remembered the Generals watching him and his brothers hobble in a line from one end of the yard to the other, a single stick of bamboo, as long as his arm, tied on both ends to either one of his ankles. To walk, the young Zānshì had to turn their toes outward, knees bent, and heels almost facing one another to move forward with a sort of tossing and swinging motion. When they fell, the Generals beat them with much longer poles of bamboo.

It had been uncomfortable, even more uncomfortable than breathing through a mask. When night fell, and it was time to sleep, Ānjìn couldn't wait for the ropes to be cut loose so that he might straighten his legs again and walk without feeling like a hobbled mule. But no one came to cut the ropes, and The Hall of Imperial Reinforcement was filled that night with the tears of frustrated young Zānshì. By morning, one boy had managed to wiggle free of his bindings. He was removed.

The bamboo poles stayed between his ankles for three summers. At the end of each season, a General cut the ropes and fitted him with a new pole to account for his growing stride. By the third fitting, he had simply learned to forget the pole. He walked with it, ran with it, ate, slept, and trained with it. When the pole was finally cut from him for good, Ānjìn seemed to have forgotten how to walk the way he used to. Not that he had any desire to do so. This was what his Emperor wanted, so this was how he would walk from then on.

He hadn't known his knees would be such a weakness, but the Rajah's men had found it. They knew how to hurt him now, which meant they knew how to hurt his brothers. He had to warn them. He would return to his Emperor and confess his failures in protecting Kāì and keeping his vow of silence at the feet of the enemy. And he would warn them all of the coming danger. If the Rajah became emboldened by learning of this weakness, he could attack, and Ānjìn's bow-legged brothers would be at the mercy of the men's harsh rods, as he had been mere hours ago.

His Painter was still working. She talked to herself sometimes while she touched him, and he wondered if she would return with him to The City. She hated his Emperor, he knew, but maybe he could convince her. He wanted to see her before taking his own life, and he wanted to offer her life as proof he had not completely failed.

Her hair fell across his face, and he opened his eyes just in time to watch her pin it back with one of her brushes. Was she painting him?

"Be still."

Ānjìn was certain he hadn't moved anything but his eyes. He wanted to tell her so, but that would mean moving his lips. So he kept silent.

"Must you watch me."

Ānjìn forgot himself and nodded.

"Be still!"

So he closed his eyes once more, and went back to spreading the pain and wondering if his Painter would accompany him home.

THIRTY THREE

"Those who came from beyond the seas with different customs, requesting imperial audiences by presenting gifts, were countless."

The Rajah's Lord was a no-nonsense sort of man, as Lords often are, and he was disgusted to learn upon arriving that his men had yet to remove the Zānshì's mask. He'd heard the rumors, but he'd also seen battle with the Zānshì and knew they could be killed, admittedly with some difficulty.

Their armies attacked only at night, and relied more on stealth and cunning than strength and ferocity. They moved like ghosts beneath the moon, but they could bleed. He had seen it with his own eyes, though the body of a fallen Zānshì always seemed to vanish before he or anyone could take a closer look.

This Lord was determined to be the one who presented his Rajah with as many secrets as could be gleaned from one of Xórong's Zānshì. So devils and diseased skin aside, he would have that Zānshì stripped in as little time as possible.

He gave the order, ignored the white faces of his soldiers, and ate a tasteless meal while waiting for the Zānshì to be brought before him.

The Lord had been informed by his men that the Zānshì had screamed when broken, that its delicate knees were a point of weakness. He tucked the information away for his Rajah and called for a pipe, wondering why it took so long for his most recent prisoner to be brought in. It wasn't until *she* entered that he understood. Women, always so difficult.

"I did not instruct you to bring her, only the Zānshì."

The soldier dragging the bloodied Zānshì dropped it to salute his Master.

"She insisted on coming, my Lord. She wishes to see the face of the creature that scarred her."

The Rajah's Lord made note of the woman's ruined throat and dismissed her with a wave.

"Watch if you like. I'll decide your fate later. You," he added, indicating the two men on either side of the Zānshì. "Place him in the center of the room."

They did as instructed. The Lord double-checked the third guard standing behind, and the six guards lining the walls of the space. One kept a firm hand on the woman's arm.

The Lord looked back at the Zānshì and sighed. He regretted wasting the soldiers for this event. He'd brought in every man on the inner patrol ring for his own protection, not that he would ever admit it, and now it looked like the woman alone could have guarded this pathetic Zānshì.

He'd obviously been broken. His white wrappings were mottled with the browns and reds of both fresh and dried blood. He sat, barely supporting himself with a single arm, his ruined legs, unable to bear any of his weight, lay splayed out to one side.

"Cut through his wrappings and get rid of that mask," the Lord instructed, the bored tone of his voice contradicting the eager, forward lean of his body.

The men on either side of the Zānshì hesitated, until another stern command from the Lord pushed their shaking hands downward, one set reaching for the Zānshì's bloodied wrappings, the other for his mask.

The man who cut through the back of the Zānshì's garments stumbled away, babbling. The man who lifted the chin of his mask dropped it to shatter on the stone floor, and sank to his knees among the shards. The Lord couldn't understand their distress until the Zānshì stood, lifted his head, and let his cut wrappings slide free.

Red eyes, rimmed in fire.

Claws the color of blood.

Lesioned, dripping skin.

The creature unfolded itself, spread its claws, and stretched, taking a deep breath, as if glad to be free of the mask that held its horrible features captive.

Two of the Lord's men immediately collapsed in prayer, hands pressed to their foreheads. The guard holding the woman shoved her in the Zānshì's direction and ran for the door.

The Zānshì beat him there.

A single swipe of his dark claws and the soldier fell, his throat a weeping red grin.

The Lord began to shake, watching as each of his men attacked or ran, both equally clumsy and futile attempts that ended in smiling throats for all.

When only one guard remained, the Zānshì drove his claws into the man's thigh and pointed calmly toward the door. Whimpering, the soldier limped away without a backward look at his Lord, who, considering the circumstances, needed a substantial moment to realize what it meant that one man had already been set free.

"One to tell the story," he whispered, remembering the way he and the other Lords had chuckled the first time they heard such foolishness. That was before the wars, before they had seen what looked like men move like ghosts, before the Lord had watched a room full of his guards die at the hands of a single creature.

When the Zānshì approached him, the Lord made no effort to defend himself, for which Ānjìn was grateful, since he'd exhausted himself killing the other men. His legs were all but finished, and the moment he slit the Lord's throat, they collapsed.

Sitting on the floor, he stretched his throbbing knees and opened his eyes, still sticky from the blood-paint the lids had been coated with.

His Painter came to his side. He gave her back the scrape-knife she'd let him borrow, which had been surprisingly sharp despite its small size. She tucked it into her hair and took hold of one of his white-gloved hands, pausing a moment to admire the handiwork of the bloody claws she'd painted onto them before pulling Ānjìn to his feet.

With her support beneath his arm, the pair were able to make it to the door, pausing only long enough for Túlià to retrieve the most respectable set of soldier robes to cover Ānjìn's blood-painted body.

There were no patrolmen left, no soldiers at all to stop their path to the stables. Ānjìn had known the bulk of the Lord's men would be patrolling his outer walls, not his inner property. The only living creatures who saw them were the horses they borrowed and a stableman who Ānjìn knocked gently over the head. By the time he woke, with no memory of the event, Ānjìn and his Painter had already reached their final challenge, the outer ring of guards.

After donning the colors of the Rajah, tossing aside his bloodied gloves, and letting Túlià wipe his face clean, Ānjìn looked enough like a fellow soldier to pass through the patrol unheeded, even with an unfamiliar woman in tow.

It was the first time Ānjin had ever ridden a horse without his mask, and the feel of the sky was enough to make him forget every ache and pain.

THIRTY FOUR

"Even the subjects and officials, with all their best efforts to praise the Emperor's sagely virtue, still could not claim to have exhausted their praises to Xórong."

"Zānshì, where did this come from?"

Ānjin looked up briefly from the fire crackling beneath his hands.

"It must have been the wind."

Túlià shook her head and returned the petal to her pocket. There wasn't a dove tree in sight, or much more than a breath of wind, for which their little fire must have been grateful. Túlià was grateful as well, to have found this place.

After crossing back into the Empire, they rode for another day before plunging off the path and urging their horses through as much undergrowth as their exhausted legs could manage. When they reached a small stream, neither horse nor human could go any further, and so they slept on the cool ground for well over a day.

Túlià had woken first, made sure the horses were tied, and taken stock of their belongings. Aside from the meager contents of her hair, they had nothing. No food. No weapons. Their horses were not even saddled.

As much as she wished to make a fire, boil water, do something, anything, while she waited for the Zānshì-boy to wake, her talents as a Painter seemed worthless outside her

Pavilion. She thought briefly of going to find food, but didn't recognize anything safe to eat, and didn't want to stray too far from her Zānshì for fear of being lost among the pathless wood.

So she had been forced to wait another hungry day before Ānjìn opened his eyes, took his bearings, and promptly began making a fire.

"Can you fish?"

"Can I what?"

"Fish," he said again, indicating the stream. "I can't stand yet."

"I've never tried."

"Try today."

Túlià blinked and stood, eyeing the stream warily. It was only a few steps away, and shallow enough that she didn't have to worry about falling in and drowning. Fish. Yes, she could fish.

Only she couldn't. And returning a few minutes later with empty hands and soaking robes, Túlià found it incredibly difficult to admit such a thing to the Zānshì with his brightly burning fire. She reminded herself that she'd gathered the wood in a pile beside him while he slept, and felt a bit better.

"I can't fish."

"You need to be faster than the fish."

Túlià sighed and returned to the stream, her hunger making her wish she could simply fill her stomach with water and be done with it. Then she saw the clams. Ancestors forgive her. But she was hungry, and she could be faster than clams.

Filling her pockets, she'd returned to Ānjìn and passed over a portion of her catch. Wincing, she watched as he broke them open, and said another prayer before joining him.

She'd found the petal stuck to the slick shell of the last clam in her pocket.

The wind. Honestly, did he think her a fool?

Túlià still wondered though, how he did it. She hadn't been close enough to touch him aside from the moment the clams passed between them, but he might have slid the petal into her pocket long before.

Even if that were the case, where was he getting them? This couldn't be the same petal as the first she'd found, days ago. It was as alive and soft to the touch as if it had been freshly picked that morning.

And what had he meant in the cart, asking her if the petal's beauty was the reason she didn't want it? Did a Zānshì even know of beauty?

"Painter."

Túlià looked up from her second helping of clams and waited while he seemed to shape an unfamiliar thought.

"Why do you…"

He trailed off, cupping his hands together and tilting his face to the sky, a clumsy mimic of Túlià's pre-clam prayer.

"I am asking the ancestors for forgiveness."

"Why?"

"Because eating clams is an insult to nature."

His dark eyes looked briefly around the trees, then fell back to the clams in her lap.

"Why?"

"When the fall season approaches, sparrows dive into streams and become clams to live through the cold. As spring season comes, they jump out of the water, regain their wings and feathers, and fly back to the trees."

Ānjìn's brow furrowed so deeply that his eyes became nearly as shadowed as when they lay beneath his mask. He didn't speak for some time, and ate no more clams. It wasn't until the sun had traveled halfway across the sky that he spoke again.

"How can your ancestors have the power to grant forgiveness? That power lies with our Emperor alone."

Túlià scoffed. "No, it doesn't."

"But it does. He told us so."

"He lied."

"Our Emperor doesn't lie!"

It was only the third time Túlià had ever heard the Zānshì raise his voice. The first shout had been moments before an arrow struck Kāì. The second had been beneath the irons of the Rajah's men. Now, if possible, he sounded more distressed.

When she answered, Túlià was amazed at the gentleness in her rough voice.

"The Emperor does lie, all the time. Your very existence proves that. He told all his people, enemies and subjects alike, that you and your kind are demons. You aren't."

"But that was a story crafted for the protection of the Empire. Not a lie."

"It doesn't matter why the lie was told. It is still a lie."

They grew silent again, the stillness broken only by a moment of shuffling and splashing when Ānjìn gathered up his remaining clams, dragged himself to the stream, and slid them carefully back into the water.

He returned and laid down as if to sleep, though his eyes remained wide open and his usually motionless hands couldn't seem to rest. Túlià truly looked at his bare hands for the first time, and noting they were perfectly normal, much like the rest of him, she laid down as well. After an hour of watching his normal hands fidget like a child, Túlià realized neither of them would sleep and grew bold enough to voice a question.

"How did you become a Zānshì?"

His hands went still, and he immediately closed his eyes. Túlià let him lay like this until her patience wore through. She tossed a stone at him.

"I know you aren't sleeping."

"Yes, I am."

"You aren't. Tell me."

He sat up and began to massage his aching legs. She'd seen him do this a few times, and wondered if it did any good, since he'd yet to do more than crawl.

"It's forbidden to discuss Zānshì secrets."

"Your face was also a secret, and I've seen that. So tell me."

"I should kill you," Ānjìn muttered, wishing for the first time since being free of it that his mask hadn't shattered. Sometimes the realization that his Painter could see him made his stomach twist up in strange ways.

"You aren't going to kill me, now out with it."

When he still didn't answer, Túlià added more wood to the fire and tossed another stone at him.

"I'm not sleeping."

She almost smiled. "I know. Answer me or I'll tell the other birds you've been eating their sparrow friends."

"You ate them too."

"But I asked forgiveness."

Ānjìn's eyes went dark again under his brow, and he began to speak.

"I started in the streets. I didn't have a mother."

"Yes, you did."

169

"I didn't."

"Zānshì, everyone has a mother. Someone brought you into this world. You may not have known her, but you did have a mother."

Ānjìn thought on this for a moment before tucking it away into the space where he kept things he wasn't meant to understand and didn't want to dwell on. The Generals had told him and the other boys that they had no mothers. He'd always accepted it.

"You had a mother, yes? And you knew her."

Túlià nodded.

"What are mothers like?"

"Tell me of the Zānshì first."

Ānjìn sighed. He seemed unable to keep from deepening the multitude of misdeeds against his Emperor. But he had failed beyond forgiveness already. Could something become more than unforgivable? Ānjìn didn't know the answer, so he tucked it away, and spoke.

In the end, it wasn't what he said that brought tears to Túlià's eyes, but the way he said it. The horrors he'd experienced growing up in The Hall of Imperial Reinforcement were terrible enough on their own, but to see the complete acceptance in Ānjìn's eyes, to hear it in his voice, to know that he truly didn't understand how much more pleasant a life of freedom, even that of a street orphan, could have been.

Hearing about the bamboo between his young ankles and seeing his twisted, bloody knees resting a few paces away were what finally sent Túlià's tears spilling over.

"Why are you crying?"

"I am thinking of my mother," Túlià lied, pulling her eyes away from his legs.

"Tell me what she was like."

170

"Like me. I have her hands and her hair. We are Sywán."

"A Sywán, in our Emperor's court?"

"Yes. It never seemed strange to me before. I didn't know the Mountain people had become enemies to the Empire."

"Did she paint?"

"Of course. She taught me everything. It was her favorite, and so it is mine."

"Her favorite?"

"Yes, painting was something she enjoyed more than anything else."

"I don't think I have a favorite."

"Well, what do you enjoy?"

Ānjìn thought for a moment.

"I enjoy your company."

"No. I don't think you understand. Look."

She held up the dove tree petal.

"This is from my mother's favorite flower. It is her favorite because she preferred it over all the other flowers. She was wearing one in her hair when she died."

"How did she die?"

"A horse kicked her at the Qixé Parade last year. Xórong likes to line up all of his possessions, women and treasure and everything else for the festival. They walk around the whole City every year. My mother and I walked behind a row of horses. They startled and kicked out when we passed a group of Zānshì. One struck her in the head. She fell across me, and by pure good fortune I wasn't trampled. The Zānshì just stood there and watched. They did nothing to calm the horses.

Kāi and I sat by my mother's bedside for two days before she left us. Xórong never came to see her. He never

171

even sent a healer," Túlià finished, her fingers curling in memory until she realized she was crushing the petal. Pulling it free, she carefully smoothed it against her robes.

Ānjìn looked from Túlià to the petal a few times before answering.

"I heard what the Tattoo said. You think someone killed her."

"Yes," Túlià whispered, running her thumb lightly over the petal. "I do."

THIRTY FIVE

"As for those who talked about Xórong according to contemporary customs, the trouble was that they pursued the expediency of the moment."

After another day of rest, Ānjìn felt well enough to sit in the middle of the stream and catch fish, a blessing, since he absolutely refused to eat another clam. Túlià cooked them on a wide, flat stone while he rubbed life back into his legs.

"Can you stand?"

Ānjìn nodded. "By nightfall."

"Will this help?" Túlià asked, handing him a sturdy walking stick she'd dragged from the woods while he'd been in the stream.

"You want to go back."

"When you are well, yes. I have to know who is responsible for my mother's death."

He nodded, testing the weight of the wood in his hands.

"Could this person want your death as well?"

Túlià narrowed her eyes at the fish she'd just placed on the fire. She hadn't thought of that. Finding answers about her mother's death would be even more difficult if the person who arranged the accident a year ago had moved their focus to Túlià. Her Zānshì could keep her safe, but judging from her mother's death, the person responsible was not one for open attack. They would attempt something more subtle and difficult to trace, like—

Like sending her on a dangerous journey to enemy-infested Mountains.

Túlià's heart began to pound. So much would make sense if this were the case. Xórong had been set against a trip to the Falls for an entire year, only to have his mind change quite suddenly. Either someone had changed it for him, or he made the decision himself. Regardless, the trip had his approval. A trip with only a single Zānshì for protection, a mysteriously leaky boat, and a dangerous Mountain people waiting at the end.

Only it hadn't been Túlià that succumbed to these threats, but Kāì. Sweet Kāì could never have been the target. She had no enemies within The City. But then, Túlià had never imagined herself or her mother to have enemies in The City either, so who could say.

Regardless, Túlià could hardly return alive and well, and begin marching about from one Palace to the next, demanding justice for her mother's death. Without proof, she would be locked up for insanity, and would likely be dead before reaching the prisons by the hands of whoever was responsible for this mess. If she wanted answers, she would have to be clever, more clever than the Emperor.

Or maybe just *as* clever as the Emperor.

It had been Xórong's idea to dress Kāì in the garb of a Princess. What if Túlià were bold enough to use his own trick, and dress herself as Kāì?

They were similar in height, and her ruined voice would not give her away, since the scar at her throat was proof enough of such a difference. Long robes would cover all but her head, and the answer to that was more than simple.

174

A mourning veil. She would return as Kāì, her face and hair covered by a white veil for the death of her dear friend and Painter, killed in the Mountains by the savage Sywán.

The thought made her heart ache. Dressing as her departed childhood companion was more than perversion, it was an insult to the ancestors, to the gods as well. But Túlià knew Kāì's spirit would speak on her behalf. She would want Túlià to find answers.

"Zānshì, I have an idea."

Ānjìn thought it was foolish, and he said so. No one could trick his Emperor. But Túlià waved him away. She was determined.

He decided to let her be. Ānjìn wanted to return to The City as well after all, and was glad his Painter would accompany him. He had to warn his brothers, his Generals, his Emperor especially, that he'd broken under the enemy. They had heard his voice. They had found the weakness in his knees. The Empire was at risk because of Ānjìn, and he needed to set things right before dying at the feet of his Emperor. Getting to The City though, could prove challenging.

"I've lost my mask."

"Yes," Túlià answered, looking at his naked face with confusion. "I know."

"I can't be seen like this. How will we move through Gāngko, find a ship, and travel back to The City without anyone seeing my face?"

"Won't you stay in the shadows, like you always do?"

Ānjìn shook his head. "My legs won't allow it. I will barely be able to walk. To move silently and stay hidden won't be possible."

"So, let them see your face. Just listen," Túlià interrupted, lifting a hand to silence him. "I know it is against the Emperor's wishes for anyone to see a maskless Zānshì, but to these people, you won't be a Zānshì."

"I don't understand."

"Look at you. No mask, no bone-knives, no white gloves. You look more a man of the Rajah with those robes than a man of the Emperor, much less a Zānshì demon. The only ways you will catch the eyes of the people we pass are with your feet and your walk. We will begin with your feet."

It took Ānjìn almost an hour to unwrap both his feet, revealing that their odd shape was due to an ungainly amount of cloth layers. The feet themselves were perfectly normal, though paler than the moon, as was the rest of him, confirming Túlià's suspicions that their time together was the first her Zānshì-boy had ever been allowed to uncover any part of himself.

"You can wrap once or twice, to protect from the earth. Now we only have to improve your walk."

She looked up, making note of how far the sun had crossed since they woke.

"Can you stand?"

"It isn't nightfall yet," Ānjìn grumbled, frowning at his legs like a child.

"We may as well try. Use your staff," Túlià instructed, moving to help him up.

She stiffened her legs, letting him use the crook of her arm as a handle. Between her efforts and the walking stick in Ānjìn's other hand, he was able to rise into a wobbly standing position.

They only managed a dozen weak steps before he collapsed.

So the next day, they tried again, managing two dozen this time.

The days took on a sort of pattern after this. Túlià would wake to find Ānjìn fishing in the stream and begin to gather wood for the fire. They walked after breakfast, rested until the afternoon meal, and walked once more before falling asleep under the stars.

Túlià did her best to direct Ānjìn in how to move more like a normal man, but her efforts resulted in a smile of all things.

"That is not how men walk," he'd said, his teeth betraying his amusement.

"Yes they do."

"I've never seen a man push out his chest like that. Also your arms swing too much."

"Anything else?" she huffed, crossing her offending arms.

"Do you mean to be stomping the ground?"

"Men are heavy," Túlià protested. "I am trying to look heavy."

"Try again."

"No. You try."

And he had, though it looked more like an infant walking for the first time than a man. An infant was better than a snake at least. Túlià was pleased, though she wouldn't have been if Ānjìn betrayed how much it hurt him to not only walk after such a beating, but to force his legs to walk in a way they hadn't been allowed to since his first bamboo pole had been tied.

Ānjìn was good at hiding pain. Enemies should never be allowed to see your pain in battle. They should be thinking of no pain but their own.

Túlià's voice caught his attention again from where she sat, criticizing him on a fallen log.

"Your walk is better but you still behave too much like a demon. Must you look like you want to kill everything in sight? Try making your face more gentle."

He tried, and now it was Túlià's turn to smile at his efforts.

"Never mind. I think perhaps if you make an effort to blink more often, that will be enough."

"Blink?"

"Yes. You stare. It's unsettling."

Ānjìn held her gaze for a full minute before blinking once with incredible intention.

Túlià sighed.

May the gods give her patience.

THIRTY SIX

"They were engaged in offering flattery in their persuasions, in order to gain advantage."

"What are you doing?"

"I've gone too many days without painting. This is the best I can manage," Túlià muttered, frowning at his interruption.

Pulling another brush from her hair, she dipped it into a mixture of ash from their fire and water from their stream to make three quick strokes across the same flat stone she'd been using to cook their fish every day.

"A snake?"

"Yes. Now quiet, please. I am praying."

"No, you're painting."

Túlià nudged him away. "I'm doing both. Go on. Practice your walking."

Ānjìn sat next to her and rubbed at his legs.

"Why are you painting a snake and praying?"

"I've already told you, I paint because I enjoy it and because it brings me peace. I pray to ask for healing so that your legs will be strong enough for us to reach The City. The snake is a symbol of healing. Painting it helps guide my prayers."

"If snakes are for healing, why did you paint one on my arm when I fought the Rajah's men?"

179

"Because snakes also symbolize immortality. Every mark I put on you that day was meant to make you appear as more than you are."

"But how can a snake represent both healing and immortality?"

"Symbols are like a language. Just as words can have more than one meaning, so can symbols. If you know the language, you can read a painting like words on a scroll."

"I can't read."

"I can. But I can't write."

"The Generals told us reading and writing are useless, along with many other things."

"Such as?"

"Calligraphy, poetry, painting—"

"Of course not! Those are the Three Perfections."

She actually agreed with the first two being useless, though Kāi had lived and breathed both for most of her life. Túlià could enjoy the occasional poem, but considered such fancy scrawls to be a bit frivolous. Painting however—

"Painting is far from useless! It has great value."

"How? You can't eat a painting, or kill someone with it. Paintings are just meant to sit there and be looked at."

"No paintings are meant to be *engaged* with."

"What does that mean?"

"It means you hold them and use them and interact with them, add to them even."

"I don't understand."

"If I were to finish a painting, let's say on a fan, I would want you to not just look at the painted fan, but use it, mark it with your seal, add a poem about how the painting makes you feel. You and the people who see you using the fan are meant to experience the painting and think on what it means. You might even honor my work further by giving the fan as a gift to someone else."

"What if the painting were not on a fan, but something harder to use, like a scroll?"

"Scrolls can be used in different ways. Hanging a painted scroll on a wall can change the feel of the room or tell visitors something about the scroll's owner. If the scroll isn't hung, you interact with it almost like listening to a story, but with your eyes instead of your ears. Imagine unrolling a painted scroll," she continued, mimicking spreading a scroll on the grass in front of them. "As you open it, your eyes move across the painting and experience the story the scroll tells you one bit at a time. And as you go, you see the seals and writing of all who have owned the scroll before you, allowing you to interact with the past through the same painted story the previous owners have read."

Ānjìn nodded slowly. "Paintings tell stories."

"Exactly. And stories everyone can read, even if they can't read in the traditional sense."

"Like your snake tells a story of healing."

"Yes," Túlià said, holding it up for him to see. "And I'll have you know, you *could* kill someone with a painting."

Now Ānjìn grew truly interested. Killing he understood.

"If a man saw his wife receive a painting of a duck, he would be well within right to kill her and the man who sent the painting."

"Why?"

"The duck is a symbol of romantic love. The husband would assume his wife was being unfaithful and punish her and her lover for it."

"But that would practically be an accident. The painting wasn't a weapon."

"What if I sent the painting because I hated the wife and wanted her dead?"

Ānjìn's eyes widened. "That's very crafty."

"Thank you."

"Teach me."

"Symbols or painting?"

"Both."

Túlià smiled. "Of course. You can't have one without the other."

Ānjìn went to retrieve his own river stone, with Túlià admiring his much steadier pace all the way. When he returned, she gave him a paintbrush from her hair and did her best to instruct him. She'd never taught anyone to paint before, and found it surprisingly difficult, like teaching someone to breathe.

Ānjìn was certainly far better at breathing than painting. His every effort resulted in something that looked as if it had been stepped on a great many times. But he never grew frustrated, and seemed to absorb the story behind each new symbol Túlià shared with him like a sponge taking in water.

"You're doing fine. This would be much easier if we had the proper tools, I promise you that."

"What are the proper tools?"

"For painting? Well, we would be using real ink for one. The finest inks are made of pine soot and glue from the horns of young deer. They come in little dried ink cakes, which we would mix with water in an inkstone."

"Can any stone be an inkstone?"

"I suppose, but inkstones are very special. Painters pass them down through generations, and people believe you can feel the spirit of the previous painter who owned it when you hold the inkstone in your hand."

"Do you believe that?"

"I used to, but after my mother died, I held every one of her inkstones and didn't feel a thing...have you finished your toad symbol?"

"No. Which one is your favorite?"

"Inkstone?"

"Symbol."

Túlià thought for a moment. "The Qìnjy. It's a pretty little bird that can be taught to speak like a person. Kāì has one in her rooms at The Palace of Refined Artistry. She rescued him from a Princess who tried to have the tiny beast cast out for only being able to say *I am forever hungry*."

Her rough-voiced imitation of the bird made them both smile.

"Was Kāì able to teach the bird more?"

"Of course not. Even despite allowing him more patience than I ever thought her capable of giving, it was always *I am forever hungry, I am forever hungry*. There were times I avoided her room when I knew the Qìnjy was awake, just so I didn't have to hear him shout at me."

"Maybe he truly was hungry."

Túlià shook her head. "Trust me. He wasn't. Kāì gave him enough sweet treats to sicken a horse. I imagine that's why he loved her so much."

Túlià's heart grew sober again, her voice drifting down into a whisper.

"I have always thought of myself as being like the Qìnjy, because the story of the bird is much like mine. I can remember a line from one of Kāì's poems.

Those who attach themselves to others are the same as the little bird; those who snuggle up to people are like the Qìnjy.

They are beautiful and can speak pretty words, but not provide for themselves. Qìnjy have to stay at the side of the wealthy and take treats from their hands to survive."

Ānjìn tried to imagine Túlià's fire-dark eyes bowing to accept a treat from his Emperor's hand, but couldn't.

"Kāì and I were both like the Qìnjy, snuggling up to the Emperor, but we were still happy because we always had each other."

"Will you paint me one? I want to see it."

Túlià shook her head. "I don't believe anyone will have fed her little Qìnjy while Kāì has been away. His cage will likely be empty when I return."

She pulled the brush from Ānjìn's fingers and tucked it back into her hair.

"I think we have painted enough for today. You need to walk. I wish to leave soon."

"I will be ready in two days."

Túlià nodded. "Two days."

THIRTY SEVEN

"But Xórong did not know that if one desires to resurrect sagely rule, one must select and employ responsible Generals and Advisers."

Leaving their little camp was another splinter of sadness in Túlià's heart, still, she was glad to be on her way back to fresh robes and a proper bed.

Her Zānshì seemed glad as well, twisting on his horse to take in everything they passed on their way to Gāngko. The moment they came within sight of people, however, he went so stiff that his mount began to stomp and complain. Even riding behind him, Túlià could tell he made every effort to keep his face hidden from the bright light of midday.

In truth, Ānjìn was terrified. He wasn't sure what it was or what it meant, the odd, shaky feeling in his stomach, but the eyes of every person in Gāngko burned against his face with far more heat than the sun.

He didn't want to look up, because if he met eyes with another, he would know they saw his face, and he would know they should die at his hand.

Ānjìn didn't want that to happen. He didn't want to kill anyone.

What had his Painter said about favorites, something you enjoy?

Well, Ānjìn didn't enjoy killing. It was not his favorite. Killing was something he knew, and something he practiced, but not something that brought him peace, like brushes and river stones did for his Painter.

He wondered if this was something else to add to the growing list of failures against his Emperor, but tucked it away. It was not for him to think on. The Painter had said he revealed no secrets by showing his face today, and he believed her, so he lifted his head, expecting to meet the terrified eyes of everyone within a hundred paces.

Instead, he saw people as people were meant to be seen. Jostling in the path, haggling for prices, chiding their children, sharing stories around cookfires. Ānjìn had never simply seen people go about their business. When his mask was near, they cowered, wept, soiled themselves, ran. At best, they would try to maintain their current task under a sort of shaking awareness that his shadow was close by and watching.

Now, instead of snatching their children away from his horse, disappearing into their homes, and barring every opening, they hardly seemed to notice him at all. He could just—

"Zānshì."

Ānjìn turned in surprise toward the sharp whisper and found his Painter had pulled her horse alongside his.

"Do you have a name?"

"A name?"

"Yes," she said, annoyed and keeping her voice to a whisper. "I wanted to call out to you before but could hardly shout *Zānshì* across the path. Do you have a name?"

"I did."

"Well tell me, and it will be your name again."

"Ānjìn."

She nodded. "Ānjìn. Try to sit on your horse a bit more...softly."

"Softly?"

"Yes. You look like you're trying to break the poor animal's back. See how that man holds the reins loosely and lets his shoulders fall. Try to ride like him."

Ānjìn did, and Túlià nodded her approval.

They rode further, steering clear of Hovels and stopping when the docks came into sight.

"We need passage on the next ship across the Xórong Sea, along with new clothes and enough food to last the journey."

"How much could we gain from selling the horses?"

"It depends on the buyer," Túlià muttered, shooing off a rather aggressive woman who was trying to cover her scar with a heavy necklace.

"I hear there's a group of travelers in tents down the way looking for horses," the woman said, raising an empty hand in hope of a coin or two.

Túlià shook her head and the woman left, tossing a sign of ill luck over her shoulder. Knowing her little blue Xié would protect her, Túlià ignored the woman and urged her horse toward the tent tops standing just beyond the furthest cart.

The closer they got, the more Túlià could see familiar symbols embroidered onto the tent fabric. Sywán.

Both Ānjìn and Túlià paused, remembering the screams of angry Mountain men as their arrows whistled down from above.

Laughter dissolved the cloud forming over Túlià's heart, children's laughter. She looked closer, her eyes finding only women and young girls moving among the tents. Sending Ānjìn a determined look, she nudged her horse closer to the Sywán.

If this was the quickest way to earn money for ship's passage, then so be it. After all, it was not these women who had taken Kāì from her. She could no more hold them responsible for the actions of their men than they could hold her responsible for the actions of the Emperor who sired her.

"Women of the Mountain," she began gruffly. "I have horses to sell, if you wish."

The eldest of the group stepped forward and bade Túlià welcome. She had silver streaks in her loose hair, and carried herself both easily and with purpose. Seeing her, Túlià couldn't help but think of her mother.

"Your horses look strong, though you look twice as tired. Rest and eat with us while we decide on payment."

Túlià nodded and slid down from her horse, watching as Ānjìn attempted to do the same. He struggled for a moment, to swing his leg over the horse's rump, and his knees buckled a bit when his feet touched the earth, but he remained standing, and allowed one of the Sywán children to lead his horse away.

They were served a simple broth, flavored with ginger and mushroom. The silver-streaked woman introduced herself as Indsè le Tufā, and watched them carefully while they ate.

"How is it," she began, "that a lady of the Empire and a Rajah's man are traveling companions."

Túlià looked at her and Ānjìn's dirtied clothes and realized they still showed enough color to reveal their supposed loyalties, in her Zānshì's case, the loyalty of the man she'd stolen the robes from. Taking one look at Indsè's sharp eyes, she decided to share as much of the truth as possible.

"We are both of the Empire. While traveling back from the Mountains we were captured by the Rajah's men. We have no other clothes to wear."

Indsè nodded. "Then we will see you fitted here. Our robes are some of the finest on both sides of the Sea.

"We couldn't accept such kindness, Cloud Mother."

Smiling, Indsè waved one of the older children over and bade her gather new robes.

"Don't mistake it as kindness, young one. It will save us some coin in exchange for your horses, yes?"

Túlià nodded, stealing a glance at Ānjìn to make sure he behaved himself before returning to her broth.

"Now I must know where a lady of the Empire learned to title me properly. Such Sywán names aren't known among your people."

"Because I am of your people as well," Túlià explained. "My grandmother came from the Mountains and my mother filled my head with her stories when I was young."

"Ah, I see. Do you know the name of her clan?"

"The Lúi. She met my grandfather at Yán sè Falls and returned with him to the Empire."

"Did you travel to the Falls to visit her family?"

"No. I am a Painter. I wished to capture the Falls in ink to hang above my door in remembrance of my mother, who passed just last year."

"Do you have the painting?" she asked, bowing her head to respect Túlià's loss. "I would love to see it."

Túlià swallowed around her scar, something in her heart shattering at having to admit such a failure aloud.

"I did not manage to paint the Falls before we were attacked," she whispered, gripping her broth bowl for strength. "It seems the space above my door will remain empty."

Not able to meet the pity in Indsè's eyes, Túlià turned instead to Ānjìn, and was surprised to find him watching her intently, his broth half-finished in his lap.

Clearing her throat, Túlià accepted more soup and inquired after Indsè's husband and sons.

"It is not safe for them to leave the Mountains," she explained. "Xórong sends his Zānshì there to collect our men almost every season now. If they are in danger of being taken from their very homes, we would be foolish to bring them down here, so much closer to his City."

"Xórong is sending Zānshì to the Mountains?"

Indsè nodded. "He needs more hands to work his farmland, so his demons take our husbands and sons. Soon it will be our aging fathers I suspect, once he becomes desperate enough."

"His farmlands? I don't understand. Don't we have plenty of farmers around the outer edges of the Empire already?"

"Yes, but they can't keep up, young one. Everything they harvest goes to feeding the wealthy in The City."

"But stealing farmhands won't make the land produce more."

"It would make the Sywán more aggressive though," Ānjìn murmured, surprising everyone with his low voice.

Túlià thought over what he said, and realized what he was suggesting. If she were a Sywán man with strong, young sons at home, and she saw travelers wearing the Emperor's colors coming up the side of the Mountain, she would most certainly attack, especially if there were Zānshì in sight.

The Sywán had attacked them because Xórong was stealing their sons. It was the Emperor's greed that killed Kāi, not the savagery of the Mountain people.

Túlià set her jaw.

"Cloud Mother, could I bother you for a white veil?"

"Of course. You lost someone in the Mountains?"

Indsè bowed her head once more in answer to Túlià's pained nod.

"I can tell you are worried for what the path ahead of you will hold. Would you allow me to ask the gods for assistance on your behalf?"

"Please. I have prayed over it many times already, but prayers from another can never hurt."

"I will gladly do so," Indsè continued, reaching to accept something from another child, "but I had more than prayer in mind."

Carefully unwrapping a small, smooth turtle shell, Indsè leaned forward and pulled a scrape-knife from Túlià's hair, making Ānjìn tense beside her until she withdrew. Scratching delicately, she began inscribing vaguely familiar symbols into the shell's belly.

"This," she explained, "is how your grandmother's people speak to the Three Sovereigns and converse with The Eight Immortals. We place our questions here, and then..." She stood, placed the turtle shell on the ground, raised her hands and eyes skyward, and brought her heel down hard, cracking the delicate shell into a handful of pieces.

Both Túlià and Ānjìn leaned in curiously, watching as Indsè sifted through the pieces, inspecting each crack and broken edge with fingers that had done far more in their lifetime than hold a paintbrush.

"There is a change coming, a change that will affect everyone who breathes. Change born of ink, fire, beauty...that is all I see here, young one. I hope it is enough."

Ānjìn stood, his eyes never leaving the small bits of shell.

"Does our Emperor know about this power?"

191

Indsè's face became hard.

"Xórong is *your* Emperor, not ours."

"Does he?" Ānjìn pressed.

"No. And I would prefer he not learn of it."

Gathering up the shards, Indsè sent Ānjìn a measured look and motioned to a child who took them out of sight.

"Thank you Cloud Mother," Túlià said, standing as well. "I will keep these things in mind as I go forward."

"I wish you safe travels," Indsè answered warmly, taking her hands. "If there is nothing else you need from us, we will dress you in the robes of our people and send you on your way."

Nodding, Túlià turned to Ānjìn, intending to signal that he accept the clothes and prepare to leave, but her Zānshì was gone.

THIRTY EIGHT

"Xórong tried to rule his Empire alone and single-handed, and therefore its downfall was merely a matter of time."

"Where have you been?"

Ānjìn wouldn't meet her eyes.

"Buying supplies."

"All night?"

"Yes."

Túlià wanted to strike him.

He was lucky the Sywán had been kind enough to let her stay with them until morning, though Indsè had refused to let her wander the dark streets alone, searching for her idiot Zānshì.

Túlià hardly slept, her heart moving between worry and hatred until the sun rose and Ānjìn stumbled back into the main tent on weary legs, a small bundle tied across his back.

"You should have told me you were leaving."

"Why?"

Why? Because she'd worried herself ill over him. Because he'd made her question every decision to trust him. Because she hadn't felt so alone since the day she'd dropped her mother's hand for the last time, or the day she'd closed Kāi's eyes.

"What did you buy?"

"What did I buy?" he repeated numbly, his eyes still on the earth between her feet.

"Yes, what did you buy with the coins from our horses?"

When Ānjìn still didn't answer, Túlià tried to take the pack, only to have him gently shoulder her away.

"I will carry it."

"Fine, but what's in it? Food?"

Ānjìn shook his head.

"Spare clothes? Medicine?"

"No."

Túlià breathed deeply and turned her eyes toward the ancestors.

"Do we have *any* coins left?"

This time, when Ānjìn shook his head, Túlià did hit him.

"How could you be so foolish! Now we will never reach The City."

Ānjìn readjusted his pack and briefly touched the place on his jaw where Túlià had struck him before nodding toward the nearest Sywán.

"Ask your Cloud Mother—"

"I am not asking any more kindness to be shown for nothing in return. We've taken enough. And I can't exactly tell the Sywán that you've spent all the coin from our horses on whatever waste you have in that satchel."

"Then we should go to the docks."

"We can't go to the docks," Túlià shouted, throwing up her hands. "We have no money for passage."

"I could work for passage."

"What?"

"I heard some of the deckhands from our leaking boat a few days ago say they worked for passage. I could do the same."

Fuming, Túlià took a moment to thank Indsè once more for her kindness, and yanked Ānjìn out into the day.

She walked quickly toward the docks, delighting in the sound of struggling footsteps as his weak knees hurried after her. She didn't slow until she noticed people staring, since even with the walking stick and dozens of lessons, he was still a sight, though hopefully not one that would make people think of the Emperor's Zānshì.

Ānjìn never shouted for her to slow. He remembered what Túlià had said about not calling him Zānshì in front of these people, and knowing she intended to hide her own face soon, did not want to call out *Painter*. He would have used her name, but she'd yet to give him permission to do such a thing. So he pushed on in silence, leaning heavily on the walking stick, balancing his bundle, and hoping he would be strong enough to work for passage when they made it to the ship.

They were still a hundred paces from the first dock when Túlià stopped, spun on him, and pointed at the nearest stacking of crates.

"Sit."

Ānjìn did, his gratitude for the chance to rest disappearing when his Painter continued walking. He got up to follow her, only to return to his crates with brow-shaded eyes when she waved him back.

Túlià began looking for a ship with women already onboard, thinking the men there would have a better chance of adding her and Ānjìn to their hired hands. She'd left him behind because she knew negotiating without him would go more smoothly, not because the sound of his pain-broken breathing had started to squeeze at her chest with every step.

She was still more than angry with him.

"What is your business, Mountain woman?"

195

Túlià looked at the deckhand with brief surprise before remembering she'd taken on Sywán clothing the night past. Normally, the Mountain features were not obvious enough in her face for people to take notice. Now, coupled with her new robes, she more than showed her Sywán blood.

Glad she'd decided not to don her mourning veil until they were closer to The City, Túlià lifted her chin and tried to hold herself like Indsè.

"I need passage for two across the Xórong Sea. I have no money, but my brother can work."

"Go fetch him then. I'll get the Captain," the man said, sending her off with a flick of his cap.

Túlià returned with Ānjìn in tow, hissing into his ear to stand straight and praying that the Captain would have pity on them.

"He doesn't look like he can work much."

"Yes but—"

"Can you?"

Túlià paused. "I don't see what use my skills would be on a boat."

"I imagine you can sew, yes?"

And that was how, one simple lie later, Túlià found herself seated in a circle with the other women onboard, a bundle of torn sails piled over her lap.

Of course she didn't know how to sew. She was a Painter. Túlià possessed even less of her mother's skill with thread than Huàjā had taken from her mother before her. Fortunately, the woman beside Túlià, hardly more than a girl really, was very kind, and after taking one look at Túlià's long fingers, began to teach her.

Being more accustomed to holding a paintbrush, blisters formed quicker than Túlià thought possible, and she cursed whatever spirit had taken over Ānjìn and led him all

196

across Gāngko last night to gather the useless contents in that fool bundle of his.

He still carried it now, even as his legs threatened to buckle under him. Yet another reason he shouldn't have left the Sywán tent. Ānjìn's knees were as strong as they could be after those quiet days by the stream, but even with no knowledge of healing, Túlià understood that he shouldn't have been using them so heavily, especially wandering out all night in the cold.

Stupid Zānshì-boy.

Ānjìn knew she was angry, Túlià could tell. She hadn't sent a word his way since they'd boarded. And after a day's worth of blisters, she had no desire to do so, no matter how many times he looked in her direction.

A few of the women had started to tease him for staring, showing decidedly less kindness than the girl who taught Túlià to sew. When they began to mock Ānjìn's shaking knees, Túlià stuck one of them with her needle.

THIRTY NINE

"He made true what has been said, that seizing, and guarding what you have seized, do not depend upon the same techniques."

A day into the journey, the Captain seemed unsure how to use a lady who couldn't sew and a man who couldn't lift anything heavy, so he set them to roping with the children and hoped none of the young ones would emerge with a needle in their arm.

Making rope was no easy task, and the children were just as unsure what to do with Túlià as the Captain had been, and as Ānjìn still was.

She had gone utterly silent, and he missed the sound of her rough voice. He spoke to her a few times, but she only twisted rope and refused to look in his direction. He was beginning to hate it.

This was how everyone treated him, keeping their face turned aside, unwilling to speak with a Zānshì, too afraid to look a devil in the eye. It hadn't bothered him when Túlià behaved this way before she'd seen his face, but now it hurt low in his chest.

A few of the men had tried speaking to Ānjìn, but he hadn't said much in return, just practiced walking more like them in an effort to please his Painter. She didn't seem to notice.

So Ānjìn worked, and he watched her, and he watched the children.

He hadn't seen much of children before now. They were very strange, somehow both loud and quiet at the same time. Their movements had no purpose, and they could talk for hours about something as silly as the wind.

They didn't speak to him much, but they didn't cower either, and they were all but determined to make Túlià smile. Watching as they jumped about her, asking after her scar and her strange robes and the blue eye tucked into her hair, Ānjìn often thought them close to succeeding. Then, she would look up and see him, his face or the bundle on his shoulders, and sink back into a frown.

Túlià finally spoke to him on the third day. Her simple acknowledgment unknowingly granted him permission to breathe normally again, and he had the children to thank for ending his suffering.

"Mountain Lady, I brought you a feather. Look, see," a small boy had said, placing a tiny gull feather on her lap.

Túlià nodded and shooed the disappointed child back to his stack of unwound rope.

"She doesn't like beautiful things," Ānjìn muttered. "Try giving her something plain."

The child had brightened and immediately began searching the supplies stacked nearby. Returning with a battered bucket, he placed it at Túlià's feet and stepped back, awaiting praise.

Túlià had looked at the bucket, then the child, then Ānjìn, then smiled. And when the Captain signaled the afternoon meal, she had motioned for him to eat beside her.

"I never said I don't like beautiful things."

"No?" Ānjìn asked, trying and failing to keep the relief from his voice.

"No," Túlià agreed, "But I understand why you would think so."

200

"What is it about beauty that upsets you?"

"Beauty is a mask," Túlià answered immediately. "People make things beautiful because they don't want to see what really lies underneath."

"Oh."

"You disagree?"

Túlià thought Ānjìn of all people would understand. His very life lay beneath a mask, though his was not a mask of beauty.

"I always thought beautiful things were useful things."

"Useful things?"

"Like my bone-knives. They had a purpose. I miss them."

"Are they really made from the bones of the first person you ever killed?"

"No."

"But they are made of human bone?"

"No. Human bones break too easily. They would make terrible knives."

Relieved, Túlià thought back to his earlier claim, that beauty was a measure of usefulness. "But the purpose of your knives was killing. Killing isn't beautiful."

"No, but it is beautiful to have a purpose and complete it."

"Like my new bucket?" Túlià asked, sliding it his way with her foot and a smile.

"Yes. Being able to hold water and not spill a drop is beautiful."

Túlià's smile vanished slowly, overtaken by the weight of her thoughts. How could beauty mean something different to Ānjìn than it did to her? Useful things weren't often dusted in gold, draped in silk, or decorated with ink.

Xórong would never hang dented buckets on the walls of his Palaces. He—

Túlià stopped.

She remembered something, something her mother had done that never made sense to her until this moment. Xórong's understanding of beauty was all Túlià had ever known, but her mother knew beauty before she came to The City, before Túlià was born. Hearing now that Ānjìn had his own way of seeing beauty, she wondered if her mother had done the same.

"Before she died, my mother used to divide her paintings into two piles," Túlià began slowly, watching as Ānjìn started back on his rope. "A pile for herself, and a beautiful pile, for the Emperor."

"She didn't find all her paintings beautiful?"

"No...No I don't think so."

"What made the paintings in her pile different from the ones your mother gave to our Emperor?"

"They made her cry."

Túlià could remember it more clearly now, her mother dabbing away tears before they could fall and spoil the ink on scrolls Túlià had only seen in brief glimpses. Paintings of people and places and faces that for some reason, made her mother weep.

"Her paintings would have been out of place on Xórong's walls. They weren't gaudy or grand. I think they just...helped her remember."

Ānjìn finished another curl of rope. "Remember what?"

"Her life before Xórong, before The City. Do you think *remembering* was beautiful to her?"

"Maybe. Maybe she enjoyed remembering her life, so things that helped her remember were beautiful, but only to her."

"Not to Xórong," Túlià added. "That's why she didn't offer them to hang on his walls. He wouldn't have found them beautiful, because different people have different understandings of beauty!"

Ānjìn gave her a strange look. "You didn't know that?"

"Oh hush," Túlià countered, taking up her own strand of rope. "You didn't know you had a mother."

Her jest was hollow though, in comparison to her heart, which seemed near tipping with the fullness of this new understanding.

People could see beauty in different ways.

It was a relief to know that she didn't have to see beauty in the same way Xórong did.

Her mother certainly hadn't. She'd broken free of the Emperor's gold-edged, gaudy beauty, and now Túlià wondered if she could as well.

"I think your mother's memory paintings would look better on the walls than the ones that hang there now."

"Which ones?"

"Jewel covered horses and the like."

"You've looked at the paintings?" Túlià asked, surprise replacing her distraction.

"Yes."

"You didn't like them."

He looked up. "I liked yours."

"How can you tell which are mine?"

"I couldn't before, but now I remember the Mountains."

Ah yes, the Mountains.

The Mountains that filled every one of Túlià's paintings. The Mountains whose tips she could just see over the walls of The Garden of Refined Artistry. The Mountains whose full forms she had, until recently, only experienced in a few of her mother's paintings, the ones she wouldn't hang for Xórong.

Maybe the truly beautiful pile was the one her mother had kept and cried over, not the one she'd offered up for the royal walls.

"The day after my mother died, he told me to paint for him."

Ānjìn nodded. He didn't need to ask who Túlià spoke of.

"He sent for me, before she'd even been properly buried, and had all mother's paint supplies laid across the floor. He wanted to know if I had her skill, or if I should be cast out of The City. I painted the moon, full and shining the way it had been the night she died. And I left. I didn't wait to see if he wanted me. I didn't care. My mother was gone and nothing else mattered. I suppose he liked the painting though, since he's kept me and my work since."

A single tear fell onto Túlià's strand of rope.

"I wonder if she would have found my paintings beautiful. *I* don't even know if they are."

"Can we—" Ānjìn began haltingly, "play a game?"

Túlià blinked the worst of the tears away. "A game?"

Her Zānshì nodded. He remembered the children speaking of games earlier, and how they'd smiled.

"Yes, a game called...Is This Beautiful?"

He lifted his walking stick as he said it, holding the sturdy piece of wood up for her to inspect.

Túlià looked it over for a good moment.

"Which sort of beautiful? Yours or Xórong's or—"

"Yours. Do *you* think it's beautiful?"

Túlià held it for a time.

Her eyes moved between Ānjìn and the walking stick she'd pulled from the woods for him. Their time by the stream felt seasons old. The staff had already begun to show wear at the place he gripped it each day.

"No."

"You're lying."

"I certainly am not."

"You are. Your face gives you away."

"Is that one of your demon skills, Zānshì," she scoffed, "can you taste when people are lying with your snake tongue?"

He shook his head. "No. I told you. The lie is in your face. All Zānshì are trained to look for it."

"Hmm. Then why can't you see when Xórong lies to you?"

"Our Emperor doesn't lie to us," Ānjìn choked. "I told you before. He would never."

"He told you that you had no mother. Did you not see *that* lie in his face?"

"I wouldn't dare look into my Emperor's face," Ānjìn whispered, still sounding horrified that Túlià would even suggest such a thing.

"Fine," she relented. "Your walking stick is beautiful."

"Why?"

"Because of what you said before, it's useful," she answered, turning her face away this time under the guise of returning it to his side.

Ānjìn nodded. "Now you ask."

"Ask what?"

"Ask me," he explained, sweeping his hand across the ship, "about something beautiful."

Túlià looked around.

"The sails, are they beautiful?"

"Yes."

"I agree. They look like clouds."

"How about—"

"The Mountain lady still has my bucket. She did like it!"

Ānjìn moved his eyes over the returning, freshly fed children, and sent Túlià a questioning look.

Túlià made a face and shook her head. Children were too noisy to be beautiful. Even so, she lifted the bucket high and said loud enough for them all to hear, "I think I will keep this bucket for a long while."

FORTY

"Consequently, Xórong's accomplishments lacked depth."

"If I could be so bold to request your hospitality once more," Túlià asked, head bowed as she stood in the open door of the dock owner who had housed her and Kāi on their first journey across the Xórong Sea.

Dockmaster Mātu, a kinder man than anyone had right to be, took one look at Túlià's veil of mourning and ushered her inside, calling for his wife and older children to make guest preparations.

Túlià sat, grateful to once again rest and have someone look after her instead of spending hours riding empty-stomached on the back of a horse or sailing on a crowded ship with work torn fingers.

Mātu's family was just as generous as before, and his children seemed blessedly more quiet in comparison to her last visit. She imagined it had something to do with her veil, which brought a hush about the house that seemed to lay across even the youngest child.

The meal was beautiful, and the conversation soft, though Túlià found it hard to enjoy either once she realized the place beside her sat empty. Kāi would not be joining her this time. But her Zānshì would not be eating outside either.

Ānjìn waited in the corner of the room, not quite in shadow, but certainly unsure. Túlià had warned him that he was to behave much differently on this occasion than he had yet. He would be expected to sit next to her at the table and make conversation, and they would continue with the pretense that he was her brother, who had decided to journey back with Túlià after hearing tales of The City while she visited him in the Mountains.

Still, it wasn't until Túlià waved him over that Ānjìn reluctantly took his place in Kāi's emptiness. He had hardly gotten settled before their hosts started on him, inquiring after their journey in ways that politely included Túlià but did not address her directly.

Túlià didn't mind. It was easy to play the part of a mourner when her heart seemed to weep every time she thought of Kāi's face. She nearly had to leave the table when Ānjìn haltingly explained her absence as the reason for Túlià's white veil, though it was Túlià's life he said was lost in the Mountains, not Kāi's.

It was harder still, to be addressed as Princess Kāi, especially by the children, who took a moment to thank her for the kindness she showed with the sharing of gifts on her last visit.

She passed the time by finding creative ways to quietly correct Ānjìn's clumsy attempts at dinner etiquette without their hosts noticing. Túlià hoped they would associate any mistakes she didn't catch with the humble Mountain life Ānjìn claimed to come from.

Aside from the odd combination of stiff and fluid movements Túlià realized she'd grown used to, Ānjìn managed to blend in fairly well, until draining his cup halfway through their after-meal tea ceremony. Luckily, Mātu's wife was more than gracious, and calmly returned his cup to brimming before completing the ceremony with flawless poise.

It wasn't until they retired near the hearth, and the children began to pester Ānjìn alone, that Túlià seemed finally able to smile again. She watched as they tugged him to the floor and asked for a story.

"I don't know any stories."

The children began to clamor and protest, making their father laugh and their mother scold.

"But he lives in the Mountains, Màmà. We wish to hear about them."

Ānjìn looked to Túlià, waiting for her nod before he began to speak.

"The Mountains are very big," he began.

Giggles spread about the children until Ānjìn's heavy brow quieted their fidgeting.

"So big that climbing them every day is enough to make your legs ache," he added, holding his walking stick up for them to see. He passed it to a smaller child, who practically glowed at the honor.

"The water there tastes sweet. And the people—"

"Are enemies," the boy with the staff finished for him, brandishing his new prize.

Ānjìn was quiet for a long moment.

"No…no, I don't think so."

"But sir," Mātu protested. "Didn't the Emperor say the Sywán had become dangerous?"

Beginning to rub at his legs, Ānjìn tilted his head and thought further.

"The Emperor…is wrong. The Sywán were kind to us, and only aggressive when they thought themselves in danger."

He looked to Túlià, who suddenly couldn't decide if the squeeze in her chest was grief, or something else. Finally finding her rough voice again, she added, "The Emperor is stealing their able-bodied to work his farms."

Murmurs of disbelief sounded among the adults in the room, their unease spreading to the children who, though they knew little of politics, could sense the discontent of parents and guests alike.

"Does he not have enough hands to work his farms?" their host asked, keeping his voice respectful in the presence of what he believed to be a Princess.

Túlià shook her head. "We were told not, by a Sywán Cloud Mother herself."

Though unfamiliar with the title, Mātu could still hear the weight it carried, and settled into his chair, silent with thought until his wife began shuffling their children to sleep.

The moment the room had cleared of his progeny, he began questioning them further on the state of the Empire, the farmlands, and Xórong's failing relations with the Sywán.

Túlià and Ānjìn could not offer much more than what they had heard, and asked him many questions in return.

"You must hear whispers of such things from all who make use of your docks?"

Mātu hesitated briefly before nodding, still keeping his eyes a respectful distance from Túlià's veil.

"Forgive me Princess, but I have, yes. I did not wish to speak ill words against the Emperor, though there have been whispers, as you say."

"Then please, speak freely."

Taking a deep breath, he passed a hand over his face and nodded once more before continuing.

"We are lucky to live here, near the water, where supplies are brought to us from afar. We do not have to work the land ourselves, but we hear those who deliver to us complain of low crop."

"Is the land not producing?" Ānjìn asked, rescuing his staff from where the children had discarded it on the floor.

"No, from what I hear, the harvest has been strong. But—" he cast another uncertain look at Túlià, and continued only after her wave of encouragement. "The City grows more every day. With much of the crop going to feed the Emperor's wealthy, those in the outlying towns struggle to eat."

So it was as Túlià suspected. Though she had not imagined the lives of those thin farmers worsening so quickly.

"How bad is it?"

Mātu stood and clasped Ānjìn's arm in response.

"I fear it will not be many seasons from now that ships begin to arrive empty at my dock."

FORTY ONE

"Alas, the Emperor never learned of his mistakes and hence grew daily more arrogant."

Just when she decided to turn in for the night, Túlià noticed one of Mātu's older children standing behind her, waiting for permission to speak.

"Yes?"

"I remember your Painter," the girl said shyly, holding up a small scroll.

"What is this?"

Túlià knew it wasn't a scroll she'd left behind on her last visit. She didn't use such cheap material in her work for Xórong.

"I have been practicing with my ink. Father thinks I am only doing characters, but after watching your Painter sit by the Sea..."

She trailed off, waiting on her toes while Túlià carefully unrolled the parchment and studied the simple, clumsy ink strokes mixed in with the girl's practice characters.

"Do you think she would have liked them?"

Túlià paused, still needing an extra moment to gather her thoughts and remember that it was her Painter's body they left in the Mountains, not Kāì. And that she was meant to be Kāì now, hidden in mourning behind her white veil.

"My Painter would have given you advice," she finally decided, to which the girl went wide-eyed with expectation.

"She would have told you not to show this to your father. Let him think you only practice your characters. Keep this a secret, paint what you wish, paint for yourself, and don't hold your hands so stiffly," she added.

"Can you show me?"

The girl flushed at Túlià's hesitation, remembering her veil and lowering her head in respect.

"Forgive me Highness, if you are too unwell."

Túlià sighed. "What is it you wish me to show you?"

"I only thought that from watching your Painter so often, you might know the proper way to move the brush."

"Go get your things."

The girl left with a smile and returned cradling her little inkstone. Spreading her scroll open, she made room for Túlià beside her on the floor and raised her brush.

"Like this?"

"No, like this. Watch my hands."

Túlià took the brush, and the child watched. She watched so silently, and with such appreciation, that Túlià forgot who she was, or rather, who she was meant to be, and just painted. It seemed that once a brush had been placed in her hand, she became a Painter again, and simply did what she loved until her mother's Mountains filled the better part of the scroll. When she sat back to let the ink dry, the sound of the child's quiet breathing finally reminded her of her place.

"Do you see?" she asked roughly, returning the brush and motioning for the scroll to be taken up.

When the girl nodded, Túlià stood, and suddenly exhausted, moved toward her room for the night. She paused for one last whisper behind her.

"Do you think I could show my mother?"

Túlià thought. Part of her joy in painting, especially after her own mother died, was to share her work with Kāì. Having someone you trusted to look over your creations with a careful, loving eye, was a very precious thing. A precious thing she had lost and would likely never regain.

"Yes. Show your mother."

FORTY TWO

"His underlings lived prostrate with fear, and flattered and deceived him in order to curry favor."

Túlià answered the knock at her door, grateful for the veil covering her frustrated mouth, and was surprised to see Mātu's wife, a look of determination on her normally gentle face.

She carried her child's scroll.

"If I may disturb you, Highness."

Túlià nodded and welcomed her in, surprised again when the soft spoken woman sat at the edge of her bed with an attitude more familiar than she'd yet seen from her hostess.

"Lǐyuè showed me her practice."

Túlià straightened, preparing to defend whatever reproach she gave. She hadn't anticipated a mother resisting what made her daughter happy.

"This is your work, is it not?"

She unrolled the scroll, displaying Túlià's inky Mountains.

"Yes."

She nodded and pulled a much more expensively made scroll from the folds of her robe, unrolling it to display the painted sunset Túlià had offered as a gift during her last visit.

"And is this your work as well?"

Her covered mouth once more dipping into frustration, Túlià realized her mistake and shook her head. She never should have picked up a brush.

"Do not lie to me in my own home, Painter. I can see how these strokes curve. They were made by the same hand. Tell me why you cover your face."

"I cannot," Túlià's rough voice rumbled out from beneath her veil. "It could be dangerous for you, and even more dangerous for me."

The woman stood. "If you are in danger, I would offer my assistance."

"I'm afraid your assistance would do little good."

"Then tell me your story. The least I may do is listen."

"What is your name?"

The woman bowed her head, "Jiùlìng."

"Jiùlìng," Túlià sighed, and pulled off her veil. "You were right to call me Painter, and I was wrong to lie, but as I said, I do it for the protection of myself and those near me."

Before she had even finished speaking, Jiùlìng's hands flew to her graceful neck, her lips parting in horror at the ragged pink scar across Túlià's throat. She'd heard the roughness in her guest's voice, but to see what caused it...

"Who did this to you?"

"When we were attacked in the Mountains, and Princess Kāi was lost, our Zānshì was unable to protect us. We—"

"Your Zānshì," Jiùlìng whispered, her hands moving to cover her mouth now. "Painter, where is your Zānshì?"

"He became separated from us in the Mountains. It is why I agreed to let my brother return with me, for protection," she added, the practiced lie coming more easily

218

from her mouth now. She could not let this sweet woman know a Zānshì had eaten at the same table as her children.

Jiùlìng's eyes narrowed at the mention of Ānjìn, her hands settling stiffly back at her sides.

"You did not mention a brother during your first visit."

When Túlià had no answer, Jiùlìng's hands began to shake slightly.

"This man, Ānjìn, is he dangerous?"

Dangerous? Of course, but not to her.

"No," Túlià said firmly. "He looks after me. We look after each other. I can say no more. Please understand."

"I...will try. But why do you cover your face and lie? You are truly mourning, I see that. But to take the place of she who you lost—"

"I hate to do it," Túlià answered hoarsely. "With all my heart, I do. But there may be more at work here than I can say. I will not put your family at risk for my secrets."

Xórong had ears everywhere, Túlià knew. If she even spoke his name in connection to what they had endured in the Mountains, it could reach all the way back to The City. Túlià needed him unaware when she arrived and began peeling back shadows to find the answers she sought.

Jiùlìng drew in a deep, calming breath and took Túlià's hands.

"If you or your brother need for anything, you will tell me, yes?"

"Yes. All I ask now is that you say nothing of this to your husband."

She nodded, released Túlià, and waited until she had repositioned her veil before moving to open the door.

"I will return with a tea for your throat, Highness, then leave you to rest."

219

Túlià nodded her thanks and sank to the floor, the weight of everything she'd done and still hoped to do, pulling her down like she carried the Mountains themselves.

May Kāì forgive her.

May the gods forgive her.

May she live long enough to do her mother honor.

FORTY THREE

"He then had elevated walks and walled roads built around his Palaces and scenic towers situated at the edges of his City."

"Painter."

Túlià nearly left her skin at the sound of Ānjìn's low, hushed voice across the room.

"I've told you not to do that, Zānshì. Over and over I've told you."

"I waited until you finished praying."

Túlià sighed. "Yes but you are meant to announce yourself *as you enter* a room, not well after, or you'll scare the spirit out of everyone nearby."

"I will try to do better."

"Good. Now did you just come to startle me or did you need something?"

"Where would you like me?"

"Where?"

"Should I stay inside, or go to the stables as I did during our last visit?"

"Didn't Jiùlìng show you to your own room?"

"Yes."

"Then sleep there, and enjoy a night in a proper bed."

"I don't want to sleep there. It's too quiet."

"Then don't sleep at all," Túlià grumbled, fidgeting with her blankets and hoping he would take the sign of her overwhelming weariness and leave. "Zānshì don't have to anyway."

"No. We do have to sleep," Ānjìn corrected. "Only not as much."

"Then I don't care what you do. Sleep, don't sleep. In your room or out. If it's too quiet, then sleep beside the Sea and listen to the spiders crawling over you."

"I would like to sleep here."

"Here?" Túlià stood so quickly she nearly pulled her blankets free of the bed.

He nodded.

"Ānjìn, you can't sleep here."

"Why?"

"Because it isn't proper."

He thought for a moment. "But you are never proper."

"I intend to be now."

"It's too quiet in my room," he repeated. "I'm used to the sounds of you sleeping."

Túlià resisted the urge to laugh when she finally looked up at his face. He was like a child after a nightmare, only without a shadow of fear in his eyes. Did Zānshì have nightmares, or were they trained free of them?

"You will have to make do."

His mouth fell with disappointment

"It's only for one night," Túlià added, more gently this time.

Ānjìn moved to crouch at the foot of her bed.

"Will you tell me a story?"

Túlià sighed. Apparently she would see no end to visitors this night.

"I will tell you one, only one story, then leave me be."

He nodded.

"What sort of story would you like?"

"Do you know how the world was made?"

He said it so quickly, and with such desire, that Túlià was surprised enough to forget her wish to be proper and sit beside him.

"Yes, of course. Why do you ask?"

"The Generals never told us," he said solemnly. "And I have always wondered."

"Well, in the beginning, there was nothing, only chaos. As the chaos lay there, for a very, very long time, it began to separate into Dark and Light, who together gave birth to a single egg. Inside the egg was P'uku, the first man. He slept for a while, then, when he was ready, he took up an axe and broke free of the egg."

"Where did he get an axe?"

"What?"

"Was there an axe inside the egg with him?"

"I suppose. Perhaps he made it himself."

"But where would he get the materials to make an axe inside of an eggshell?"

"I truly don't know. I've never thought about it before. May I go on?"

Ānjìn nodded, though Túlià could tell he wasn't satisfied with her answer.

"When the egg broke, a light substance flowed out of the shell and up above to form the sky. Another, heavier substance fell down below to create the earth."

"But—"

"No Ānjìn, I don't know what the substances were made of or how they formed the earth and sky. That is simply how the story goes. Now, when P'uku stepped out of the egg and saw the sky above and the earth below, he stood between them and held them apart while they grew. He grew as well, and when it was time for him to die, his breath became the wind, his eyes became the sun and moon, his hair became the stars, and his body became the Mountains."

"But how—"

"Ānjìn, if you keep interrupting, you won't hear the rest. P'uku's muscles turned to fields, his blood to rivers, his veins to roads. His skin became the flowers and trees, and his bones became jade and pearls. In this way, the world was fully prepared for The Three Sovereigns to arrive and fill it with people and animals."

"How did they make people?"

"That is a story for another time. Now Ānjìn *please* go to sleep. I'm tired."

He stood, frowning with thought as he moved to leave.

"And don't come back in here to stand over me like a nightmare-eating *Món* while I sleep."

Ānjìn's far deeper frown showed that was exactly what he'd intended to do, and after he shut the door and Túlià finally shut her eyes, she realized the room did feel a bit too quiet without him.

FORTY FOUR

"He filled the Palaces with curtains and hangings, bells and drums, and beautiful women, each assigned to a particular post and forbidden to move about."

Ānjìn didn't like his bed, so he slept on the floor and thought of Túlià's story.

Even though it confused him, he knew her tale was far better than the one he'd tried to share with the children when he spoke of the Sywán Mountains.

Mātu and his family were kind. Ānjìn had wanted to please the children, and they did seem pleased with him. He could think of a great many stories they would not have been pleased to hear.

Stories of battles and blood and all the smiling throats he'd left behind. Throats that hadn't been given the chance to heal like his Painter's.

He remembered the words of his Generals each time they faced an enemy.

No mercy. None left alive. No man or animal, child or mother spared. We are snakes in the grass. We are ghosts in the night. We are Zānshì, and they will fear our Emperor's name.

Ānjìn had never seen a true battle, like the ones spoken of by the older Zānshì who fought in the Emperor's wars of joining when he wished to bring together a single united nation. That fight had been won before Ānjìn was born.

Now, he and his Zānshì brothers left The City only to settle disagreements with those few, small, remaining bands of people who resisted their Emperor's rule. And, as he'd recently learned, to kidnap Sywán men and boys. Ānjìn had never participated in one of those ventures, and he was glad of it.

His first time leaving The City had been a trip to a farm on the far outskirts of the Empire. He'd been sent with one of his brothers. They were to burn the farm, its fields, animals, and people.

No man or animal, child or mother spared.

They had separated, one to burn the home, one to burn the stables.

Ānjìn had been tasked with burning the stables. He latched the door and lit the thatched roof, listening to the screams of the family as his brother completed his own task nearby.

He hadn't known how quickly a stable could catch fire, or how long it would take to burn. The animals seemed to live well past what he expected. Ānjìn had never heard an animal scream before.

Just before the roof caved in beneath the weight of so many flames, a horse managed to jump free of the latched door. He danced between Ānjìn and the crackling stable, his mane and tail heavy with soot. It had amazed him, he remembered, for his manner to be so frightening that a fear-mad animal would choose the fire at its backside over running past his silent, masked form.

While Ānjìn watched and did nothing, his brother had moved in past him, severed the thick tendons of the horse's legs, and stood over its body until the stable's flames moved across the grass and set the animal alight.

When they returned to The City, his brother told their Generals how Ānjìn had hesitated, watched, stood by in silence while a horse nearly escaped his reach.

He had been punished with a heated ring on every finger, a sampling of the fire he should have dealt easily at the farm. With the placement of each ring, he silently repeated his wish for forgiveness, his desire to do better, and his new certainty to never fail his Emperor again.

Ānjìn didn't think Mātu's children would have liked that story.

Ānjìn didn't like that story.

It was the first time he'd failed his brothers, his Generals, and his Emperor. They had watched him since that night, searching for the moments he hesitated, the moments he held back, the moments he did not smile beneath his mask at the sight of spilled blood the way many of his brothers did.

Ānjìn had never been worthy of his Emperor, he knew. But now he would return, he would beg forgiveness, he would warn everyone, and he would die. It was all he could hope for.

Checking to be sure his satchel lay safely within reach, Ānjìn closed his eyes and slept.

FORTY FIVE

"He erased doubt and established laws, so all would know what to shun."

It felt good to have a task in the morning to keep him from stumbling through the bows and goodbyes he knew his Painter must be hating at the moment. Children were not her favorite. Despite this, he'd come to realize they all seemed to enjoy her very much.

Ānjìn had risen before dawn, not able to stand the quiet of his room any longer, and slipped out to the stalls to begin preparing for their journey. Túlià had said she wanted to leave soon after the morning meal, a meal he hadn't minded missing since his stomach was still full from last night's banquet. Did people always eat so much?

He had long since finished hitching cart and oxen when the sound of children moving around outside signaled the meal's end. Túlià met him in the yard, her veil and the stern words of the children's mother the only things that kept their little hands from Túlià's fresh set of robes. She hated it, he could see, being in the Emperor's colors again, though he'd noticed her Sywán garments tucked carefully among their provisions.

Bowing in the direction of the house, and bowing once more after she'd finished checking that he'd properly tied down their things, Túlià let Ānjìn help her into the cart.

He snapped the reins and breathed deeply, enjoying, as he always did, the somehow still new feel of the sun on his bare face. Ānjìn pitied Túlià, trapped in the cart and hidden beneath her mourning veil. He was both unsurprised and incredibly glad when she called for him to stop, emerged without her veil, and moved to ride beside him.

"It's too hot in the cart," she explained, climbing up to sit on his narrow bench behind the oxen. "Besides, this road is hardly traveled. We shouldn't have to worry about anyone seeing my face, and if another cart appears on the horizon, I'll shut myself back up in that hot little box until you tell me it has passed."

"Hmm."

"What?"

"You have returned to not being proper again."

"I'm sure I have no idea what you mean," she said, snapping open a fan and doing her best to keep the heat away.

"It would be proper to ride in the cart."

"Do you want me to ride in the cart?"

"No."

"Good."

They traveled in contented silence for a time before Túlià used her fan and long fingers to motion toward the oxen.

"These are the same oxen that pulled us the first time?"

"Yes."

"Oh. I thought you ate them."

Ānjìn threw back his head, and laughed. Yes, he laughed. He laughed until it hurt, then his Painter began to laugh as well.

"You thought I *ate* them?"

"Yes."

230

"*Both* of them?"

She nodded, wiping away tears.

"How could I possibly—"

"I don't know!" she cried, bringing on a fresh wave of laughter.

It felt so good, so good to laugh with her. He couldn't remember the last time he had, and to share it with her, with the warm sun on his face, was something more than precious.

This, Ānjìn decided, was his favorite.

"That was before, I suppose," Túlià continued. "When I still thought you were a monster. I told Kāi, mostly in jest, that you'd spent the night in the Dockmaster's stables to eat our oxen. When we didn't see them the next morning, we became certain that's what you'd done."

"Do you still think I'm a monster?"

Túlià sobered at the question and looked him over carefully.

"No."

"Why? What changed?"

"I've seen your face," she explained. "You don't look like a monster."

"But you still called me Zānshì, for a time."

She nodded, stowing her fan. "Yes. I was still unsure then. You could have been a monster on the inside."

"Inside?"

"Yes. Some people may not look it, but are monsters beneath their skin."

Ānjìn thought for a moment.

"I would like a new game."

"What sort of game?"

"A game called, Is He a Monster?"

"Women can be monsters too, but yes, I'll play. How does it go?"

"I will give a name, and you tell me if the person is a monster."

"Alright. Give me a name."

"The Rajah's Lord."

"Yes. Monster."

"Why?"

"He was going to kill us. He had his men beat you. They are monsters as well."

"But they all acted for the will of their Rajah and the good of their people."

"That doesn't matter."

"It does. You used to think the Zānshì to be monsters, but we do the same, for our Emperor and—"

"I still think the Zānshì are monsters. I said my mind had changed about you, not the rest."

Ānjìn wasn't sure how this made him feel. Proud that he'd earned her trust? Disappointed that she still feared his brothers? But she should, shouldn't she? Zānshì were made to be feared. It was a part of them, one of their most important duties to their Emperor.

"I am confused."

She sighed and thought, her long fingers twisting together until she spoke again, more carefully this time.

"Being a monster…is a choice, or, maybe not a choice, exactly. There are evil spirits, creatures born with darkness who can't escape it. For people, I think, being a monster is a choice. The men who beat you could have chosen not to, but they hurt you anyway, and I believe they enjoyed it. They chose to have hatred in their hearts, and that makes them monsters."

"Are you a monster?"

232

She turned wide eyes on him. "Why would you ask me that?"

"You hate our Emperor."

"He may very well be responsible for my mother's death," she answered, shocked that he expected any less from her.

"But you hated the Emperor before you learned of that. And you hate the entire royal family, aside from Kāi. They can't all be responsible."

Túlià couldn't seem to decide between being angry or broken. Ānjìn began to wish he hadn't asked. But he needed to know.

"You just don't understand," she finally murmured.

"I want to. That's why we're playing."

"It isn't a game! None of this is a game. My mother is dead. Kāi is dead! I've lost them all to monsters and they will never come back to me!"

"Túlià—"

"The Zānshì at the parade stood by and did *nothing* while my mother was trampled by horses. You stood by and did *nothing* while Kāi bled out in my arms. I have never been more alone, and I have monsters to thank for it!"

She was weeping now. Tears of anger, grief, and frustration braided together into sobs that stained her cheeks and made her ribs ache from gasping.

"Stop the cart."

Ānjìn stopped. He waited until she slid down and returned to her proper seat behind him before reaching for the comforting weight of the satchel strung across his back and silently urging the oxen forward again.

233

FORTY SIX

"The first law: anyone who used antiquity to criticize the present would be executed along with his family."

When they made camp for the night, Túlià needed over an hour to gather enough courage to leave the cart. Even then, she couldn't look Ānjìn in the eyes until after she'd eaten beside the fire he'd made for her.

Something was different about him. She noticed as soon she did manage to look up. It took her a moment to understand that it was because he wouldn't look back at her.

But he was always looking at her. He never seemed to stop. Every time she glanced his way, his eyes were on her, studying, watching, protecting.

She'd hated it once, but now she couldn't fathom why. It was as though he'd put his mask back on, but worse somehow.

"Thank you, Ānjìn, for the fire and meal."

He didn't answer. He didn't move. He might as well have been dead too.

What would her world be like, she wondered, with Ānjìn dead?

Because Túlià wasn't alone.

She'd realized it as soon as her tears had cooled in the cart. The silence. Ānjìn had always been silent, but it was a new kind of silence not having him beside her. She'd felt it in her empty room the past night as well.

It was still silent now, an awful silence that pushed against her ears like cold water.

How could she feel so alone with another beating heart merely a stone's throw away?

Noticing the pebbles beneath her feet, Túlià had an idea.

When the first pebble bounced off Ānjìn's arm, and he raised his dark eyes, Túlià thought he might actually kill her.

She tossed another pebble.

This time, he batted it aside and watched her the way she was used to.

She tossed a third pebble. He caught it.

"What are you doing."

"I believe I am apologizing."

"Is this a new game?"

"No," she tossed another pebble. "Apologizing is when you admit to being wrong, and feel sorry for it."

"I know what apologizing is."

"Am I doing well?"

"I don't think so."

"Will you forgive me anyway?"

"For what?"

"For blaming you. What happened to Kāì wasn't your fault, it was mine. I can't bear to live with it, so I blame others, and I blame you. I am most likely doing the same for my mother. Her death could very well have been an accident."

"But if it wasn't, then your hatred for our Emperor would be justified, and you wouldn't be a monster."

"Yes. That would be easier, so it's almost what I would prefer. I suppose I am a monster then."

"Hm."

"You don't think so?"

236

"I think if you can choose to hate, then you can choose not to, and I think you will choose not to."

"Then you have greater faith than I do."

Ānjìn added more wood to the fire.

"Will you tell me about her?"

"My mother?"

"Your Kāi."

Túlià smiled.

"She wrote poems, and her calligraphy was simply gorgeous. We complemented each other because of it, that she could write but not paint, while I could paint but not write. My mother said that most Painters were Scholars who had become well versed in calligraphy, and if they had free time enough, would teach themselves to paint using the same style as their characters."

"Is that not how you learned?"

"No. Nor my mother. She taught me the way her father taught her, tracing the shapes in ink that we saw with our eyes, not letting our hands depend on the old, practiced motions you learn while making characters. She said learning to write would poison our fingers. It was what her father told her when she was small, and I was glad, because then it didn't matter that Xórong wouldn't allow me a tutor. Only the chosen Princesses are awarded such luxuries."

"Then how did Kāi learn to write so beautifully?"

"She was promised to the son of a Scholar at her birth. The Scholar's son didn't care much for writing, so Kāi became a sort of stand-in pupil. Her role only grew stronger when the son died of fever before they could be married, and through his mourning, the Scholar tripled her lessons in an effort to forget the loss of his son. They stayed very close."

"Did she take on poetry at his insistence?"

"No, she always liked the way the characters looked on the page more than what the words said, but the moment she heard whispers that Xórong enjoyed the occasional poem, she had the Scholar teach her until she became quite good."

"You had poetry on some of your paintings, yes?"

"Yes. That was Kāì. Or Xórong."

"The Emperor wrote on your paintings?"

"Of course. I told you paintings are meant to be viewed and touched and added to. At the very least, he would always contribute his seal to my work."

"And you didn't mind the intrusion?"

"I wouldn't have, if it were anyone but Xórong. Seeing how he marked my paintings as his own reminded me that I belonged to him as well."

"But not in the same way that you are Kāì's."

Túlià nodded in agreement and smiled. "No, her involvement I agreed to and enjoyed. Kāì's poems made my work more beautiful. Her words on my paintings made the scrolls into something we shared, not something she took or claimed. That's how it is meant to be."

"What did she write about? You mentioned her bird, the Qìnjy."

"Yes, Kāì absolutely adored writing about birds of all kinds. It was perfect because they fit just so alongside the Mountains I painted. She used to sit in my Pavilion and talk to me while we worked, writing about the birds she watched flying by. A rosefinch got tangled in her hair once, and she insisted on removing it herself. She wouldn't let me call one of the servants to help because she thought they might be too rough with the little thing. Luckily, he loved the sound of her voice and sat perfectly still until she had him free."

Ānjìn laughed, a much quieter laugh than his first, earlier that day. Túlià decided she liked his laugh, and wanted to make him laugh again the way he had before, with his eyes closed and his head thrown back, careless and just…happy.

So she told him the story of the day she and Kāì had convinced the head Gardener to let them paint a row of elephants around the edge of the central fountain, just inside The Gate of Divine Authority. Kāì had dropped an ink cake into the fountain, fallen in while trying to retrieve it, and splashed Túlià for laughing at her efforts. By the time they made it inside, both were drenched. Their robes had to be thrown away, their skin held the ink for three days, and the fountain spewed black water for half a season.

Needless to say, neither Túlià nor Ānjìn could hardly draw breath through their laughter by the story's end.

FORTY SEVEN

"The second law: any official who observed or knew of violations and failed to report them would be equally guilty."

"Where should I sleep tonight, Túlià?"

"You realize," she answered, smiling, "I never gave you permission to call me by name."

"I decided permission wasn't necessary. You never asked before using my name."

"I did."

"No, you said *what is your name*, not *can I use your name*."

"Well, I don't have to ask. You're a man. I am a proper young woman."

"Why is it you only seem to be proper when it suits you?" he grumbled, gathering up his bedding. "And how far away must I sleep tonight?"

"As far as you like, but stay on your side of the fire."

He nodded. "And no standing over you like a nightmare-eating *Món*."

Túlià laughed. "Yes, none of that please."

Ānjìn smiled and passed her an extra blanket. "Your laugh, is it beautiful?"

"It might have been once, but not anymore. Now I imagine it sounds a bit like I'm choking."

Ānjìn was quiet for so long that Túlià raised up from the comfort of her bedding to look over at him. He lay very

241

still, on his back, hands clasped against his chest, staring at the sky.

"What is it?"

"Apologizing is when you admit to being wrong?"

"Yes."

He sat up as well.

"I was wrong to cut you."

"Why did you?"

"My training demanded it. But as you said, it was still a choice, and I made the wrong choice."

"You didn't kill me though."

"No, I didn't."

"Did your training demand that?"

"You saw me in a weakened state. Zānshì aren't allowed to be weak. You could have told someone, so yes, I should have killed you."

"Zānshì aren't supposed to get ship sickness."

He nodded. "I needed to make sure you stayed quiet. I told myself afterward that I didn't kill you because it would have brought more questions than letting you live. But now I think I was just too weak to take your life. So I took your voice, or I tried to. You healed well."

"I don't miss my voice. I hardly notice the roughness anymore. And besides, you could have taken my fingers. That would have been worse than dying."

Ānjìn thought for a moment.

"Are you afraid to die?"

"No."

"Why?"

"I will get to see my mother again, and Kāi, and all of my ancestors."

"Hm."

"Are you afraid to die, Ānjìn?"

"What is it like, the place you go after you die?"

"My mother described islands of Paradise where righteous souls live in golden palaces with the gods. There is always plenty to eat and drink, and pain and sickness can't reach anyone there."

"But you said there are spirits born of evil. Where do they stay?"

"In the underworld, where the ruler of darkness watches over layers of judgment chambers below the ground. Each chamber holds a different punishment for a different sin."

"What sort of punishment?"

"Beheading, burning, boiling in oil, that sort of thing. It's not a happy place."

"Oh."

"But if sinners learn to regret their evil and ask for mercy, they can drink the elixir of forgetfulness and be reborn into the living world for another chance at a better life."

Ānjìn was silent for a long time. When he finally spoke, it was not what Túlià expected.

"I have no one waiting for me."

"You could," she answered carefully. "You might simply not know it."

"I know *something* waits for me, but if it's not family, then it must be something bad. Punishment, like you said."

Now it was Túlià's turn to be silent. She didn't want to speak until she was certain she had the right words for her Zānshì-boy.

"...My mother's people believe we will meet all those who care for us after death. And for those who care that still live once we have died, we will sleep, and wait for them to join us. It's why we are buried with provisions, to sustain us

243

while we wait in this world to cross over into the next with our loved ones."

"Why are you telling me this?"

"Because even if there is no one in your past waiting for you, there could be someone in your future who *you* may wish to wait for."

Ānjìn's dark eyes became heavier somehow.

"But what if there is a person who doesn't want me to wait for them?"

"Well," Túlià smiled, "there is hardly anything they can do to stop you, is there."

The shadows over his eyes retreated, banished by the light of his slowly growing smile.

"Even if they are incredibly stubborn?"

Túlià threw a much larger pebble and settled into her blankets.

"Being stubborn is a good thing."

"I never said it wasn't."

"Some would consider it a strength, in fact."

"And I would agree."

"Go to sleep, Ānjìn."

FORTY EIGHT

"The third law: anyone who was blasphemous against the Empire would be subjected to Tattoo."

When the edge of The City came into sight days later, Túlià retreated to the cart, donned her white veil, and waited for the wheels to stop. Ānjin was supposed to vanish the moment they passed over the moat and through The Gate of Resolute Separation, and vanish he did. They would find a place to meet again in The City, after he had covered himself once more in Zānshì wrappings and mask.

Túlià heard his fingers pass lightly over her door and counted to eight before emerging, her hands outstretched to passersby. Thanks to her veil, it wasn't long before a woman took pity.

"What befalls you, Lady of Xórong?"

"My driver, he has deserted me. Please, the Emperor expects my return at The Hall of Obedience before nightfall."

The woman nodded. "I have a son, young and strong, to drive your oxen. I will fetch him if it pleases you."

Túlià bowed in thanks, and while she waited for the woman to return, caught the attention of a girl wearing the colors of Xórong's serving class.

Worn thin and travel weary, Túlià had no desire to be bothered, no desire to explain away her rough voice to dozens of curious Palace-goers. So, to avoid repeating such tiresome and painful explanations, she whispered into the serving girl's ear, her words like the wings of a secret fly plucking at the strands on a spiderweb of gossip.

The girl slipped away, practically running for the servants' quarters in the South Three Houses to inform its residents of the death of Xórong's Painter at the hands of the Sywán.

By the time the woman returned with her dimpled son, Túlià suspected the loose lips of the serving class had already spread her announcement between Palaces faster than any messenger. Her tale would hopefully reach every ear by the time she arrived, and keep anyone from questioning her veil or voice, the latter of which she intended to use as little as possible.

Túlià's new driver smiled bashfully at the ground beneath her feet, helped her into the cart, took the reins, and guided her oxen to The Gate of Refined Artistry. After thanking him, Túlià made her way inside.

It took every bit of her concentration to walk as much like Kāì as she could recall, with smooth, silent footsteps, folded hands, and graceful spine. Resisting the urge to adjust her veil every time she passed another person, Túlià wasn't able to breathe again until she finally made it to her rooms.

Then, breathe she did, deeply and with immense gratitude. There was nothing like the familiar smell of your own space after being away for days upon days.

"Anything else, lady?"

Túlià started, frowning beneath her veil at the servant she'd directed to unload the cart. He had been the only one there to receive the returning Princess Kāì, which had saddened but not surprised Túlià. Kāì was never really a Princess, so her return didn't warrant much fanfare.

Dismissing him, Túlià stood alone in the windowed space of her private rooms.

She and Kāi's dwellings lay side by side in The Palace of Refined Artistry, only a short walk from the nearest garden, which housed The Pavilion of Refinement, where Túlià composed collection after collection of paintings, just like her mother before her.

Now, as much as she wanted to fall into her own bed and sleep for days, Túlià couldn't risk being found dressed as Kāi in a dead Painter's rooms. It would have raised questions. Steeling herself, she stepped around the crane-painted screen she'd gifted Kāi three seasons ago, and entered her companion's quiet, empty space.

Túlià had always considered Kāi to be just that, a companion. They had agreed long ago not to refer to one another as sisters. Their closeness, the bond they shared, was a choice, not a title imposed on them by blood. Túlià also never thought of Kāi as someone who served her, though as a personal Attendant, she was much higher ranked than a mere servant. Only blood daughters could become Attendants, and they most often served the Princesses.

Indeed, Kāi had served one of the Princesses nearly all her life, spending what free time she had in The Pavilion of Refinement with Túlià and her mother. It wasn't until after Huàjā had passed, and she'd been offered the role of Painter to the Emperor, that Túlià had the power, little though it was, to insist Kāi come to stay with her.

She'd needed the company more than she'd needed someone to keep her day-to-day affairs in order, but Kāi had done so willingly and with love, making the year after her mother's death more bearable than she'd thought possible.

As a show of gratitude, she'd encouraged Kāi to begin adding poems to the works Xórong didn't wish to mark himself, and both women had delighted in seeing their combined efforts on the painted fan of a Princess or a screen set out in the gardens.

Túlià walked among Kāi's belongings, which somehow looked almost as lonely as she felt.

An unfinished scroll lay on her desk, open to a poem.

Is it possible that life can last forever? Worried and sad, my tears wet my garment. The noble bird soars over Mountains, while swallows and sparrows rest among lower forests. Dark clouds becloud the front yard. A bland zither tone saddens my heart. In the lofty Mountains there are honking cranes. How could ever I follow them?

Kāi hadn't given in to Xórong's spoiled sense of beauty either. Túlià realized that now. She had found beauty in poetry, in watching Túlià paint, even in her awful little Qìnjy. Kāi had her own understanding of beauty, an understanding free of the obsession, envy, greed, and competition that Xórong pushed on everyone else within the walls of The City. And Túlià loved her for it.

She managed to read the poem through, dry eyed and smiling, until she turned and saw the Qìnjy cage, its once-vibrant resident lying still and silent at the bottom.

FORTY NINE

"At court they began to disapprove in their hearts."

Túlià slept very little that night.

In the end, she couldn't bear to lie in Kāì's bed. Gathering a few blankets, she'd piled them on the floor and spent hours counting the many unthinkable consequences of what she'd done and still intended to do.

She would have ten days, ten days before her mourning period ended and her veil had to be removed. Ten days of walking The City as Kāì to learn all she could about her mother's death.

Even in mourning, however, she would be required to earn her place. With Túlià dead, Kāì would be given to a new *Mistress*. The word felt strange in Túlià's thoughts, since she had never considered herself such to Kāì, but a new Mistress was indeed who she would soon be assigned to, a spoiled, gold-dusted young thing to order her here and there. She would likely be instructed to visit the Advisor before morning's end. Xórong did not tolerate laziness from his lower court.

Ānjìn would spend the next ten days among his brothers and Generals with a task no less difficult than her own. When they'd parted, he still intended to tell everyone of what his torture had revealed to the Rajah despite the risk of great punishment. He'd said it was his duty to warn the Zānshì of the potential threat to come. And though it pained her to protect Xórong in any way, Túlià recognized the importance to Ānjìn, and also knew that to protect the Emperor was to protect his people.

Curious, Túlià had asked how Ānjìn would speak to his Generals, since she now knew about his vow of silence, and wondered if Zānshì were allowed to speak to one another.

He had shown her, to Túlià's amazement, that the Zānshì had a language all their own, spoken not with lips and throat, but with their hands. He'd demonstrated a few words while they sat behind the oxen, and waited patiently until she could coax her long fingers into the motions herself. A language of finger shapes. Xórong had thought of everything, though Túlià could hardly imagine a group of white-masked Zānshì standing in a circle, in secret, making such delicate movements to one another. It was almost...haunting, and she wished to someday witness what she considered to be something akin to a performance.

A knock at the door interrupted her morning meal, fulfilling her prediction of a quick summons to the Advisor when she opened it to find one of his personal servants on the other side.

Straightening her veil, Túlià followed him through gold-rimmed gates and flowered gardens, ignoring the whispers from passing servants who smelled of seed soap and yellow rice wine.

Much like Kāi's rooms were situated so near to Túlià's and The Pavilion of Refinement where she worked, the Advisor's private rooms and workspaces adjoined the Emperor's Hall of Ensuring Contentment, though Xórong used it more for entertaining guests than hearing the pleas of his people. The Hall was filled, just past tastefully, with as many of his treasures as could possibly be fit inside. The best he kept for himself in his more private spaces, of course, but this collection was meant to garner the envy of visitors from far-off lands. It still held a few of her mother's paintings, the sight of which, as always, tugged at Túlià's heart. She saw none of her own though, and wondered briefly if they had been covered or removed due to her recent death. It certainly wasn't Xórong's way of thinking to do so, but perhaps there was someone here with enough respect for the spirits to cover her work.

The Advisor to the Emperor was a frenzied sort of man, who always looked as though he needed more than a day of rest. He was charged with the inner runnings of The City, and acted as more of a glorified servant than a true Advisor, since Xórong insisted on handling all other affairs of the Empire himself. This meant the Advisor did less in the way of guiding the Emperor's choices and more to organize the servants, kitchens, baths, and everything else that stayed strictly within The City walls. Now, with her old Mistress dead, Túlià veiled as Kāi had become one of the Advisor's duties.

Despite being summoned, Túlià had to wait behind three others. They all complained of the same thing. The food for the Emperor's end-of-season banquet was late arriving. Túlià thought of Dockmaster Mātu's prediction and wondered if the delayed food came from having to send carts to all edges of the Empire to collect enough harvest to supply such a feast.

When it was her turn, the Advisor did not look up from his scrolls until she answered his request to speak her name, and then, she was certain only because of her scar-roughened voice.

"Skills?"

"Embroidery and calligraphy," Túlià lied.

"Will your voice improve?"

"It isn't likely."

"Then go to Princess Xiàná. She prefers her Attendants be silent anyway."

Túlià's stomach twisted.

"Xiàná? Are you certain there is no one else?"

He shook his head. "No one willing to hear your voice. The other Princesses already have Attendants besides. Princess Xiàná has just dismissed her last Attendant for walking too closely behind her."

"Advisor—"

"You will be silent and Princess Xiàná's, or sent to the kitchens, where you can rasp at the servants as much as you like."

Túlià felt her face heat beneath the veil. Of course it had to be Xiàná, who she hated nearly as Xórong's equal. Remembering Ānjìn's words about monsters and the choices they made, Túlià took a deep breath and bowed her head.

"Princess Xiàná. Thank you, Advisor."

He waved her away, and she managed Kāi's walk all the way to his doors before reverting to the frustrated stomp she usually adopted on The City paths.

Túlià would not have access to the places she needed to search if she were confined to the kitchens. Servants could certainly slip about between Palaces and eavesdrop unnoticed, but Túlià had never been good at sneaking. Ānjìn had told her as much. And she wasn't familiar with the secret paths of The City the way a servant would be. She could hardly learn them in ten days either. As an Attendant, she would be able to enter places in plain sight that no servant would ever be allowed.

It had to be Xiàná.

FIFTY

"Outside they debated these laws in the streets."

"**Y**ou must be still, Princess."
"My name is Xiàná."
"Yes, Princess Xiàná, I need you to be still or I cannot paint your portrait."

It wasn't often that Túlià saw her mother's patience wear thin, but it was more than thin now, thanks to Xórong's most recently chosen Princess.

Despite being new to her life in the high court, and barely past eleven summers, Princess Xiàná already carried herself like someone who expected her orders to be followed, and followed quickly.

"Princess, please. Your father has requested a portrait of you. He intends it as a gift. But I cannot continue if you don't stop fidgeting.

A handful of servants moved to Xiàná's side, readjusting the many layers of her silk robes, tucking away long strands of loose hair, and dabbing fresh powder onto her cheeks.

The Princess coughed and waved them away, smudging the bright red of her lips with sleeves so long she seemed to lose herself in their gold edges.

"I don't want my portrait to be painted."
"But your father—"
"I don't care what the Emperor says," Xiàná cried.

Túlià's mother took a deep breath and stood from the half-painted scroll laid across her table.

"*Maybe if you come to look at the painting, Highness, and see how pretty you are, you might change your mind.*"

Princess Xiàná waded through the bunched fabric of her robes to reach the table and peer down at Huàjā's carefully inked lines.

Túlià remembered admiring what she considered a remarkably perfect likeness of the Princess's delicate features, but Xiàná hadn't seemed to think so.

"*I hate it. Stupid Painter woman! Throw it away and start again. This time, make it look like me!*"

FIFTY ONE

"It became a mark of fame to defy the ruler, and was regarded as lofty to take a dissenting stance."

"My dear Kāì, wait, please!"

Túlià pulled herself from the memory of Princess Xiàná's spoil-pinched face and went still until she saw who had stopped her on the way to her new Mistress's rooms.

"Scholar Lóshī," Túlià sighed. May the spirits forgive her.

"I heard everything," he said softly, losing his relieved smile at the sight of her veil. "Forgive my joy over your return. It is hardly appropriate given the circumstances, but I am so glad my little poet made it home safely."

"As am I, Scholar, though it came at such a cost. I miss Túlià more every moment."

"Of course. You alone know how deeply I understand such a loss. And I see the rest of the whispers were true as well, though I hoped against it. Your voice, dear poet, does it cause you much pain?"

"Hardly any now, though I suppose my words will only be beautiful on parchment from here forward."

Lóshī chuckled and apologized immediately, inclining his head toward her veil. "Forgive me again, but it is true. Your calligraphy may very well surpass even the writings of the Emperor himself."

"And I have you to thank for it," Túlià murmured, bowing in return. "Now if you will give me leave, Scholar, I must continue on to my new Mistress."

He smiled again, this time with brief confusion.

"New *Mistress*? An odd word to hear from your lips, as is *Scholar*. You have only ever called me by name. I know you must suffer, but is something else the matter—"

His words stumbled as he took her hands, hands he spent seasons training to write characters worthy of the eyes of the ancestors themselves, that now opened like unfamiliar flowers against his palms.

Well, not entirely unfamiliar.

"Túlià?"

She shook her head, trying to pull away, but his grip had become iron.

"Túlià, what does this mean? Where is my little poet? Where is Kāi?"

"She is—lost," Túlià choked, "Lost. But Scholar, please. You must listen."

Lóshī's breath began to shake, his hands tightening past painful around Túlià's wrists.

"Lost? Lost? Not my poet. Not another. The gods cannot take another from me!"

He sank to his knees, shaking his head and weeping, still refusing to release Túlià.

"Scholar Lóshī, please. You will bring the Zānshì. You must quiet yourself."

"How can you be here? How can you, in her robes, in her place!"

"I do it for my mother," Túlià hissed in his ear. "My mother, who cared for Kāi like a daughter herself."

"Huàjā?" His eyes cleared for a moment. "Gone as well. How could we have lost so much?"

256

"Yes, my mother is gone. And I want to know why."

"Why?"

"I do not believe it was a mere misfortune," Túlià whispered, still bending quietly to his ear. "I have heard otherwise."

He began shaking again and pulled her down to kneel in front of him.

"The Hall of Written Illumination. There are records. Túlià, what happened to Kāì? Who took her from us?"

Túlià bowed her head, remembering that day, the blood, the Zānshì, the Sywán, who fought only to protect themselves.

"It was…an accident. A terrible—"

"You lie! I can hear it even past the roughness of your voice! You—"

He jerked and slumped forward. Túlià braced instinctively, expecting the weight of his body, but instead, he was lifted up and away, leaving her on the floor, in the shadows of the two Zānshì who had knocked him silent.

FIFTY TWO

"The lesser officials lead in fabricating slander."

The first thing Ānjìn had done after leaving Túlià was to find a special place where he might tuck away his satchel. He would have ten days, according to his Painter, and hoped to do what he must with the contents before seeing her again.

Ānjìn did wish to see Túlià one last time, to pass on anything he discovered about her mother before he was brought to his Emperor and ordered to die.

Then he would sit for her in the place where spirits waited.

The second thing Ānjìn had done was to stay in shadow until midday, when the rooms in The Hall of Imperial Reinforcement would be emptied for inspection. The moment the Generals passed through, he slipped inside and donned a new set of white wrappings.

And a mask, of course.

He shivered when it touched his skin. Was this how it felt to hate something? Was this how Túlià felt about his Emperor?

Was this how she felt about the Zānshì? About him?

But she'd said once he died, there was nothing she could do to keep Ānjìn's spirit from waiting for her, no matter how stubborn.

So he would wait.

Ānjìn chose to think of this, not of his own breath trapped behind the mask, and went to find a General. There was always one beneath the nearest turret, watching from the perfect position to study both the training grounds and the smooth cycle of patrols relieving one another from duty on The City walls above him.

Emperor Xórong had demanded constant watch over the entire City, no easy task due to its size and complexity. He wanted to always be aware who came in, who came out, and what his visitors did while they stayed.

But no General stood there now. He would only have left if his Emperor called a meeting. And Ānjìn knew where that meeting would be.

He could go.

If Ānjìn's crimes against his Emperor were already past forgivable, attending a Generals-only meeting could hardly make things worse. Besides, he wanted something, some piece of information, however small, to offer Túlià when they met again. He doubted to learn anything about her mother at such a meeting, but the emptiness of the space beneath the turret scratched at him.

So he went.

The Generals were permitted to speak in their Emperor's presence. They wore black masks, with no seal over their mouths, and carried black bone-knives instead of white.

Meetings with the Emperor were not scheduled, and occurred only at his request, always in the same place, a small room tucked between The Hall of Imperial Reinforcement and The Palace of Unrequited Symmetry.

When he arrived, Ānjìn began automatically searching the walls, looking for one of Túlià's painted hanging scrolls, but there were none. The room was strangely bare.

"If there is nothing else…"

Ānjìn watched as the man kneeling before his Emperor was pulled away, red-eyed and quiet.

A Scholar?

Why would the Generals be called to meeting for a Scholar?

"What would you have us do, Highness?"

Emperor Xórong turned to the General and made an easy movement with his hand. "Nothing yet. This is a small threat, hardly a threat at all, in fact. I will wait until I know more, and direct you then."

A threat.

The Rajah.

Ānjìn's heart jumped.

How could the Emperor dismiss his errors so easily? The weakness he had displayed in front of the Rajah was a threat fully grown. It was no surprise to Ānjìn that the Emperor knew of his failings already, but his information was flawed, and his Empire was in danger.

Ānjìn stood, straightening out from crouch and hiding place, and made his way to the center of the room. Kneeling, he held out his hands, requesting to speak.

Hisses of disapproval and cries of outrage gathered across his shoulders, but Emperor Xórong held them back with his eyes.

"If this Zānshì risked death to be here, and was then foolish enough to reveal himself, what he has to say might be worth hearing."

He nodded to one of the Generals, who watched Ānjìn's rushed fingers through the holes of his black mask, and interpreted the movements for their Emperor.

"He says he was patrolling the border and heard rumors that one of our Zānshì had fallen into the hands of

261

the Rajah. The Zānshì was tortured, and the Rajah's men found weakness in his knees. He apologizes for his interruption, but could not wait to inform you of the danger. He worries the Rajah may attack and use this information against you."

A half-truth.

A half-lie.

Ānjìn had lied to Emperor Xórong. But he did it for Túlià. He would see her again, then confess every falsehood at his Emperor's feet.

It was a long time before Xórong spoke.

"Have this Zānshì whipped for his interruption."

FIFTY THREE

"In upper circles, Xórong's authority became compromised, and in lower ones cliques began to form."

When the Zānshì took Scholar Lóshī away, Túlià half expected to feel their gloved hands as well, but they let her be. She hadn't been the one to cause a disruption.

The Emperor hated disruptions.

Lóshī would likely be held in solitude until he calmed. If he could regain control quickly, word of his fit in the halls may never even reach Xórong. Túlià didn't want to think about what would happen if it did.

Would Scholar Lóshī tell Xórong the truth? If he gave up her secret or shared her plans, Túlià would surely be discovered, questioned, and most likely imprisoned for deceit. She would have no hope of finding answers in a cell.

Keeping her eyes on the floor until the Zānshì had taken Lóshī well out of sight, Túlià stood, and was surprised to find herself shaking.

"No," she muttered, taking long strides toward The Hall of Written Illumination. "They are only men. Only men."

She knew that now. So why did she still fear the Zānshì? Why did her body still seize motionless at the absence of sound they seemed to carry with them like a cloud of smoke?

They were only men. One of them could have been Ānjìn, for all she knew.

But she did know. Ānjìn hadn't been there with her. Túlià was certain. She would have felt something. Or he would have shown her somehow, given her some sign.

The Zānshì were only men, but they were still warriors, still duty-bound to their Emperor, so she still had more than every reason to fear them. Knowing their secret gave her no true advantage. Even after seeing Ānjìn's face, the worst she had been able to do was hit him with a pebble and strike him once. She regretted the latter, but also knew that if he'd truly wanted to stop her hand, he could have done so easily.

Even though Túlià had a Zānshì of her own now, he was only one against an army of men masked as demons, and she was running out of time.

She had to assume Lóshī would share her secret, had to assume the ten days she'd given herself to find answers dwindled with every step she took. She needed to find Ānjìn, send him a message somehow, to warn him of what happened, but first, The Hall of Written Illumination.

Túlià had never heard of whatever records Lóshī mentioned, and didn't know if they would have any relevance to her mother's death, but it was the only piece of information she'd gained so far. Her new Mistress could wait a few hours more, since Túlià now had none to spare, so she lowered her veiled face past the Zānshì pair guarding its entrance, and stepped through the Gate of Written Illumination.

Aside from the hush of two Scholars moving about the space, lifting, opening, and reading scrolls, the Hall was quiet, and strangely empty.

Túlià had been expecting boxes, stacks of boxes, with scrolls spilling from every one, but she could have removed

264

the entire contents of the large room in perhaps a dozen armloads. It wasn't until she selected a scroll that Túlià was struck by its familiarity.

One of her works, an ink painting of her mother's Mountains with a tiny marble pavilion barely discernible at its base.

Xórong had, as always, marked the upper left corner with a poem.

White dew grows on the marble steps, and in the long night, soaks into my stockings. But now I let the crystal curtain down, and gaze through it at the autumn moon.

Why was it here?

Is this where her works had been moved in light of her supposed death? She'd noticed a few of them missing from the walls, but there were so many in front of her now, enough to make her want to check every rolled bit of paper and silk to see if the contents of the room had all been created by her hand.

Túlià moved to look through a row of hanging scrolls strung between free-standing frames that had been none too gently pushed together against the furthest wall. Stepping behind the first towering, shadowed, Mountain scene, she ran straight into a smaller, robed figure and nearly went sprawling.

"Princess Xiàná?"

Steadying herself and adjusting her jewels, Túlià's new Mistress regarded her through dark eyes rimmed with gold dust.

"Who are you? What are you doing here?"

"Your Highness," Túlià stammered, hastily remembering the role she'd assumed. "I have been searching for you. I am your—"

"What is wrong with your voice?"

Túlià bowed even lower, remembering what the Advisor had said about sending her to the kitchens.

"An accident. Forgive me for speaking."

"Speak long enough to answer my questions. How did you find me?"

"I did not realize you were hiding, Mistress, or I would not have looked so hard."

"I am not hiding," she huffed, pointing at a ring she'd dropped in the collision until Túlià picked it up. "Even so, you will tell no one you have seen me here. I should have you imprisoned for this."

"For coming to The Hall of Written Illumination?"

Xiàná stiffened at her insolence.

"The Hall of Written Illumination and its adjoining Pavilion are off limits to the serving class."

"Even for a blood daughter?" Túlià asked, standing.

Xiàná's eyes narrowed.

"Who are you?"

"Kāi. I am to be your new companion. Your new, silent companion."

"Well you are hardly silent."

Though she'd aged to twelve summers now, it seemed the time since her tantrums at Huàjā's expense had not granted the young Princess any new sense of maturity.

"I intend to begin silence as soon as you stop asking questions, and as soon as I ask one of my own. What were you reading?" Túlià asked, producing the small scroll she'd rescued from the folds of Xiàná's skirts while retrieving her ring.

The Princess's face became a new shade of pink.

"I was not reading anything. The Emperor forbids his chosen daughters from learning to read."

Túlià blinked beneath her veil. She'd never heard of such a law, and the Princess certainly looked like she was lying. When Túlià opened the scroll, she half expected to find another of her paintings, something the Princess could have enjoyed without knowing how to read. But this scroll was filled with nothing but delicate rows of carefully stroked characters.

"So, you weren't reading, Princess?"

Xiàná drew back her hand, but stopped even before Túlià realized she had been planning to strike her.

"It is only out of respect for your mourning that I do not punish you. I will hardly be so lenient when your veil period has ended. Now gather my things and come."

"Yes Mistress," Túlià murmured, watching with interest as Xiàná slipped out from behind the hanging scrolls, nodded to the nearest Scholar, and made for a little door at the back corner of the room.

They snuck into a smaller, busier space, where a half dozen Scholars hastily filled scroll after scroll with oceans of dark characters, while a tall man at the front of the room recited what Túlià guessed were messages or new laws from the Emperor to be recorded.

When she slowed, Xiàná grabbed her wrist and pulled, leading her through another set of doors, then another, until they were outside and on their way to Túlià's original destination that morning, Princess Xiàná's rooms.

It wasn't until she shut the doors behind them and cleared out her other servants that the Princess spoke to Túlià again.

"You will not say a word to anyone about my presence in The Hall of Written Illumination or I will have you horribly punished. Do you understand?"

Túlià nodded. "But how did you learn to read if it isn't allowed?"

Xiàná tucked the scroll into her vanity chest and motioned for Túlià to adjust her tightly pinned hair.

"I told you, I cannot read."

"I saw you, Highness."

Pushing her hands away, Xiàná frowned. "You are truly awful at this. My face is being mussed by your clumsiness. And your voice is offensive to me."

"I am aware."

"And mistaken," the Princess insisted. "I know every ridiculous rule the Emperor makes for his Princesses, and reading is most *certainly* not allowed. Keep your sleeves out of my powder!"

Túlià repositioned herself and reached for the hairpins once more. "You don't refer to the Emperor as Father?"

"Only to his face," Xiàná muttered, nodding at a pearl-inlaid hairbrush.

With growing surprise, Túlià lifted the brush and decided to push further. This was a side of Xiàná she had never seen before. Sneaking into The Hall of Written Illumination, knowing how to read, disrespecting the Emperor?

"Do you...hate him?"

"Hate him?" The Princess spun toward her, blossom-pink lips pursed with frustration.

"Of course I don't hate him," she began with false sweetness. "I am not allowed to hate him, just as I am not allowed to learn to read, and not allowed to wear what I like, and not allowed to remain in my rooms when he invites his disgusting guests to run their eyes over me like a horse in a parade."

"But, but I thought—then why do you work so hard to gain his favor?"

Xiàná shook her head in disbelief. "Because without his favor, don't you know where I would be?"

Túlià's silence was answer enough, and Xiàná tipped her chin toward the nearest open window.

"Cast out. The Emperor sends his unwanted to the streets."

FIFTY FOUR

"The ordinary people who wore coarse clothes, who did no harm to the government, or disturbed the masses, began to whisper."

*B*rother, did you attend the Qixé Parade this year past? There was *a painter who—*

The Zānshì turned away before Ānjìn's fingers had even completed the question, ignoring his inquiries as had every Zānshì before him. Ānjìn knew why, but it didn't stop him from trying.

Brother, the Qixé Parade—

Again, for the dozenth time, he was answered with the sight of his brother's back moving stiffly away from him.

It was the whipping.

The smell of his blood, the sight of it crusting the white cloth across his shoulder blades, marked him as a disobeyer. Ānjìn had done something to displease their Emperor. His brothers didn't need to know the details of his offense. They didn't care. Knowing that he'd failed in some way was enough.

He had been confined to the training yard and Enforcement Hall because of it, since no one was allowed to see Zānshì blood. So Ānjìn would remain in the circle of his brothers' judgment until he managed to scrub his clothes clean.

He had heard of such a punishment, and could recall only one pink-stained set of robes walking around the yards very early in his training. He had never been sure if the whipped Zānshì managed to finally wash his stains free, or if he simply disappeared.

Either way, such a task had taken seasons to complete, and Ānjìn didn't have seasons, he had days. Nine days until he would say goodbye to his Painter, kneel before his Emperor, and confess his betrayals, every last one.

Until then, he would do all in his power to gather information for Túlià, though the sight of his blood like a red flag in the wind seemed to have stripped what little ability he had to find answers.

When the sun drifted low behind the yard walls, Ānjìn resigned himself to a night of scrubbing, and began to move toward the fountain simply because he could think of no other—

"Zānshì."

The black mask of a General appeared beside the fountain and motioned for him to follow. "Return to the room of punishment. Our Emperor has a task for you."

Ignoring the pain in his back and knees, Ānjìn re-entered the space where his Generals had tied him down, bared his skin, and whipped him bloody. He had suffered, but the pain was nothing compared to the Rajah's irons against his legs.

No Generals filled the room now, only the one who led him and a soft looking man who knelt on the floor. It was a Scholar, the same he'd seen weeping at the Emperor's feet.

"Zānshì, this man holds information our Emperor seeks. You are to recover that information. Break him quickly."

Ānjìn nodded, and the General left.

"Please, please. I have already...already told everything I know. There is nothing—"

The Scholar had to pause and wipe clean what was left of his mouth before speaking again, but Ānjìn didn't let him. Stepping forward, he raised his bone-knife and struck, blunt end first, into the tender space behind the ear.

Three strikes, increasing in pain, then give your prisoner a chance to speak. Three more strikes, this time drawing blood, then another chance. Continue in this method until answers come forth. Most prisoners do not make it past the fifth strike.

The Scholar howled, muddling the voices of the Generals in his mind, and Ānjìn watched as he made silly attempts to drag himself away.

Break him quickly.

Why was this Scholar being tortured? He was not a warrior. What threat did he pose to the Emperor? And the sound he'd made when Ānjìn struck him...he was in pain, real pain.

In training, Ānjìn had been taught to bear pain. The pain of fire against his skin, water in his lungs, metal cutting into bone. Pain was something he could tuck away and forget, or it had been, until he'd been given a different kind of pain.

Was the agony of the Rajah's irons against his legs the same as the strike of his bone-knives to a Scholar untrained in the ways of burying the hurt of his body?

Ānjìn thought of all the prisoners he had made suffer in the past, all the people he'd broken. Most of them were not warriors either, and though he hadn't enjoyed it, Ānjìn had done what his Emperor required of him. He had never truly understood the power of pain, not until, with the bones of his knees in near splinters, he had wished for death.

Pain became something new to him that day.

The suffering had been too great to spread. And now, with the Scholar making the same sounds at his hands as Ānjìn had at the hands of the Rajah's men, he realized all pain was agony to people who had not been trained to control it. People like those he had tortured in the past. People like the poor Scholar before him now.

And he claimed to have shared all he knew.

Looking at his mangled body, Ānjìn believed him.

If most men gave up their secrets before the fifth strike, this Scholar was either unreasonably strong, or his claims were true. He had nothing left to share.

Crouching beside him, Ānjìn slid a single bone-knife between the Scholar's ribs, pierced his heart, and waited until the blood stopped flowing before he left the room.

FIFTY FIVE

*"The Empire was already in rebellion, but the ruler had no loyal
Advisors left to inform him of the villainy."*

"You wish to return to The Hall of Written
Illumination? Why?"

When Túlià failed to offer an answer, Princess Xiàná
stood, leaving the mirror behind to sit at her window and
enjoy a bit of fresh air.

"There is hardly anything of interest there anyway. The
Emperor has most of it burned."

"Burned?"

She frowned, pushing a poorly pinned lock of hair out
of her eyes.

"You are truly the most awful Attendant I have ever
had. And yes, burned. The Emperor made a new law ages
ago that everything *impractical* in The Hall of Written
Illumination should be burned. It is nearly always empty,"
she continued, trying to salvage what she could of her hair,
"since the Zānshì come in once every half season or so to
burn the next batch. What you saw in the Hall today will not
be there for long."

"But why are there so many of my—so many paintings
there? Does Xórong burn those too?"

Xiàná's delicate brows lifted.

"Yes, *Xórong* burns almost everything in that room, as I said. And good riddance. His awful Painter doesn't deserve to have her work on display."

Túlià swallowed. She knew it. She knew the Princesses hated her. Kāì had always chided her for saying so but—

"She's the reason we're all miserable. As if the Emperor didn't make our rules of life clear enough, she had to paint pictures of them on a scroll hung across the walls of our leisure rooms."

"What?"

Xiàná regarded her with frustrated disbelief.

"Are your eyes as ruined as your voice beneath that veil? Surely you must have seen her work there. *Admonitions of the Court Instructress*, she called it, yards and yards of silk painted to show just how a proper Princess should behave. The Emperor loved it, of course. He mentions it at nearly every evening meal as a sort of standard to hold us to."

"I thought you hated the Painter for her competition."

"Competition?" Xiàná scoffed. "Favor for the Emperor is always a competition. Why should we hate her for that? It is what we live every day."

Túlià sank onto the nearest cushion, and thought.

"Do all of the Princesses feel this way about the Emperor?" she finally asked.

"Of course. Our *Father* is simply a better alternative, though not much better, from whatever brothel would snatch us from the streets should we lose his favor and be cast outside The City walls. So we stay and we primp and we dance and we smile, and we do our best to live up to the impossible standards his Painter strung across our rooms."

"I didn't know what he wanted them for."

"Excuse me?"

Túlià stood. "I didn't know Xórong was going to hang my work on your walls. He commissioned a scroll filled with your daily activities. He was very particular. The Princesses dressing, washing, caring for their hair, playing their instruments. This scroll, are there characters near the works?" she asked, ignoring the confused slump in Xiàná's mouth.

"Yes, lines of characters separate each painting, telling us in great detail how we ought to behave to best please him. It is a double insult of sorts, since none of us are meant to be able to read it anyway. But how did you—"

"He added them after. I swear on the ancestors. It's what he always does to my work, as a claiming of sorts. He puts his own mark, his own message, though it's usually nothing more than a harmless poem."

Xiàná stood as well, her eyes hot with anger.

"Well this scroll was far from harmless. Why are you here, Painter? Are you not meant to be dead?"

Túlià shook her head, searched the room for listeners, and lifted her veil when she felt certain they were alone.

She held one other certainty in that moment. Princess Xiàná was a potential ally, and a powerful one at that. For the first time since forming her half-mad plan, Túlià felt she had gained a foothold.

"I am not dead. Take me back to The Hall of Written Illumination and I will explain everything."

"I knew you weren't an Attendant," Xiàná said smugly. "A horse boy could manage pins better than you. Why should I go anywhere when I could simply scream for help and have you imprisoned for deceit?"

"Because I am beginning to learn that I'm not the only breathing body in The City who hates Xórong. I came here seeking answers, and if I find what I believe to be true, then

I intend to hurt him. I am offering you the chance to help, or, if you wish, to simply pretend you never saw me."

"Hurt the Emperor?" Xiàná's perfect lips gave a very un-Princess like smile. "How may I be of assistance, Painter?"

FIFTY SIX

"How pitiful!"

"I am entering the room."
Despite his efforts to do everything Túlià had asked of him in the past, to not startle her and calmly announce his presence, she still jumped when Ānjìn stepped into her space.

But she'd called him here. He'd seen the dove tree branches on her windowsill. How could someone who expected him still be startled?

Standing just inside, he looked around the room with interest until his eyes settled on Túlià.

"You look worried."

"Something happened today," she began, stopping when she saw his blood-soaked robes.

"Who did this?"

"A punishment, one I deserved. Are you in trouble?"

"I'm afraid Xórong will learn of my search, or at least find out I am not Kāì."

"Did you speak to him?"

"No, but—Ānjìn, do you have to wear your mask here?"

He nodded. "I don't want to, but I think it would be best."

Sensing her frown, Ānjìn reached for his mask and nodded at her veil.

"Alright, but only if you join me."

She did, and both delighted in a brief moment of free air before Túlià's frown returned.

"I spoke with Scholar Lóshī, the man I told you about, who as far as raised Kāì. He knew his little poet too well to be fooled by my clumsy attempts to mimic her, and all but lost his mind in full view today."

"Did he hurt you?"

"No. The Zānshì took him away. I know he will be briefly imprisoned but I fear he will be questioned as well. He has lost so much, his son and now Kāì. I don't know if Lóshī would be strong enough to protect me from Xórong's inquiries, especially if the Emperor suspects me already."

Something began to twist in Ānjìn's stomach and the pain in his knees grew slightly worse.

"A Scholar?"

"Yes, I don't know where the Zānshì brought him. I assume the lesser confinement. An old Scholar like Lóshī hardly deserves the lower cells. What is it?"

Ānjìn looked tired. He felt tired. He seemed to feel everything more intensely when he was with Túlià, as if she made him remember that he was simply a man. This reminder was often refreshing, as it allowed him to just be. Not a Zānshì, not a demon, just Ānjìn. But the things he felt now were thick and unpleasant.

"Túlià, your Kāì's Scholar, I think I killed him."

Seeing his pain, Túlià motioned for him to sit, moving cautiously for his sake and hers.

"What do you mean? How could you have killed him?"

"There was a Scholar being questioned in the Generals' room. I attended to gather information about your mother. The Emperor had him taken away just after I arrived. I was

280

whipped for attending, and was later offered the chance to earn forgiveness by questioning the Scholar."

Túlià stiffened.

"And did you…question him?"

"I struck him once. But I couldn't go on. I was certain he didn't know anything of value. I knew he wouldn't be let go, and I knew he had nothing left to give, so I killed him."

"How."

"A knife in the heart."

Túlià shook for a moment, took a deep breath, and then released a long sigh.

"He would have been killed anyway?" she asked, carefully beginning to examine the blood marring Ānjìn's back.

"Yes, and suffered more beforehand."

"You did him a mercy?"

"I tried."

"Then…there is nothing else to say. He will join Kāi."

The pain in Ānjìn's body released like a great flood, as though a dam he never realized he'd built had sprung leaks at her words.

"I wish I had learned something about your mother."

"I didn't learn much either, though Scholar Lóshī did tell me before he was taken that there might be some information about my mother in Xórong's records. I searched a bit today, and made an interesting ally. We will continue tomorrow. Did you know Xórong has been burning a great many of my paintings?"

"No."

"I saw some among the scrolls in his Hall of Written Illumination. My ally told me just about everything stored there is burned in regular batches."

"All of it?"

"Everything Xórong considers *impractical*."

Ānjìn looked around the room, taking in the stacks of supplies, inks, scrolls, brushes, paintings completed, half completed, and just begun.

"Will he come here next, to take any of these?"

"I hope not. Xórong has never set foot in my rooms, or my mother's Pavilion, and I pray he never does. It was her space, and mine, and Kāi's. It carries their memories."

"Do you remember telling me about the Three Perfections?" Ānjìn asked.

"Yes. Painting, calligraphy, and poetry. Why?"

"If the Emperor finds your paintings impractical, he might find the other Perfections impractical as well. Will he take and burn Kāi's poems?"

Ānjìn watched as Túlià's face worked through a dozen emotions that somehow ended with her smiling down at him.

"It's possible. Will you help me hide them?"

He nodded, followed Túlià into Kāi's rooms, and made sure to turn his back each time her tears needed a moment alone with the poem-filled scrolls.

FIFTY SEVEN

"How could Xórong reframe his commitment, when his original ambitions proved impossible to attain?"

"So you didn't hate my mother's work?"

"Of course not," Xiàná muttered, standing on her toes to reach a higher shelf. "I only hated portraits."

"Why?"

"Because I was new to this life and didn't understand what was expected of me yet. I abhorred wearing all that finery. It was itchy, heavy, and terribly uncomfortable. I am used to it now, but I wasn't then."

"I don't understand how your physical discomfort made you demand my mother repaint your portrait half a dozen times."

"Because I hated the way I appeared in them. I hardly recognized myself beneath all that gold. And every time I saw my own portrait, I was reminded that I could never look the way I wanted again, that I would always be a doll for the Emperor to do up however he liked."

"I owe you an apology," Túlià murmured, meeting Xiàná's eye through the stacked scrolls that stood between them in The Hall of Written Illumination.

"Do you?"

"Yes. I always believed you to be spoiled."

"Well that I certainly am."

"I mean I thought you enjoyed being spoiled, that you were as ugly inside as you are beautiful outside. I was wrong. You are just as much a prisoner to Xórong as I am."

"Yes."

Her soft, clipped answer gave the sense that hearing how the Emperor's Painter used to think of her had bruised Xiàná's young heart, so Túlià attempted to change the conversation, hoping the Princess would one day be able to forgive her misjudgment.

"Have you found anything useful?"

"If by useful you mean old law scrolls and memoirs from dead Scholars, then yes, there are dozens of them," she scoffed, sounding more like herself.

"But can we *use* them?"

"I am still unsure what you mean by that. What are we looking for exactly?" Xiàná asked, brushing dust from her gold-edged sleeves.

"Most specifically, something about my mother. But I would be happy with any sort of secret we can use against Xórong."

"Well there must be secrets here, even if I have never come across them in my reading. I don't imagine he would go to so much effort to have these things burned purely for the sake of *impracticality*. There must be something he doesn't want us to—"

"Daughter, how did you find your way here?"

Túlià's heart seemed to stutter and fail for a moment, and the two Zānshì who flanked their Emperor did nothing to calm her fear of being caught. Taking a deep, calming breath, she followed Xiàná's lead and swept into a low bow, remaining bent even after the Princess had straightened for a proper greeting.

"Father! Oh how good of you to come help me look in the midst of your busy day," she exclaimed, her words so convincingly sweet that Túlià feared she would tell Xórong what they had truly been looking for and ask him to join in the search for his own demise.

"Look for what, little flower?"

"My kitten, the one you had brought in from the Rajah's lands. He's wandered off. My servants and I have been looking since before morning meal."

Xórong began to play with a lock of her hair, twisting it around his fingers while he sent a few condescendingly helpful looks around the room.

"He doesn't appear to be nearby, sweet daughter, and I am afraid my true purpose in being here is a bit more serious."

"Is something wrong, Father?"

"Nothing to worry yourself over. My Zānshì have simply told me that more visitors than usual have been entering this place, and I wanted to investigate."

"Oh but Father," Xiàná giggled, "It is only a few dusty bits of silk and paper. Why you even guard it is above me."

"I'm sure it must seem silly to you, flower, but trust me, there are important records here, not meant for enemy eyes."

"Oh my," the Princess whispered, her own eyes widening as though at the mention of a Palace scandal. "What sort of records?"

Xórong gave her hair one last tug and lowered his voice to a whisper as well.

"You won't tell anyone, will you daughter, if I give you a quick look?"

Xiàná shook her head and giggled into her sleeves as she followed Xórong to one of the shelves she and Túlià had been sifting through only moments ago.

While her father made a show of selecting the proper scroll, Xiàná motioned Túlià over to arrange the long folds of her robe.

Grateful to be able to move again, Túlià hurried to obey, grateful also for the Princess's cleverness and subtle attempts to keep Túlià close to hear whatever Xórong revealed.

"This scroll," he said, spreading it open on a nearby table, "details my plans to move The City."

The room fell silent, Xiàná's giggles fading away into shock.

"Father?"

"I know, I know. But there is no cause for alarm," he answered, tweaking her chin and sweeping his other hand across the heavily marked scroll. "I know you can't read it, but trust me little flower, this will be a good thing."

"Why? Why move your beautiful City, Father? This is our home," she added, briefly nudging Túlià with a slippered foot to set her hands arranging the robe folds once more.

"It is, and it has served us well. I'm afraid we have simply outgrown it. Just as your missing pet would outgrow the pillow he sleeps on and require a new one, we require a new City."

"And we will all move with you, Father? You must promise me."

"Of course. We will stay together. I wouldn't dare leave a single one of my flowers behind, though it would be best if you did not tell your sisters of this. I don't want to upset them."

286

"I will keep silent," she whispered, smiling now, at the prospect of a secret. She leaned over the scroll, her eyes wide and innocent. "Does it say where the new City will be, Father?"

"No no no. That is a secret for my eyes only. Your Emperor is too clever to write down such a valuable piece of information anywhere. It stays in my thoughts, and mine alone. You can be sure of that."

"Will all of your common people come with you? An Emperor must have subjects to rule, after all."

Xórong chuckled at her feigned eagerness.

"I hope they do. They will have to, in fact, since the old City will be leveled into farmland."

"But Father," Xiàná gasped. "What of all your beautiful buildings?"

"Pah, they are hardly beautiful, especially in comparison to my exquisite daughters. It is you and I and the rest of our family that matter. *We* are The City. The people have been a bit restless lately. They need a reminder that where we go, they must follow. We are not bound by silly buildings or tied to land. We can move as we please, build where we please!"

"Oh Father, that does sound wonderful. When do you plan to—"

"Little flower, is this your new Attendant? She seems awfully dull, though she might be beautiful beneath her veil. We will have to see in a few days, won't we. Stand," he added, addressing Túlià now. "Tell my daughter how many days are left in your time of mourning."

"Seven, your Highness," Túlià murmured, bowing to both of them.

"Well my goodness, let us hope her face is more beautiful than her voice," Xórong laughed. "What is her name, daughter?"

"I've forgotten. What is it again?"

"Kāì, Mistress."

"Oh yes, Kāì. She used to belong to that Painter. Do you remember, Father?"

"How could I forget? Such a tragedy to lose her," Xórong murmured, his eyes running over Túlià. "And a great pity so much of her work is to be burned."

"Burned?" Xiàná gasped. "But Father, I thought you loved your Painter's pretty Mountains?"

"I do. I do. But sadly, we cannot bring everything when we travel to the new City, and I will find a new Painter there as well, so we will hardly need these old-fashioned works. Now come flower, leave this boring place and return to your rooms. I will send someone to help locate your pet."

"Thank you Father," Xiàná murmured happily. "You are more than good to me."

FIFTY EIGHT

"Soon, a Rajah advanced on the Emperor's City."

Xórong would build a new City.
Túlià's eyes refused to shut that night.
Xórong would level the old City.
She watched light from the rising sun creep across Kāi's floor.

It was why he needed more farmers, why he had been kidnapping Sywán men, why the usually peaceful people had attacked her and Kāi the moment they saw strangers wearing the Emperor's colors ascending their Mountains.

Xórong said he was moving The City to prove to the people that he and his family had greater worth than mere buildings and streets. After speaking to Dockmaster Mātu and hearing his predictions of empty ships, Túlià knew better.

The Emperor wasn't moving his City by choice, but out of necessity. The farmers at the Empire's edge could no longer feed the growing population of wealthy in The City they surrounded. Xórong needed new farmland and the earth beneath The City had never been tilled. It would likely be rich enough to sustain the royal family until the end of his reign at least.

The new City would likely be built somewhere higher, on rocky ground, useless for farming. There were dozens of places to choose from, but Túlià was more concerned for the Sywán than for the secret location tucked deep into the Emperor's head.

How many more men and boys would he take? How many Sywán lives would be lost in the taking? The City was grand and sprawling. A few handfuls of kidnapped Sywán would hardly be able to work so much land.

Would Xórong dare attack the Mountains in full force?

The soil there didn't offer much in the way of harvest, but if Xórong gained control of the Mountains, taking Sywán to work his new farmland would be far easier than—

Túlià rose from the straw mat she'd placed beside Kāì's bed, but sank back to her knees as sickness overtook her.

The Mountains, home to a dwindling people who were the last to practice the old ways and religions Xórong had banned. The Mountains, where so few men and boys remained to defend it, taken by Xórong to work his fields. The Mountains, which offered little in the way of fertile ground but boasted a lofty view of Xórong's sprawling lands.

The Mountains.

Túlià had refused to give up Xórong's Zānshì secret to the Rajah in an effort to protect the innocent lives of the Empire's people, and she stood by that decision, but the scales had changed, and it was this new balance that twisted her stomach into sickness.

Xórong would build his new City in the place where Túlià's grandparents fell in love, the place where good, strong Mountain folk like Indsè le Tufā lived and laughed and told the stories of the ancestors. An entire people ripped from their home and made to toil as slaves in the Emperor's fields, watching while he and his wealthy grew fat on the Sywán's labors and lounged in the shade of their sacred Falls.

Túlià could not allow this to happen.

She had seven days, only seven days…but who could she tell? Even with a Zānshì and a Princess on her side, she could never hope to—

Footsteps passed by just outside Kāi's window, taking the path to The Garden of Refined Artistry. Relieved, Túlià stood, leaving the safety of the familiar space, and did her best to follow silently through the trees.

She thought it might be Ānjìn. She wanted it to be Ānjìn. And she nearly called out for him until the figure entered her mother's painting Pavilion. The sight of his moonlit face beneath the thatched roof sent chills all the way to the soles of her bare feet. Numbly, she waited at the bottom of the Pavilion steps like a scolded child until he noticed her.

"Ah, Painter, have I woken you? I hope you don't mind my late visit."

Túlià watched as Emperor Xórong moved to a hanging scroll and ran his ringed fingers over the sweeps of her mother's Mountains. It wasn't until his hands stilled that she realized she had left her veil at Kāi's bedside.

FIFTY NINE

"His subjects bowed their heads, hung halters from their necks, and pleaded for their lives."

"I was always able to tell the difference between your work and your mother's," Xórong continued, selecting another scroll from a nearby drawer and opening it with obvious admiration. "She had a much greater gift for subtlety."

He moved to the worktable, which stood proudly near the center of the Pavilion, and began to play with Túlià's supplies, testing the end of a brush against his wrist, weighing an inkstone from one hand to the other.

"I want you to paint me."

When Túlià didn't answer, Xórong gestured patiently at the space before him. "A chair, here, if you don't mind."

She did as he said, too numb to resist, bringing the chair and pulling a fresh scroll from her mother's stacks. Túlià spread it on the table, readied her ink, and watched as Xórong made himself comfortable.

Even seated, he seemed to command the space. Her space. Her mother's space.

Túlià painted.

He stood after a time, moving closer to look over her shoulder and inspect the work's progress.

"No, no this won't do. You must include the surroundings, the contents of the Pavilion. Start again."

Túlià started again.

She knew what this was, a mark. Like his seal. Like his poems. Xórong marked her art, like he did all of his possessions, as his own. And now, with this portrait, he claimed ownership of her Pavilion, her mother's Pavilion, and everything it contained.

Túlià's hands began to shake, and she wondered if this was how Kāì's Qìnjy felt at the time of his death, trapped and alone, tiny heart fluttering to a standstill.

Xórong kept silent, and simply watched her. He said nothing about Túlià's missing veil, nothing about her deceit, nothing about—

"Tell me, for I am curious, however did you manage to survive crossing my Sea in a ship filled with more holes than a poor man's robes?"

When Túlià didn't answer, Xórong moved close again, nodding in approval at her work before returning to his chair.

"I thought drowning would be a fairly clean death," he continued. "But I suppose if you preferred to die another way, you could hardly have told me as much."

"The crew," Túlià said roughly, surprised at the sound of her own voice. "The crew was strong. They bailed water for days."

She felt removed somehow, as if she could be nothing more than a Painter in that moment, her hands and eyes obeying his wish for a portrait, her mouth obeying his demand for an answer.

"Ah, the crew," he closed his eyes and nodded. "I should have provided you with fewer men. What happened after you reached the shore?"

"Did your sources not say?" Túlià asked, feeling a brief twist of pride at her disrespect before the numbness regained hold of her body.

"Oh yes, though I always wonder at their accuracy. I would like to hear from you."

Hands folded, he smiled expectantly, like a child awaiting his nightly story.

"We left our Zānshì in Gāngko, hired guides, and rode up into the Mountains."

"You dismissed my Zānshì? How strange. I wonder what could have brought on such a reckless decision," he scolded, his eyes settling heavily on the scar at Túlià's throat.

"We were attacked. Kāi was lost, as were our guides. I escaped, made my way back to Gāngko, and rested until I grew strong enough to return to The City."

"What an interesting turn of fate," Xórong murmured, watching Túlià's long fingers move across the scroll. "That your death was the intention of the entire journey, yet you were the only one to return unscathed. Well, mostly unscathed."

Again, his gaze returned to her throat.

"My dear Painter, you never said what became of the protection I sent with you."

"I did not see my Zānshì again."

"*Your* Zānshì?" Xórong asked, mock confusion covering his face.

Túlià swallowed and cursed herself miserably. Her last hope of living past this encounter dissolved away like a drop of ink in the Xórong Sea.

"Painter, you know the Zānshì are demons. You must be careful to keep such an insult from their ears. I proclaim my absolute control over the creatures, but I have recently come to terms with the knowledge that this is…not always the case."

He knew. Of course he knew.

He knew about Ānjìn. He knew Túlià had brought a Zānshì back to The City with her. He knew she had seen his face. But how? It was maddening, the power he had, the seemingly endless web of loyal lips who fed him Túlià's every move.

The numbness had become so strong now, that Túlià could hardly focus on Xórong's words. She was amazed her hands could still hold the brush, that her work, though half finished, already looked to be one of the best portraits she'd ever made.

Túlià had perfectly captured the way Xórong carried himself in her space. The way his eyes suggested both indifference and a fierce hold on the viewer. The way his body, while not seated in the middle of the scroll, still managed to be the overpoweringly central detail of the scene. The way his arms, despite being folded comfortably, appeared to open and claim every object in the Pavilion. Even the set of his shoulders, which echoed the lines of the largest hanging scroll in the space, seemed to declare that it was he, not Túlià's mother, who had created the beautiful painting behind him.

"You were careless, both of you. Did you honestly not think I would hear the cries of a grief-stricken Scholar, the sound of pins dropping from the hands of a useless Attendant, or the whisper of a Zānshì's fingers inquiring after an unfortunate accident at the Qìxé Parade?"

"Was it an accident?"

Túlià waited, motionless. Even her fluttering heart seemed to pause for Xórong's answer.

"Sweet Painter, of course not. Have you finished my portrait?"

SIXTY

"Because of it the Emperor ate but did not enjoy the taste."

urn them.

Ānjìn faltered, his eyes moving between the heap of scrolls at his feet and the torch offered to him by an impatient, white-gloved hand.

Burn them, Zānshì. By order of our Emperor.

Two of his brothers stood with him, stiff and still, aside from the one who signed his instructions. Even though their bodies gave away nothing, Ānjìn could sense their disapproval when his fingers moved in question.

Why?

Because our Emperor demands it.

Ānjìn looked at the piled scrolls again. Many had fallen open. Some still hung, partially ripped from their standing frames after such rough handling. He could see enough of the careful strokes to tell they belonged to his Painter.

He couldn't burn them. Of course not.

Painting was Túlià's favorite.

No.

His brothers were visibly agitated now, and grew even more so when he flinched at the crisp *hiss* of the torch being thrust between scrolls.

The Zānshì who had set the heap aflame nodded at the third, who reached carefully into the fire.

You disobeyed a direct order from our Emperor, Zānshì. You must be punished.

He signaled the other Zānshì again, who had pulled a thick, burning scroll from the flames.

Hold out your hands.

Ānjìn did. He deserved it, didn't he?

The third Zānshì placed the scroll in Ānjìn's outstretched grasp and returned to his place across the fire.

You will remain this way until the scrolls have stopped burning and think on your disobedience.

Ānjìn nodded, already willing the heat in his palms to spread over his whole body, lessening the pain he knew would only grow stronger once the scroll burned through his gloves.

The other two Zānshì, seeing that he intended to obey this time, ignored him, and began to speak across the flames with silent hands.

Is this the last batch of burnings?

No. There are more, and still scrolls from the Scholars our Emperor wishes to be rid of.

The third Zānshì's mask flicked toward Ānjìn for a moment.

Did our Emperor say why?

We do not question our Emperor's reasons. But I hear the burnings will soon be less.

Yes. The Painter is dead. She will not be able to produce more work to feed the fires.

Noticing the scroll in Ānjìn's hands had burned low, the Zānshì who ordered his punishment motioned for a fresh one to replace it.

Ānjìn found himself unable to focus on spreading the pain, and simply ground his teeth, watched the Zānshì, and thought of his Painter, wondering if there would be dove tree branches across her window that night.

Her work seems much like the last Painter. I assisted some of those burnings as well.

They were mother and daughter, the first answered. *Did you not see them at the Qixé Parade?*

Ānjìn's heart began to burn more fiercely than his palms, which had long since lost the protection of their wrappings.

No. I did not attend. I was on sentry that night.

You missed a show. The old Painter died beneath the horses we spooked. The daughter was meant to die as well, but the mother used her own body as a shield for protection against the hooves.

Foolish.

Agreed. Then we had to suffer another year of seeing the daughter's useless work covering our Emperor's walls.

An inconvenience, the second Zānshì nodded. *They only provide more shadows where enemies can conceal themselves.*

Ānjìn's jaw cracked, bringing both Zānshì's eyes to him.

Not useless. Not an inconvenience. Túlià's work was beautiful.

The first Zānshì replaced the smoldering scroll in Ānjìn's hands with a third and returned to his position across the fire.

Ānjìn's eyes never left him.

SIXTY ONE

"He found no pleasure in tending to matters of court while he waited for the Rajah to arrive."

"You only allowed me a trip to the Falls to kill me and make it appear as an accident?"

The numbness had left Túlià's body. Her painting was finished, but her anger had barely begun.

"Of course. An accident here in The City, so soon after the one I caused your mother, might have drawn the wrong attention."

"And Kāì, did you intend for her to die as well?"

"I had no quarrel with your Attendant, though I was certainly more willing to risk her life to the dangers of such a trip than one of my true Princesses. They are delicate flowers you know."

In other circumstances, the thought of fire-eyed Xiàná as delicate would have made Túlià laugh in Xórong's face, but now her frustration was too great. Hearing him refer to Kāì and his Princesses as though some were his daughters and some not, made Túlià wish to send a paintbrush through his throat. They were all connected by their royal blood, her, Kāì, Xiàná, and the rest. They should have been equals, friends, sisters the way sisters ought to be, but Xórong had destroyed any chance of that by pitting them against each other as rivals, raising some higher and leaving the rest behind to serve those he'd chosen.

But he hadn't been successful, not completely.

Túlià had found her closest friend in Kāì, a new ally in Princess Xiàná, and had even bonded with one of Xórong's prized Zānshì. His rule was not as complete as he desired, and despite his strutting about, they both knew Túlià had slashed holes in the Emperor's carefully spun webs in ways he now had to dance about to repair.

If she were to die today, she would do so happily, knowing her last moments of life had served as a thorn in Xórong's side. Until then, she still had answers to seek.

"Why did you choose Kāì to accompany me? The lower court has dozens of women who could have served as your false Princess."

"Because you loved her," Xórong answered simply. "I knew you would be more likely to agree on a trip with her. And I knew Kāì would enjoy both the prospect of pleasing me and the chance to dress up a bit."

Túlià watched, seething, yet still outwardly calm as he motioned her aside to add his customary poem and seal to her completed work.

"Why did you kill my mother, and try to kill me?"

"Well, you can die knowing it was no fault of yours. The answer lies in your blood."

"The Sywán."

"Ah yes, clever Painter. You and your mother share Mountain blood, which sadly, despite the unique beauty it produces both in face and skill, is not something I can have within my walls any longer."

"Because you are moving The City?"

He smiled and nodded. "Why yes, exactly. I'm afraid I don't want to divulge the exact details, but—"

"You intend to attack and enslave the Sywán to work the old City land while taking their home in the Mountains as your own. I imagine having sired a daughter with Sywán blood in her veins would bring unwanted attention during a time when you will be trying to convince your people that the Sywán you've enslaved are enemies, or mere animals, or perhaps *monsters* even."

The brush in Xórong's hand stilled for a moment before he composed himself and continued painting the sleek characters of his poem on Túlià's scroll.

"I correct myself. You *are* partially at fault for your misfortune. Tell me, why did you insist on praying to the oldest gods in existence after I very clearly created laws against it."

"The gods of my people—"

"Yes, your people, your mother's people. The blood you both hold from them was problematic to my future plans. I hated to lose Huàjā's beautiful work, but her death was completely necessary, I assure you."

"I was meant to die that day as well."

"That was my hope. When you survived, I decided to see if you possessed your mother's skill. I was a bit greedy, I admit. I missed Huàjā's paintings already and told myself if you had the same gifts, I would keep you on for another year, just to have one last taste of Mountain beauty hanging on my walls. You made it worse for yourself though."

"How so."

"If possible, your brush strokes were even more beautiful than your mother's, to the point that I had well made up my mind to keep you, blood aside. I started spreading the rumor that you weren't my daughter at all, only a skilled Painter I'd added to my court. People believed it, with many thanks to you in that regard," he added.

Of course. Túlià, in her hatred, had delighted in focusing the attention on her role as the royal Painter, not

305

on her status as the Emperor's daughter. She had introduced herself as such, and in doing so, had actually supported Xórong's efforts all along.

"You said you'd decided to keep me on. How did I make it worse?"

"Your paintings. You absolutely *insisted* on painting Mountains in almost every case. Your mother at least had variety."

"The day of my last viewing," Túlià murmured. "I painted Mountains on every single piece. Scrolls, fans, all of it, to honor the anniversary of my mother's death. That was why you changed your mind about letting me go to the Falls, wasn't it? A room filled with Sywán Mountains was too much, especially so near to the time you intended to attack. You had to rid yourself of me quickly. So you sent me to the Falls on a leaky boat with only a single Zānshì for protection and hoped I wouldn't return."

"Oh I more than hoped. And I do *hope* you see how much fate worked in my favor on this journey. You survived my boat, but nearly died at the very place you'd been wishing your whole life to visit. Tell me, did you manage to paint the Falls before your mother's people attacked?"

Túlià's scrape-knife met his throat, ending the half formed smile that stretched across Xórong's face, for she had realized, the moment her numbness cleared, that he had been foolish enough to come here without his Zānshì.

"The Sywán attacked us because *you* goaded them with your kidnappings. My mother's people are kind, peaceful, and wise, and I do not blame them for protecting their husbands and sons against your Zānshì. In regard to fate, I hardly see how it worked in your favor since, despite everything, I am here, alive and well, with my knife at your

306

throat. The foolish journey you sent me on will end in your death, not mine."

"Hmm," Xórong began, strangely unconcerned that his neck would soon resemble Túlià's. "You mentioned the Zānshì. That reminds me. I believe I have something of yours."

"What?"

"Yes, you brought something back from your trip. That Zānshì who mysteriously left his post at your bidding and allowed you to ascend the Mountains on your own, which goes against my direct orders. What can be said about a Zānshì who doesn't follow orders, I wonder. In my mind, for all intents and purposes, that means he is...off."

"Off?"

"Yes, there was an incident, many years ago, with a Zānshì who seemed disinclined toward my wishes. I ordered him watched, and when my Generals told me recently that he has made little progress since then, I made certain he would be the one to accompany you. I hoped he would either die on the boat or return to me, confessing his failure to protect the Princess, at which point I would order his death."

"You threaten me through him? Well you can hardly order his death after I've killed you."

"I will not die today, Painter, and neither will you. I've changed my mind."

"How merciful of you," Túlià hissed, pressing the little blade deeper into his throat.

"No, I will kill you tomorrow. I am curious about something, you see. Do you think, if placed before a crowd of Zānshì, you could select yours? They are meant to be identical you know."

Túlià had wondered that herself, but it didn't matter now. She could kill Xórong, summon Ānjìn with her dove tree branches, and they would both be free of The City before anyone noticed the Emperor was missing.

But the moment she positioned herself to do just that, four identical bone-knives pricked Túlià's ribs simultaneously.

Zānshì.

So, Xórong hadn't left them behind.

SIXTY TWO

"If Xórong fell before the law and were executed, it would make no more difference to his people than one hair off nine oxen."

Túlià was confined to her rooms in The Palace of Refined Artistry.

Xórong himself escorted her there from the Pavilion, bringing his Zānshì in case she decided to attack again, though he clearly didn't expect any more outbursts from his Painter since he'd allowed her to keep the scrape-knife she'd taken to his throat.

"You will remain here," he'd said, standing in her doorway. "I leave my Zānshì with you just to make certain you don't try anything foolish."

Túlià didn't intend to. It seemed all of her foolishness had run out, quickly taken over by the returning numbness. She had only one last wish.

"Promise me you won't hurt him."

"I'm sorry?" The Emperor looked surprised, an expression Túlià was not used to seeing on his proud face.

"I will do as you say, and choose my Zānshì in front of as many common people as can fill your grand courtyard. Make an example of me all you want, but once I've chosen, let my Zānshì go free."

Xórong thought for a moment, his face serious, then nodded.

"Alright, but only if you succeed. Choose the wrong Zānshì, and I will kill you both immediately. Please do understand though, that even if you do succeed, I will still execute *you* the following day. You've challenged my authority, and as I said, an example needs to be made."

Túlià nodded. Xórong turned to leave.

"You've forgotten your portrait, Highness," Túlià murmured to his retreating robes, the weight of her numbness pulling respect, of all things, from her lips.

He smiled at her over his shoulder. "Keep it, and put it with the rest of your things to be burned. I'm afraid it isn't your best work, Painter."

And he left.

Standing in the middle of her rooms, Túlià wondered if she might be able to weep.

No tears came.

She considered shouting curses to the Zānshì outside her door.

No words came.

Moving to her table, Túlià unrolled the scroll. The numb, Painter half of her soul couldn't seem to forget Xórong's words. She needed to see if the last portrait she would ever create was truly inadequate.

It wasn't.

Her mother would have been proud.

And disgusted.

Disgusted to see Xórong's arrogant form painted so that his shadow of ownership laid claim across every part of their Pavilion.

Again, wishing she could find the strength to weep, Túlià moved to the shelf of precious things in the far corner of the room and carefully took down her mother's favorite inkstone, which belonged to her father before her.

Returning to the table, she held it against her chest and tried to feel something more than the awful numbness.

Nothing came.

No words to her lips, no prayers to her thoughts, no tears to her eyes.

She simply stood there, still and silent, her empty gaze blurring the edges of the scroll.

It helped, she realized, to focus on her mother's painting, hanging softly in the background of the Pavilion behind Xórong's possessive shoulders.

Running her thumbs lightly over the inkstone, Túlià didn't move for a long while, until, with something akin to a Mountain breeze against the heart, her gaze sharpened.

Gathering the necessary supplies, she bent over Xórong's portrait, and began.

If this was truly to be her last painting, it would do far more than burn.

When she finished, Túlià waited for the ink to dry, rolled up her final work, and opened the doors of her rooms.

"You. Take this to Princess Xiàná."

The Zānshì looked at her, his eyes dark and unfamiliar beneath the mask.

She could see them of course, his eyes. You could see any Zānshì's eyes, as Túlià had learned, so long as you were willing to lift your own eyes above their misshapen feet. Most people wouldn't, and she was counting on the fact that her open challenge would take the Zānshì off guard.

He blinked under the heat of her stare and reached for his bone-knives in an effort to frighten her off.

"You listen," Túlià hissed, stepping close enough to breathe his air and press the end of her painting into the Zānshì's chest. "You listen and you look at me, *boy*. I know you aren't a devil. I know you aren't a demon. And I know

311

you probably haven't even passed your first shave. If you don't take this painting to Princess Xiàná *right now*, I will tell your Emperor that you failed to deliver his most recent portrait to his favorite daughter's chambers. Then won't he be *so* disappointed in you."

The Zānshì visibly faltered, his hands fluttering from the scroll in Túlià's grip to the bone-knives strapped to his back. Finally, he took the scroll, opened it enough to show his fellow Zānshì, who seeing that it was nothing more than a harmless portrait of their Emperor, nodded in agreement.

Túlià waited until her painting's unwilling messenger rounded the corner before returning to her rooms and breathing deeply for the first time since she'd felt the prick of bone-knives against her heart in The Garden of Refined Artistry.

She could only wait now.

Sitting at her open window, Túlià wished she could call for Ānjìn, but there would be no way to speak to him without her guards overhearing.

She knew Xórong would most likely not uphold his end of the bargain. What reason would he have to keep Ānjìn alive after her execution? She knew only that the Emperor wouldn't let his people see Zānshì blood spilled, meaning Ānjìn would be taken away from the grand courtyard to die.

Hopefully, in that time, he might escape.

SIXTY THREE

"To them, he was nothing but a mere ant now."

F ailure to cover his face.
Failure to kill the Painter.
Failure to hold against the Rajah's Lord.
Failure to keep the secrets of the Empire.
Failure to…

The list went on.

Each grievance seemed to pull Ānjìn closer to the underground chambers of spiritual punishment Túlià had described to him.

"Do you deny it?" the General intoned.

Ānjìn bowed his head.

He was guilty of all of this and more, but it was his Emperor's words that brought Ānjìn the greatest pain.

"Zānshì, I am disappointed."

Of course he was. Ānjìn had failed his Emperor in every way, and he was lucky to be called for his confession before he could commit any further treason.

Still, he couldn't help but think of Túlià and the satchel he'd hidden, wondering if his Emperor would grant him the last request of retrieving it. But Ānjìn knew he had run out of time. There was nothing he could do now but die and wait.

313

Túlià couldn't keep him from waiting. He would see her again.

"You will have to be punished, of course," his Emperor continued.

Of course. Ānjìn reached for his bone-knives, offering them up in his palms like the burning scrolls he'd held the night before.

"But not yet."

Ānjìn paused, the knives already halfway to his heart.

"I require one last task from you, Zānshì. It will not reverse all the wrongs you have done, but it will certainly improve my memory of you."

Ānjìn stowed his knives and touched his masked face to the earth at his Emperor's feet. Anything. He would do anything.

"Tomorrow, I will have a gathering. All of the Zānshì. Most of the people. And the Painter."

Túlià? Why his Painter?

"She has committed many crimes against me as well, and I need to use her as an example. With my people watching, I will give her the opportunity to choose you from the line of Zānshì. You may even give her some sort of sign, to ensure that she picks you without mistake. When she does, I will give the order, and you will take your life while she watches."

Ānjìn raised his eyes, meeting the Emperor's gaze for the first time in his life, and addressed him aloud.

"Will you let her go free?"

Snarls of outrage echoed from the Generals, and a few managed to strike him before the Emperor's lifted hands sent them back.

"I will."

314

SIXTY FOUR

"Xórong was kept for the sport and amusement of the Rajah.

Túlià entered the gardens with her head held high, wearing the Sywán robes she'd been given by Cloud Mother Indsè. She had stowed them away on the journey and smuggled them into The City, not able to part with something so precious. Túlià wanted Xórong to see them before he killed her, and she wanted to wear them when she died.

Indeed, his obvious disapproval at the sight of her robes when he arrived to escort her to the gardens was all the incentive she needed to give her courage to face the day.

She had done what she set out to do. Princess Xiàná would make certain her last wishes were fulfilled. Túlià could die in peace, especially knowing that whether she succeeded or failed in choosing Ānjìn from his brothers, she would die and he would have a chance to escape.

There was a certain calm, she realized, in accepting that the future was set regardless of her actions.

Xórong left her at the edge of the very same fountain she and Kāì had once filled with ink, and mounted the steps of The Hall of Divine Authority to sit comfortably above everything he owned.

The Emperor certainly cut an imposing figure. His Palaces rose behind him. His gates towered before him. His daughters and wives gathered on cushions at his feet. His

315

servants stirred the air near him with fans. His Zānshì stood in rows on the sprawling staircase below. His people moved restlessly in a great heap, gathered all around the spectacle, and his Painter waited on a fountain's edge, in the middle of it all.

Xórong lifted his hand, and the courtyard went silent.

"My people, this foolish daughter of the Mountains has come to me claiming to *know* one of my Zānshì."

Gasps and whispers joined the exotic butterflies that spilled over from the gardens and fluttered through the heat-thick air of the main courtyard, as Xórong's people turned to their neighbors and asked what this could possibly mean.

"Worse," he continued in a voice that, despite its soft nature, had more command behind it than any shout, "she claims she can choose *her* Zānshì from a crowd of his identical brothers."

The whispers increased in intensity and seemed to brush against Túlià's ears as she stepped down from the fountain and began the long journey toward the foot of the steps.

Of course Xórong couldn't have just placed her near the Zānshì at the start. He wanted a spectacle. He wanted his people to gawk at her for as long as possible.

When she reached the first row of waiting warriors, Túlià's heart remained strangely calm.

They were only men, after all.

She began to walk among them, close enough to touch. And when she'd reached the third row and still sensed nothing of Ānjìn, she did begin to touch them, hoping to feel something beneath the stiff flesh of an arm or shoulder.

No Zānshì reacted to her hands, though the people certainly did, rumbles of shock and uncertainty pressing against the silencing blaze of Xórong's eyes. Túlià wondered if this had been part of his plan, for his gasping, shuffling citizens to see her breathe the same air as a supposed demon and survive. She hoped her comfort in the presence of his warriors was as much of a discomfort to Xórong as it was to the crowds he'd gathered.

She'd just reached the end of the seventh row when something made her pause.

Túlià retraced her steps, following a change in the air that teased stronger than the slowly intensifying whispers.

Dove tree petals.

One of the Zānshì, who stood just as motionless as the rest, smelled as if he had bathed in them.

Túlià smiled.

"After I choose you, we will be separated," she whispered. "Promise me—"

"Have you chosen?"

Turning toward Xórong's impatient voice, Túlià nodded.

"I have."

He stood, and the people went silent, straining to hear his response.

"Let it be known," he said, opening his arms to encompass all he owned, "that despite this foolish girl's claims, I alone am in complete control of the Zānshì."

"Demon," he continued, "Do as your Emperor commands, and end your life."

The Zānshì fell to one knee, lifted his bone-knives, and plunged both into his own heart.

Túlià screamed.

SIXTY FIVE

"He was treated the same as the musicians and jesters, and made light of by the new court."

Ānjìn had tricked Emperor Xórong. It was easier than he'd expected, especially after realizing what he should have known already. Much like Túlià reminded Ānjìn that he was simply a man, she had also told him from the start that Xórong was the same.

A man who lied.

A man with weaknesses.

A man who could be tricked.

Once he'd seen the lie in Xórong's eyes when he promised to spare Túlià's life, Ānjìn spun his trick fairly quickly, thanks to a memory he had long since tucked away in the place for things a Zānshì was not meant to understand.

An accident, early in his training.

While he and his young brothers stood in a line for Xórong to look over his newest batch of warriors, the boy next to Ānjìn had fallen, his legs weakened by the still fresh pain of the bamboo pole between his ankles, and knocked Ānjìn to the ground with him.

They landed in a heap at Xórong's feet and lay there, trembling, waiting for punishment.

After having them yanked upright by the Generals, Xórong had looked both boys over and ordered Ānjìn to be beaten.

Red-faced beneath his new mask, Ānjìn began to speak with clumsy fingers, indicating to his Emperor that it was the boy to his left, not he who had caused this disrespect.

Xórong had scoffed, ignored his pleas, and doubled his punishment.

Then, Ānjìn hadn't questioned it, as he had already been told his Emperor's judgment was completely just, always and unfailingly so.

Now, he knew differently.

Not only was Xórong unjust, he was unable to tell his Zānshì apart.

It had been clear to all at the time of the incident that the boy had fallen into Ānjìn. But the moment they became tangled at his feet, Xórong could no longer distinguish one masked boy from the other, and delivered unfair punishment with false certainty.

Ānjìn knew now, with true certainty, that if Xórong was unable to distinguish his Zānshì as boys, he most certainly would not be able to distinguish them as men.

This, coupled with Ānjìn's understanding that neither he nor Túlià would be allowed to live, sparked the beginnings of something in his mind. It seemed there was only one course of action left for him to take if he wished to save his Painter's life.

Xórong might not be able to distinguish his warriors, but Ānjìn certainly could.

All he'd needed was a dove tree.

SIXTY SIX

"But a great man would not be bent."

*H*e *died quickly,* Túlià told herself.
He looked well.
He wasn't tortured by his brothers.
Ānjìn was at rest and waiting for her.
She should be grateful it had not been worse.
Why wasn't she grateful?
Because she'd never felt more alone. Because even despite knowing Xórong would likely go back on his word, Túlià had been foolish enough to hope otherwise. Because Túlià had wanted to be dead by now as well, and could not fathom why she wasn't.
She'd lost Huàjā, her patient mother, Kāi, her sweet companion, and now Ānjìn…
Ānjìn. What had Ānjìn been to her?
A friend. An ally. A Zānshì. Her Zānshì.
Ānjìn was her Zānshì and he always would be. Just as he taught her to believe in her own kind of beauty, Ānjìn had learned to become his own kind of Zānshì. He was still a warrior, still as fierce as any demon, but his loyalty to the Emperor had become devotion to her, his bone-knives protective instead of cruel, his face lifted to the light of the sun, free from the mask that had trapped him in darkness since Xórong took him from the streets.

Túlià thought of Ānjìn, his head tipped back with laughter, enjoying her company, the fresh air, the stories she offered up like dove tree petals between them, and her heart grew heavier than an empty inkstone.

Desperate for distraction, she thought of her last painting, how easy it had been to convince the Zānshì guarding her door to carry it to Princess Xiàná.

They had taken one look at the scroll and probably thought it foolish. The harmless last wish of a silly girl. But it wasn't harmless, and neither she nor Xiàná were silly girls. Her new Princess ally would know what to do. She would see that the portrait was delivered to its true recipient. Until then—

"I am entering the room."

Túlià jumped. Then she cursed him. Then she cried.

"Why are you crying?" Ānjìn whispered through the bars. "I did all of this so you wouldn't be hurt."

"All of what? What did you do?"

She reached for his hands, but pulled back at the sight of his burned flesh. So he had been tortured.

"I don't understand, Ānjìn. Xórong said he wouldn't kill you, but then I watched you die!"

"Xórong lied. And I didn't die."

"Yes I can see that. So whose blood is being scrubbed off the steps of The Hall of Divine Authority?"

"Another Zānshì."

"You let another Zānshì die?"

He nodded. "Túlià, this Zānshì was there the night Xórong had your mother killed."

"Are you certain?"

Ānjìn nodded again.

322

"I heard him speaking about how he spooked the horses at the Qìxé Parade, then stood by and did nothing. His words were cruel."

"You knew Xórong planned to make me choose, so you tricked me into choosing someone else?"

"Yes."

"But that is…it's so—"

"Clever?"

"Awful!"

"Oh."

"Ānjìn, I thought it was you!"

"I know. I'm sorry. Xórong said if I took my life the way he wanted, that he would let you go free. He lied. I knew if I died on his steps, he would kill you soon after. I couldn't let that happen."

"So you did what? Stuffed another Zānshì like a dove tree dumpling and sent him in your place?"

"No. I knocked him over the head and rubbed him down with petals. Then I woke him up just in time to attend the gathering so he would have no way to wash the smell off beforehand."

Túlià drew in a deep breath and swallowed as much of her anger as she could manage.

"Why didn't Xórong know it wasn't you who died today?"

"Because he can't tell us apart."

"What?"

"He can't tell the Zānshì apart. He never could."

"Then I am proud of you," Túlià laughed, surprising them both with the sudden warm sweep of happiness that filled her. "It would seem our poor Emperor is growing lazy in his old age."

Ānjìn smiled and let his scarred knuckles touch hers against the bars.

"Let me help you free of this place. I will find the keys and we can leave."

Túlià's heart leapt at the thought, then stilled.

"Ānjìn, Xórong will realize you tricked him, especially if he finds my prison empty. He will send his Zānshì across the Empire looking for us. I don't want to live in fear for the rest of my life."

"Then what would you have me do? I won't leave you here to die."

"You will leave me here," Túlià said. "But not to die."

After everything she'd learned about Xórong, everything she'd seen, the display he'd put on today, his Zānshì, how he ran his City and ruled his people, Túlià had an idea.

"Take a horse. Travel to the Dockmaster's house where we stayed. Wait for me there. I will be along in a few days."

Ānjìn pulled his mask away.

"Promise I will see you again if I leave."

"Is this one of your demon skills?" Túlià whispered, "to read my face for lies?"

"Túlià, promise."

"I promise. But even if things go wrong, you'll wait for me?"

He nodded.

"Of course."

And he left.

Túlià sat alone in the quiet cell, deep in thought, until the prison guard came to deliver her evening meal.

If all it required to trick Xórong was to take advantage of one of his weaknesses, then Túlià intended to do just that.

"I wish for an audience with the Emperor."

SIXTY SEVEN

"A great man would not die in vain."

Ānjìn had never cursed before, but he did now. Dockmaster Mātu's older children had very much enjoyed teaching him a few words, and giggled every time he released one. He'd finally been forced to send them from the room, realizing that his task required silence and concentration. If only his hands weren't so badly burned.

He had been lucky though. Lucky to steal a horse and slip past the other Zānshì, fooling them with a mask he removed as soon as he'd left their sight. Lucky that after he'd burned his white robes and buried his mask, Mātu's family had taken him in, offering room, clothes, and food.

The lady of the house had seemed reluctant at first, to have him there, but when he'd bowed low and explained that Túlià had sent him and that she would be joining him in only a few short days, she'd agreed to share her home for a third time, and had relaxed even more when Ānjìn's claims came true with the arrival of a messenger.

"A cart will come one day behind me bearing a prisoner bound for exile. I was sent ahead to secure passage for her on a ship."

Ānjìn had done his best to answer the family's questions, assuring them that Túlià's crimes against the Empire were minor and that she would be no danger to them. He explained how she had taken Kāi's place to discover more about her mother's death, but that the Emperor had learned of her deceit and decided to have her exiled because of it.

Apparently, this was just the sort of story the children had been begging for on his last visit, because not one of them took their little eyes off Ānjìn during its telling. Their parents seemed spellbound as well, and all agreed by its end that they were excited to see the Painter again, though saddened to hear it was sweet Princess Kāi who had been lost in the Mountains.

Ānjìn continued to let them believe he was Túlià's brother, since he imagined they might be frightened to learn what he had once been. Such knowledge could put them in danger as well, which was why he also shared nothing else about he and Túlià's time in The City, or beforehand.

Joining Dockmaster Mātu on the small vessel he'd selected to bear Túlià away, Ānjìn helped the other deckhands prepare to leave, which they intended to do as soon as she arrived. Ānjìn did his best to blend in among them, knowing Túlià would likely be escorted by a pair of Zānshì who might identify him from afar.

When the day of his Painter's arrival finally came, Ānjìn could hardly breathe. He forced himself to look busy, to keep his eyes on his work and avoid the sight of the Zānshì who accompanied her. It wasn't until the cart pulled away and Ānjìn heard the children shrieking that he let his gaze return to the house.

A lone, robed and hooded figure stood before the Dockmaster's property, watching quietly as older children took the hands of those younger and wrenched them inside. Mātu and his wife appeared, though they didn't make it past their stoop before slamming the door shut. The windows

328

soon followed, all except for the last, from which an unseen hand tossed a bit of what looked like meal scraps before shutting as well.

SIXTY EIGHT

"A million changes were all the same to him."

Túlià hadn't expected it would hurt so much. The reaction of Mātu's family was everything she knew it would be, but the ache in her chest caught Túlià off guard. Steeling herself, she moved toward their door and knocked lightly. She had thanks to give, and it mattered not if they were well received.

"Dockmaster Mātu? Lady Jiùlìng? I only wish to thank you for your kindness. For taking in Ānjìn and I, caring for us, sharing your home, and granting us safe passage on your ship."

Túlià was met with silence.

She waited.

One of the younger children began to cry.

"Dockmaster Mātu? Please—"

"You have your scraps, once-woman. Take them and go," he barked from behind the door, the unfamiliar cruelty in his kind voice was echoed by the frantic whispers of his wife.

"Don't speak to it, Mātu. You will bring ill fortune on our home."

"Take the children to the back room," he murmured in response. "I will wait here with my knife until she has gone."

Yes, it hurt. It hurt a great deal. It hurt more, somehow, than the procedure itself.

Túlià had expected the pain then, though the humiliation was something new.

To be stripped of her robes, laid out on a table, and pricked with a thousand needles had made her wish she'd thought to ask Ānjìn beforehand how he managed to handle suffering so neatly.

Túlià imagined she would have made her Zānshì-boy proud though. She hadn't screamed or begged, only wept silently, unable to wipe the tears from her eyes thanks to the ties at her wrists and ankles.

Looking toward the ship that awaited her, Túlià wondered what Ānjìn would think of his Painter now.

SIXTY NINE

"At his death, the world would not rank Xórong among those men who were able to die for their ideals."

The moment his Painter boarded, gasps of shock and fear moved outward from her in waves, as deckhands made signs of protection and whispered to one another from the far edges of the ship.

Look, look!

Once-woman.

Tie her down!

Get her off the ship!

Coils of tightly spun rope, much like the great lengths Ānjìn and Túlià had twisted together with the children of their last voyage, began moving across the deck like snakes pulled by the hasty hands of the crew.

Stay back.

Once-woman.

Stay back!

Ānjìn began to run, cursing his knees as he moved from the far end of the ship to where the ropes were being flung at his Painter.

These ropes were well made, not twisted by children, a broken Zānshì, or a rough-voiced Painter. They had real weight, and when they struck Túlià, they served more as a weapon than a way of restraint, knocking her to the deck and drag-burning across her already tender skin.

She cried out and fought back, straining to reach the paint knives she'd decided to keep always in her hair, despite knowing none would be strong enough to cut her free of such thick restraints.

"Túlià!"

Ānjìn reached the first crew member and broke both his hands with one quick sweep of the same staff his Painter had pulled from the woods to aid his aching knees.

The rope fell away, and he moved on, breaking another set of hands before Túlià's cries brought him to her side.

"Stupid Zānshì-boy," she managed, gasping with pain and shaking her dark, hooded head. "If you break them all, who will sail the ship?"

"Túlià?"

She wouldn't look at him. Why wouldn't she look at him? Was it the ropes?

Ānjìn turned, still kneeling beside her, and cracked his staff against the deck hard enough to startle the last few ropes from the remaining unbroken hands.

"Túlià. Are you hurt?"

"I'm fine."

"What happened? Why did the crew attack you?"

"They were frightened. Mātu and his children were as well."

"I don't understand. Why would they be frightened? They're treating you worse than a Zānshì."

He watched her shoulders tighten and fall.

"Túlià?"

She sighed, deeply, and drew back her hood, pulling gasps from the lips of the deckhands who stood watching from a wary distance.

Someone had…done something to his Painter. Ānjìn wasn't sure what until the strange, yet still familiar face spoke to him in Túlià's rough voice.

"I told you Xórong wouldn't let me leave The City alive. I knew too many of his secrets. Well, the moment I said so aloud, I realized there might be a way. A long, painful, humiliating way, but a way all the same."

"Who did this to you?"

"Xórong. Well, he didn't hold the needles of course. He has a man trained especially for that purpose."

"Why?"

"Because I wanted to be free of him. If Xórong's greatest concerns were that I keep his secrets and be horribly punished to save his pride, then I knew this would be perfect. So I went to him, and asked to become…this."

Tattoo.

Once-woman.

Keep away from us.

Ānjìn watched the whispers settle on his Painter, weighing down her proud spine, her eyes, the curve of her mouth.

"Túlià—"

"The Inkman was very creative. I told him to treat me as if I were a painting, and he seemed to enjoy the prospect. And Xórong loved the punishment of course. I've heard it's worse than death to become a monster that people flee from in the streets. He knew no one would listen to the ravings of a Tattoo, so his secrets and his pride were safe."

"Túlià—"

"I don't think it looks too bad, besides. My robes cover the worst of it. I have this lovely, snarling *Taote* across my brows to keep me company always. And I still have my fingers of course. A few Tattoos won't get in the way of painting. Also I—"

"Túlià. Can I show you something?"

She nodded, doing her best to ignore the whispers and stares of the deckhands behind him as Ānjìn pulled a familiar satchel from his back. Reaching into it carefully, he produced a single, smudged scroll.

Kneeling on the deck in front of her, Ānjìn spread it open, pinning down the ends carefully with his burnt hands while she bent to study it over his shoulder.

A lone Mountain stood rough and proud in the center, surrounded by the tilted trunks of a dozen dove trees at its base. A waterfall began at the peak, dripping down the Mountain's far side before splashing into an ocean filled with open-mouthed clams and the flashing eyes of Túlià's little blue Xié.

"The Mountain is a symbol for you," Ānjìn murmured, "but you have to keep going."

She followed his voice to the far edge of the scroll and unrolled it further, forgetting the deckhands as she knelt beside each new story, spreading the silk until it stretched from nearly one side of their ship to the other.

Túlià's knees began to ache from crawling, but she hardly noticed the pain. Every piece of her focus fell on tracing the sweet, untrained ink of Ānjìn's work with her long painter's fingers.

She touched the stars over her and Kāi's sleeping heads, joined by the Sun and Moon children of her stories. She touched her mother's Pavilion, with a single, dark inkstone resting beneath its thatched roof. She touched a little Qìnjy, singing next to the Cloud Mother's unbroken turtle shells, which were decorated with every Sywán symbol Ānjìn had been able to remember from their tents. And she

336

touched the scroll's end, which held two figures, recognizable only by their mask and scar, sitting side by side, painting on river stones with the soot of their bright little fire.

The painting was a mess of ink that would have wrinkled the nose of every wealthy art lover who used to fawn over Túlià's work back in The City. They would have turned away in disgust, not wasting the time to decipher each precious, clumsy symbol her Zānshì-boy had included. But this painting wasn't for them, it was for *her*.

"Ānjìn, bring me your hands."

He did.

They were burned.

Ink stained.

Túlià could feel them shaking.

He must have worked for days.

"You made this?"

He nodded.

"In the Sywán tent, you said you wanted a painting of the Falls to hang above your door."

When Túlià didn't answer, Ānjìn shifted, placing himself between her and the whispers, sitting so that all she could see were his eyes, reflecting the light from the wide stretch of water behind her.

"Is it beautiful?"

"Yes," she whispered. "It's the most beautiful thing I've ever seen."

SEVENTY

"They would believe simply that his wisdom was exhausted and his crime great."

At first, when Princess Xiàná opened the scroll Túlià sent her, she was confused.

Then she understood.

Then she laughed.

Xiàná held her stomach and laughed like she'd wanted to since Xórong selected her, and she knew she'd never be allowed the freedom of such trivial things as unrestrained joy again.

Freedom.

The thought sobered her.

She would need help.

The servants couldn't be trusted. Too many of them owed their fear-fed loyalty to Xórong. Her sisters, on the other hand, were less willing to shake in the Emperor's shadow. She could count on at least a few to assist in the tasks of the coming days.

Xiàná had realized two things upon opening the scroll. First, she knew its true, intended recipient. Second, she knew much more could be done to prepare once it had been sent.

So, after wrapping the scroll in the special packaging reserved for Xórong's high court, she sent it by way of a trusted messenger from an outlying town. Then, it was time to find her sisters.

They didn't laugh at Xiàná, as she thought they might because of her young age. She was grateful they took her words seriously as they had in the past, which was more than their father had ever granted any of them.

Well, he would take them seriously now, if not very soon in the fast-approaching trials.

Every Princess left the leisure rooms that day with a new sense of determination, fondly touching the edge of Túlià's *Admonitions* scroll as they passed. Each shared a fresh respect for the Painter their little sister had spoken so highly of, and each wished to see her last aims fulfilled.

When they heard she had been set free, Tattooed but free, they were overjoyed, and could hardly keep their secret smiles covered at Xórong's table during the evening meal. Afterward, with their Painter safe and her package sent, it was time to leave The City.

That night, under cover of darkness, the Princesses left the prison of their walls in pairs. Hidden behind the guise of common robes, they echoed their father's tactics and sent whispers of their own fluttering to the ears of the nearest towns.

Make ready.

War is coming.

Take what you can and flee.

Many were filled with joy, some with fear, some with disbelief, but most, like the Princesses, with determination.

Long had the people wished for change. Long had they waited for a spark.

Now, it would seem that spark had been set, by a Painter of all things.

So the common people prepared.

And they waited.

SEVENTY ONE

"Xórong had been unable to escape penalty and in the end had gone to his death."

"You mean to tell me you used all our coin from the Sywán on paint supplies, then carried them around on your back until a few days ago?"

Ānjìn nodded, looking more than pleased with himself. He stood carefully so that Túlià was protected from every whisper and stare by the Sea at her back and his sturdy form in front. Despite his bent knees, walking stick, and simple dress, Ānjìn still very much cut the figure of a warrior. The deckhands recognized it now and Túlià was grateful, since his dark eyes were all she needed to keep her attackers at bay.

"Can I see them?"

"My Tattoos?" Túlià went pink. "Of course not."

Ānjìn smiled. "You're being proper again."

"Well I'm hardly going to drop my robes in front of an entire ship."

"Give me your hands," he said, mimicking her earlier demand.

She did, letting her sleeves fall back enough for him to admire the dark creatures twisting up her arms.

"Beautiful," he said simply.

"Why?" she muttered, tugging her hands free. "There is hardly anything useful about having demons inked into your skin.

"They set us free, didn't they? And just think, no unruly child will ever bother you again."

Túlià bared her teeth at his teasing, but only succeeded in making him laugh at her ferocious expression.

"You look more like a warrior than I ever did. I am beginning to think you won't need me to protect you anymore."

"I certainly won't," Túlià agreed. "Though I will need you for two other things, and two things only."

"Oh?"

"First, I will need you to hang a scroll above my door."

This time, when Ānjìn looked at the painting she cradled against her chest, his wide smile was not born of teasing.

He nodded eagerly. "I will. What is the second thing?"

"The second thing," Túlià said, becoming suddenly somber again, "is to be my company."

Ānjìn would do that. He would do that gladly. But he didn't understand why his Painter looked so saddened by the idea.

"Most Tattoos," she continued, whispering now, "do not live past a year of being inked. They are driven mad by the cruelty of strangers and the loneliness of abandonment until they take their own lives. It is part of the reason why Xórong agreed to let me go. He didn't think I would live long enough to spread his secrets, even if anyone were willing to listen to the mad ramblings of an exiled once-woman."

Ānjìn remembered how Túlià had looked, standing alone at Dockmaster Mātu's door, listening to the screams of his children and having scraps tossed out to her like a dog.

He knew what it was like to be treated this way and felt no surprise at learning those who had not been trained for such a life could hardly bear to live it.

"Does this mean I can stay with you?"

"Of course it does, stupid Zānshì-boy. How are you meant to be my company and hang my painting if I leave you behind?"

SEVENTY TWO

"Why?"

As fate would have it, though Túlià would never know, the very moment her and Ānjìn's boat touched the far shores of their exile, her package touched the Rajah's hands.

It looked innocent enough.

A scroll.

A painting.

A gift.

A gift from Emperor Xórong, no less.

It was of course, the very same portrait Túlià had painted of Xórong, the last work she'd ever created for him, packaged in Princess Xiàná's careful wrappings.

In the portrait, Xórong posed comfortably among the contents of her mother's Pavilion.

But Túlià had changed one very small thing.

The hanging scroll, her mother's, the one that nearly covered the Pavilion wall behind Xórong, the one his shoulders had proudly claimed ownership of, was different.

Originally, the painting had shown far off rows of Mountains bearing hundreds of innocent little sprigs of apricot blossoms. In Túlià's new version, however, the hanging scroll displayed a map of the Rajah's Kingdom with its cities, towns, farmlands, and his Capital especially, covered in angry red flames.

The insulting image was joined not only by Emperor Xórong's seal, but by a poem as well, written in his own hand.

The fleet-footed stallion cannot be harnessed with the worn-out nag.
The phoenix does not fly with the flocks of little sparrows. No more
so, therefore, does the worthy man stand side by side with the
unworthy.

Upon opening the scroll, the Rajah was at first confused, then insulted, then enraged.

"Xórong dares to call himself a stallion and myself a nag, his Empire a phoenix compared to the unworthy sparrows of my people! He means to burn us to the ground! Well these sparrows will not burn easily!"

Crumpling the scroll, he called for his Lords, his Advisors, and the soldier who had recently returned, babbling mad from the edges of the Kingdom, claiming to have seen the face of a Zānshì.

If Xórong could dare to be so bold, the Rajah would be bolder. And indeed, it was not long until the flames Túlià had painted lit the torches of the Rajah's people and then the edges of Xórong's farmland.

When the Rajah reached The City, the surrounding towns had already been emptied of those who had long wished to be free of Xórong's reign. Warned by the very Princesses he had chosen, they fled for safety, leaving behind only those who either supported their Emperor or those who were too afraid to step outside his shadow.

Among those who stayed, of course, were the Zānshì.

But the Rajah was ready for them.

When Xórong's demons left the walls of The City and prepared to cross the moat that separated their Emperor

346

from his common people, the Rajah gave one simple command.

"Archers, aim for their knees."

To those who watched, it quickly became clear that Emperor Xórong wouldn't have the chance to build his new City after all.

SEVENTY THREE

"Because all his past actions had brought this on him."

"Are you sure you don't want me to sell that one?"
Túlià followed Ānjìn's inquiry to the space above
their door where he'd hung her painted scroll. In truth, the
work was much too long to be confined to such a tiny bit of
wall and stretched around the entirety of their little cottage,
so that no matter where Túlià stood she could enjoy it just
overhead.

"That one is not for selling," she said, making him
smile as he did every season before he left to deliver her
latest batch of paintings to the town a few leagues down the
road.

Their seaside cottage was the perfect place for Túlià to
paint in silence. Even though the people of the Islands were
not as affected by her Tattoos as the people of the Empire,
she still preferred to avoid their stares with her face to the
water, where she could have peace and quiet.

Ānjìn loved traveling to town and walking among the
people without his mask and white robes, carrying nothing
more than his Painter's work and a staff to steady his knees.
The people always seemed to know when he was coming,
and had been gathering to greet him since the first day.

He'd made it clear at Túlià's bidding that these
paintings were meant for all. Not just the wealthy or the
noble, but anyone who wished to purchase.

The coin from those who could afford to spare it paid for the paints and supplies Túlià needed, while the baskets of bread, folds of cloth, and other treats from the farmers and craftsman were plenty to keep Ānjìn and Túlià taken care of until the next season.

When Ānjìn returned the following morning with a smile on his face and his arms overflowing with bundles, Túlià could just see the tips of her mother's Mountains over his shoulder, shining in the clear light of the rising sun far across the sea.

It was truly beautiful.

THE END

Paintings, Poems, Texts, and Other Sources of Inspiration

Paintings

Ni Zan, *Six Gentlemen*, 1345, Yuan Dynasty, 24 ³⁄₈ x 13 ⅛, Shanghai Museum of Art

Guo Xi, *Early Spring*, 1072, National Museum of Taipei, Commissioned by Emperor Shenzong, Northern Song

Fan Kuan, *Travellers Among Mountains And Streams*, ca 1000, Hanging Scroll, ink and color on silk, 6¾ ft x 2½ ft, Northern Song, National Museum of Taipei.

Wang Meng, *The Simple Retreat*, Yuan dynasty ca. 1370, Hanging scroll, ink and color on paper, 53 ½ in x 17 ¾ in

Ma Yuan (active 1190-1220), *Mountain Path in Spring*, National Palace Museum, Taipei

Gu Kaizhi, *Admonitions of the Court Instructress to Palace Ladies,* Tang Dynasty, Silk, 130 in x 9 ¾ in, British Museum, London

Poems

"Mountain Travels" by Du Mu

Inscription for Guo Xi's *Early Spring* by the Qianlong Emperor

A famous couplet by Wei Zhuang

"Poems of My Heart" by Ruan Ji

"Marble Steps Complaint" by Li Bai

Texts

Canepa, Matthew P. " Distant Displays of Power: Understanding Cross-Cultural Interaction Among Elites of Rome, Sasanian Iran, and Sui-Tang China." Ars Orientalis 38 (2010): 121-154.

Chang, K.C. "Urbanism and the King in Ancient China," World Archaeology, 6, 1 (June 1974): 1-14.

Chuan-Ying Yen, " The Decorative motifs on Tang Dynasty Mirrors," Cleveland Studies in the History of Art, 9 (2005) 1-10.

Dorinda Neave, Lara C.W. Blanchard and Marika Sardar. *Asian Art* (2015)

Hung, Chang-Tai. "Oil Paintings & Politics: Weaving a Heroic Tale of the Chinese Communist Revolution." Comparative Studies in Society and History 49, no. 4 (2007): 783-814.

Lee, De-nin Deanna. " Chinese Painting: Image-Text-Object." In A Companion to Asian Art and Architecture, Rebecca M. Brown and Deborah S. Hutton Eds. (Malden, MA: Wiley-Blackwell, 2011): 563-579.

Liu, Bo. " Deciphering the Cold Sparrow: Political Criticism in Song Poetry and Painting." Ars Orientalis 40 (2011): 108-140.

Musillo, Marco. "Two Careers: The Jesuit Memoir of Giuseppe Castiglione Lay Brother and Qing Imperial Painter." Eighteenth-Century Studies 42, no. 1 (2008): 45-59.

Pik, Chan Lai. " Jade Spiders and Praying Mantises of the Western Zhou Dynasty: Reconstructing an Ancient Cultural Mindset." Ars Orientalis 41 (2011): 165-185.

Sima Qian's *Records of the Grand Historian (Shiji)*, Created during the Han Dynasty in 94 BC

Other

The Mausoleum of Shinghuandi, The First Emperor of China, Qin Dynasty

The tomb of the Marquise of Dai, who died in 186 BCE

Author Jordan Renee has been obsessed with books for as long as she can remember, and fondly recalls spending childhood car rides staring out the nearest window and crafting stories to pass the time. She first started writing these stories down in high school, and completed this particular novel during her senior year of college, where she managed to scribble a chapter here and there between classes. Jordan graduated with a double major in English and Art History, and continues to spend her free time squeezing in a bit of reading or writing whenever possible. You can also find Jordan at the nearest rock climbing gym, treasure hunting in one of her favorite antique stores, or spending time with her family, whose antics consistently provide loving inspiration for the characters and stories she creates.

Made in the USA
Middletown, DE
31 March 2022